EXCELSIOR

12-82

For Ann
with great affection

Bob Williams

EXCELSIOR

An historical novel of Lake Minnetonka

by

Bob Williams

JAMES D. THUESON, PUBLISHER

Minneapolis

JAMES D. THUESON, PUBLISHER
Box 14474 University Station
Minneapolis, MN 55414

DEDICATED TO PATTY
whose roots, heart and home
are in Excelsior.

Prologue

EXCELSIOR and the Lake Minnetonka area are modern-day suburbs to the Twin Cities. The little community's proud heritage comes from Minnetonka's heyday in those years around the turn of the century. To recreate that Excelsior today, one would have to combine the beauty of Minnesota's north woods, the excitement and fashion of a major city, and the hotels, the horse and buggy and the charm of Mackinac Island. Now, through the combination of historical fact and fiction, we can once again stand on the shoreline of Lake Minnetonka and see the steamboats filled with summer visitors from around the world departing and docking at EXCELSIOR!

City Of Saint Louis

It was the largest boat ever to have sailed on Lake Minnetonka when it was launched in Wayzata on July 9, 1881. The *City of Saint Louis* would eventually become a sister ship to an even larger steamboat. Advertised as *The First Boat In America To Be Lighted By Electric Lights*, it carried 1500 passengers and was based at Excelsior.

Photo, courtesy Minnesota Historical Society

White House Hotel

One of the oldest and best-known hotels in all Minnetonka, the *White House* was located at the foot of Water Street in Excelsior on a grassy bluff overlooking Excelsior Bay. From its veranda, guests watched the famous steamboats dock at the municipal landings with their loads of vacationers and visitors so important to the story of *EXCELSIOR*.

Lake Park Hotel

One of the largest hotels on Lake Minnetonka, the *Lake Park Hotel* was built in 1879 in Tonka Bay at the end of the M. and St. L. Railway's line to Lake Minnetonka. The *Lake Park* boasted beautiful parks, groves, flower gardens and a special pavilion for musicals and band concerts for its guests and visitors from other hotels in *EXCELSIOR*.

Belle of Minnetonka

The *Belle of Minnetonka* was the granddaddy of all Minnetonka steamboats and the largest to ever sail the historic lake. Originally known as the *Phil Sheridan*, the huge riverboat was launched at Lake Minnetonka on July 3, 1882, and carried as many as 2,500 passengers as it left Excelsior to meet trains across the lake at Wayzata and make stops at famous Minnetonka hotels.

Photo, courtesy Minnesota Historical Society

Hotel Lafayette

The *Lafayette Hotel* at Minnetonka Beach was the most famous of all the hotels located on Lake Minnetonka. Visitors from around the world were guests at what was known as the finest summer resort hotel west of Saratoga. And it was advertised as *The Only Hotel On The Lake With An Elevator!*

MATTHEWS-NORTHRUP-CO.
BUFFALO.N.Y.

Trinity Episcopal Chapel

Trinity Parish was founded in 1853 and eventually moved from a log church on St. Alban's Bay to Excelsior in 1862 where this *Trinity Episcopal Chapel* was built. Above the chancel are the words, *Surely The Lord Is In This Place*, and they brought special meaning to those in the story, *EXCELSIOR*.

Photo from the author's collection

Excelsior's Waterfront

This was one view of EXCELSIOR'S waterfront as seen from the *White House Hotel*. The photograph has become popular because it pictures the three largest steamboats of the day (from left to right) the *City of Saint Louis*, the *Hattie May*, and the *Belle of Minnetonka*.

Photo from the author's collection.

The G.A.R. On Mainstreet

Veterans of the Grand Army of the Republic posed for this photograph along Excelsior's main street, Water Street, before a holiday parade. Thousands of visitors would later line the street in time for the Fourth-of-July parade in the story, *EXCELSIOR!*

Photo from the author's collection

EXCELSIOR

Saturday, July 2, 1887

1

THE PURSER'S REPORT listed a total of 352 passengers for the seven-mile trip across Lake Minnetonka from the little town of Wayzata on the north shore of the big inland lake to the larger, yet small, town of Excelsior on the south shore. The total did not include the fourteen local youngsters, all boys, who had been allowed to hitch a ride aboard the big side-wheeler on its trip over to meet the Great Northern Railway's *Western Star* passenger train. And even though the steamer boasted a capacity of 1500 passengers, the morning's fare, mostly vacationers on their way to Excelsior resort hotels, was a better-than-average load for a Saturday morning.

EXCELSIOR

It was a warm Minnesota morning with a clear sky and very little wind. The sun, which had shone just barely above the trees massed along the uneven shoreline on the early-morning trip across the lake, had now risen into a clear field of blue sky and the morning sunlight sparkled on the bright red letters across the portside paddlewheel box. In the most ornate showboat printing of the day, the words *City Of Saint Louis* were spelled out in letters two feet high.

Some thirty-four feet above the main deck of the steamer which was fashioned after the riverboats of the day, the skipper of the *City* stood at the starboard windows of the wheelhouse where he was checking over the purser's report for the morning run. The report was standard procedure for boats belonging to the Lake Minnetonka Navigation Company and, at the bottom of the yellow form, the young man signed, "John Stark, acting captain, July 2, 1887."

John was officially classified as a pilot for the Navigation Company but he had been serving as "acting captain" ever since Captain Jess Williams had slumped over his dinner in the boat's dining room during the first week in June. The old captain died of a heart attack and the company had sent a request to Pittsburgh for an experienced Ohio riverboat man as the new captain. But he still hadn't arrived after four weeks. In the meantime, the twenty-four-year-old Stark, already the youngest pilot on the lake, was now the youngest captain—at least for awhile. Almost every pilot on Minnetonka, regardless of his age, would have traded places with John Stark, just to be aboard the *City*, the second largest steamboat on the lake. Yet John Stark was not completely satisfied with his new job, or with his old one for that matter. It wasn't that John was not aware of his youthful accomplishments. He had grown up on this lake and knew it as well as anyone and better than most. But all of his life he had longed to be the skipper of his own steamboat, even if it were only one-third the size of the famous *City*

The young pilot filed the purser's report in the wooden wall file at the rear of the wheelhouse and turned to remind the wheelman, Dick Blake, of the unmarked sandbar located one-hundred yards off the shore of Big Island on the starboard bow. "Watch for the bar just beyond that clump of trees, Dick," said the young captain.

"I can see it already, John," came the answer from the wheelman.

"After you pass it, you'll have clear sailing until you're ready to make your turn into Exclesior Bay."

"I'm catchin' on," came the reply.

Blake was twice John's senior but was unfamiliar with Lake Minnetonka, having arrived this spring from Read's Landing where he had piloted at Lake Pepin on the Mississippi river. Satisfied that everything was in order, John stepped outside on to the top deck and let the screen door slam behind him. There was very little breeze, he thought. His white cap with the black visor hid most of his long wavy blond hair, and his sun-bleached eyebrows and eyelashes made his strong features appear more sun-tanned than they really were. Like all of the boat captains working for the Lake Minnetonka Navigation Company, he was clean-shaven, but he wore no official uniform. The only mark of distinction for the string of boat commanders was the captain's cap with the company seal sewn on the front, above the visor. John had tried to look the part, however, and as usual, was wearing a clean white long-sleeved shirt, open at the neck, and a pair of khaki trousers. Somewhere he had a navy-blue jacket which he had purchased by mail-order from the W.T. Moore Company in Chicago, but he only wore it on special occasions and on weekends to impress the passengers who might doubt his authority because of his youth. Had he known the load was this heavy, he would have worn the blue coat this morning.

The young captain leaned over the starboard rail of the *City* and looked aft toward the churning paddlewheels. The main deck was crowded with its new load of passengers, catching their first breath of fresh air since they had begun their vacation journey in the stale atmosphere and stuffy surroundings of the latest 1887 Pullman cars. Most of the visitors had come from the south—Memphis, St. Louis, New Orleans, Jefferson City, and St. Jo. Their vacation trip was a major project not only in miles but in numbers as well. Besides mother and dad and the children, a traveling family brought many of their black servants, maids and nurses. For some, the trip across Lake Minnetonka to Excelsior was their maiden voyage. But for many, the 40-minute ride was the last leg of an annual trek to a month-long summer vacation, the end of the monotonous train ride and the beginning of an endless round of playtime events. Mothers could shop the resort hotels and local stores and stroll daily in their finest Eton suits and tailored dresses. Young ladies, dressed in white pique dresses or bright plain knickerbockers, would make it a point to be seen often on the tennis courts, the beaches, on the bike trails, sipping afternoon iced tea, and arranging "by-chance" meetings with the eligible young men on a holiday. There were even more likely prospects from the large corps of local young men who spent most of their daylight hours in jobs necessary in making the tourist business successful in Excelsior and neighboring communities.

Fathers, perhaps a wealthy banker from the east and a successful retailer from the south, found time for daily fishing in Lake Minnetonka, an opportunity to visit with other vacationers, some elegant living and dining, and a chance to just plain loaf. Children, on the other hand, didn't have time to loaf. There were too many things to see and do—boats and rafts, wilderness and unexplored paths, swimming and sailing, livery barns and horseback riding, baseball games and fireworks. And the end of each day found almost every youngster so exhausted that parents had no trouble enforcing rules about bedtime.

The sidewheeler was churning past the eastern shore of Big Island now. The island was located in the middle of what was known as the lower lake of Minnetonka and had been discovered along with the lake itself in 1822 when a scouting party from the United States Army fort on the Minnesota river had stumbled on to the virgin waters. Among those in the group of white men was young Joe Snelling, son of the commandant of the fort which was to carry the Snelling name through the rest of Minnesota history.

John Stark's eyes searched along the dense foliage along the shoreline of the island, only a hundred yards away, catching a familiar little channel or inlet which he had explored as a youngster. He had spent all twenty-four years of his life in Excelsior and a good share of those years had found John sailing the lake and seeking out every sand bar, every good fishing field, every secret inlet and hiding place. His thoughts took him back to his boyhood days. As a youngster, he had rowed an old flat-bottom boat seemingly hundreds of miles over the lake with his boyhood chums, especially Emmet Markham. Once they had loaded the old rowboat with used lumber and laths from the old Miller house, which had burned down, and started out for Big Island to build a shack.

"Johnny," shouted young Emmet. "The boat's leaking back here!"

"Jesus Christ! Start bailing! You and Willy take those tin cans and bail. Andy and I'll keep rowing."

The boat continued to fill with lake water and the two bailers found themselves losing the race with the leaky boat-bottom. "Keep bailing, keep bailing!" shouted John. "We'll head for Gale's Island instead!" But they didn't make it. The water level had risen to put the old rowboat under and still the young boys bailed and rowed, sitting in water up to their bottoms and watching the lumber float out over the stern of the boat and drift away with the waves.

The thought of little Andy Ross who was now the manager of the White House Hotel in Excelsior, reminded John that he would meet his boyhood friend and Mr. George Wolfe after lunch today to discuss the Fourth-of-July race between the *City* and its sister ship, the newer and larger *Belle Of Minnetonka*. George "Pinky" Wolfe was a member of a corps of those scroundrel gamblers who invaded Excelsior each summer. But those who knew Pinky well also knew that he was a man of his word and that he possessed a well-camouflaged quality of integrity and fairness that was clearly lacking in most of his professional bretheren.

The bright red and white riverboat had now passed the southern tip of Big Island and off the starboard bow, a mile and half away, John could see Sunrise Point on the tip of the area known as Lake Park or Tonka Bay. It was truly the first spot in the lower lake to catch the initial faint rays of the sun across Excelsior Bay each morning. Off to the left, passengers had their first view of the southern mainland and Excelsior. Rising up beyond the shoreline was a series of high bluffs, dotted with hotels, villas and boarding houses, half-hidden among the heavy growth of trees which were everywhere. Near the eastern end of Excelsior Bay lay the municipal docks and landing where the *City* and eighteen other steamers docked daily with their loads of visitors. Just beyond the docks was the White House, and its appearance in the distance reminded John once more that his meeting with Andy and Pinky Wolfe was a most important one. Should he win the duel race with the *Belle* on Monday, he could become a boat-owner himself. Mr. Sampson had already promised to sell him the *Hattie May*.

"What the hell do you want to fool around with this old tub for, John, when you're already runnin' the best boat on the lake?" Mr.

Sampson had asked. He smiled, because he already knew the answer, and in John Stark, he could see himself thirty years ago.

"I just want to own my own boat, Mr. Sampson," replied John. "I know the lake and I want to be my own boss."

"You put up half the money after the Fourth, John, and it's yours. You can pay me the rest next year after the tourist season is over."

"It's a deal, Mr. Sampson," and John Stark shook hands with the elderly gentleman with the long grey hair and the handlebar mustache.

Yes, a victory on the Fourth would provide winnings to carry out his life-long hopes for his own boat, and then he could ask Rose to become Mrs. John Stark.

The *City's* steam-whistle prompted John to glance at his pocket watch. It was 10:55 and they would be docking in less than ten minutes. Yes, this holiday weekend was a most important one, he thought. Most important, indeed!

2

THE SIGNS on either end of the depot which was located just off the main street read EXCELSIOR and, to visitors arriving by rail, it was the end of the line—the destination for summer vacations. The depot was painted a bright green and, although the front of the building was at ground level along the railroad tracks, it was high enough to load freight on to the Hoag Dray Line wagons on the rear side. In the winter, the waiting room was empty and cold and old Herb Johnson only kept the small pot-belly stove going in the telegrapher's office to keep him warm during his daily hours. In the summer, however, no stove was necessary. The temperature in the waiting room rose with

33

the warm sun of April, became hot by the end of May, and was almost unbearable during the summer. Only in Herb's office did the windows work properly and, even then, the stale air was noticeable to everyone who entered—except Herb. He had been depot agent for the Minneapolis and St. Louis Railway at Excelsior ever since the railroad had built the track west from Minneapolis, some eighteen miles away. And although this was the end of the line for most of the daily trains, some went on along the spur line to nearby Tonka Bay, four miles away where the passenger trains would make a turn-around at the Lake Park Hotel, also owned by the railroad company.

Herb looked out through the windows by the telegrapher's desk and watched the impatient Emmett Markham standing along side the tracks. He knew why the young newspaperman was here to meet the train. "He's waiting for the Blair family to get here on the 10:25 and he's going to have to wait a hell of a lot longer," he thought. Yes, it was that time of year all right—the week of the Fourth of July when the Blair family arrived for their month-long stay at the White House, also owned by the railroad. In fact, the Blairs had visited Excelsior ever since T.J. Blair had become an official for the M. and St. L. and had taken charge of visiting the railroad's hotel properties. The Lake Park Hotel at Tonka Bay was larger and newer, but the Blairs simply liked the village of Excelsior better and the young Blair boys had more opportunities to get into trouble at this lakeside village.

Emmett B. Markham stood on the red brick paving which surrounded the depot and extended along the tracks to the main-street crossing thirty yards away. He was a handsome young man, dark-haired, and strong features, accented by a square jaw and a large cleft in his chin. His eyes were those of a newspaperman—searching, probing, weighing facts and sights, yet capable of deep, tender feeling. His grey suit was accented with navy piping and he had worn a fresh white shirt and string tie for the occasion. The coat and tie would come off as soon as he returned to the print shop.

As a boy, he had come down to the station often during the summer to watch the M. and St. L. passenger trains arrive with their loads of visitors—fancy dresses, umbrellas, fresh men's suits, canes, starched shirts, tall hats and luggage and luggage and luggage. Some of his young buddies had helped pull the bright-colored express carts with the wooden wheels after they had been loaded from the baggage car. But young Emmett would come just to see the trains arrive. Then it was back to his father's newspaper office to melt more lead and to distribute more type back into the cases so the printers could start all over again with a new edition of *The Minnetonka News*. The *News* was published year-around but after the first of September, Excelsior lost its summer visitors and settled down to a quiet little town for the winter. That's when Emmett and his father would pack up each year and head back east to Fall River, Massachussetts, to the newspaper plant and printing firm there. Every summer brought Emmett back to Excelsior, though, and by the time he was eighteen, he was already the fastest type-setter in the shop and was taking on some of the reporting and advertising duties for the *News*. When he was graduated from Brown University two years ago, he had decided that he wanted to run a weekly newspaper more than anything. So he headed back to Minnesota.

The distant and familiar sound of the whistle from the *City of Saint Louis* prompted Emmett to lift his watch from his vest pocket to check the time. It was 10:55 and the morning passenger train was already a half-hour behind schedule. It was late, and it was carrying the most important passenger in the world. It was bringing Hillary Blair back to Excelsior—and to Emmett. It had been almost a year since he had kissed her goodbye as they stood on this very same red brick. Emmett could remember shaking hands with Mr. Blair who boarded the train for the return trip to St. Louis. Hillary's two younger brothers peered through the windows of the Pullman, pressing their noses up against the glass, and Hillary's mother stood on the first step at the rear of the car.

"Hurry up, you two, and get the goodbyes over with," she pleaded, "or we'll have to leave without you. Your father may be a vice president but they wouldn't hold this train for the president himself." Emmett and Hillary had been oblivious of the urgency and kissed once more before the lovely young woman had pulled her hands from his clasp, turned and boarded the train. It had been the third such agonizing parting of the two young people in three summers at Excelsior and it was by far the most difficult. Emmett had vowed then and there that he would not let her go the next time.

The dots and dashes of the telegraph key interrupted Herb

Johnson's day-dreaming for the moment and he automatically
shifted his concentration to the message as it split the stuffy air of the
depot. Herb had been listening to the sounds so long that his mind
could accept whole paragraphs of code, almost without effort. Now
the key had gone dead again and Herb decided that he had might as
well add to the misery of young Markham standing outside. He
pushed open the screen door and shuffled down the brick walk
toward Emmett.

"Morning Emmett."

"Morning Herb."

"Hate to tell you this, son, but you've got a mighty long wait
ahead of you if you're lookin' for the 10:25."

Emmett's heart sank. He had hoped that he could be here when
Hillary came, but time was running out on him this morning and he
had to meet Mayor Bertram for lunch at the White House at 11:30.

"How long will it be, Herb," he asked.

"There's been a delay somewhere the other side of Minneapolis
and I guess it will be afternoon before she gets in. Maybe one, one-
thirty."

The handsome young man frowned for a moment. He had
already been concerned about Hillary's arrival before the train was
late. True, they had never written very much to each other, but she
hadn't answered his infrequent letters since last fall. And although
the Blairs always arrived each summer at the same time, Hillary had
always let Emmett know on just which train they would be. There
had been no letters and no such note about this year's arrival,
however, and Emmett had to check with the hotel to see when the
Blairs would be getting into Excelsior.

He thanked old Herb and turned to start down Excelsior's main
street which was bedecked with American flags in honor of the
holiday weekend. The White House Hotel was two blocks away,
overlooking the lake, and there was no use being late for the meeting
with the mayor. Emmett would need the official program schedule of
the events for the holiday weekend which was about all that was left
to set in type for the special Fourth-of-July program. He would
simply have to miss meeting Hillary at the station. But he promised
himself that he would never let her go again once she arrived. Then
he smiled as he started down the main street. He'd offer to give up his
own independence—on, of all days—the Fourth of July!

36

3

LAKE MINNETONKA'S sprawling shoreline extended some two hundred miles in and out of nearly fifty bays, and the lake was divided into two general areas—the Upper and Lower Lake—which were connected by a small, narrow channel about thirty yards wide and two hundred yards long. The channel was known as The Narrows, and was the shortest route from the Lower to the Upper Lake—hence, the most popular one for the many steamboats which sailed Minnetonka in the 1880's.

Nestled into the very southern shore of the Lower Lake was the bustling little community of Excelsior. It had been founded in 1853 by a group of pioneers from the east who had formed the Excelsior Pioneer Association in New York and who had headed west, overland to the Mississippi and then up the river to St. Paul and Minneapolis and on west to Lake Minnetonka. The little band of easterners had been led by men like Geroge M. Bertram and the Rev. Charles Galpin and they had chosen a site of high bluffs and sloping landscape to the waters' edge for their settlement. These were not ordinary pioneers. For the most part, they had the benefit of a good education, a fine background of eastern families, and in many instances, a moderate amount of wealth to go along with their position in life. And when they arrived at their new home in Minnesota on the shores of Lake Minnetonka, they wasted no time in putting all of their special talents and heritage to work. From the beginning, two important segments of community life had been established in the little town. Churches and schools were established the same year in 1853. The Rev. Mr. Galpin organized the Excelsior Congregational Church that year. By 1870 the congregation had grown to the point that a new church building was needed—and constructed on high ground across from the school, overlooking Excelsior's two-block long business district and Excelsior Bay just two blocks to the north.

In Excelsior's first year, Trinity Episcopal Church was also born. A log church was built across the bay at nearby St. Alban's and in 1862, a new building was built for Trinity in the heart of Excelsior. Pioneers also added a stockade around the little chapel to protect residents of the community in the event that the Sioux uprisings to the south reached Lake Minnetonka that year.

The Rev. Mr. Galpin was also busy organizing schools in the new little community and before long, a log cabin school was making steady progress. By 1858, the little town of Excelsior was doing very well for itself, and although it grew steadily over the next two decades, it did not reach its greatest success and popularity until the 1880's. Now, in the peak of the summer season of 1887, it was the busiest commmunity in the state of Minnesota outside of Minneapolis and St. Paul. Excelsior had become the most important point on Lake Minnetonka and, from there, visitors and their accompanying business success spread to all parts of the lake. All major steamers made Excelsior's waterfront the starting point for their trips and the town was served by railways—the Minneapolis and St. Louis, and the Minneapolis, Lyndale and Minnetonka. Between them, the timetables called for twelve to fifteen trains daily. The community also boasted the latest in telegraph and telephone connections and was serving its residents and visitors with two mails a day. A Methodist Church had been added to the religious life of the community, too. There were grade schools, an academy, a newspaper, three general stores, a hardware store, three hotels, some eight or ten boarding houses which were appropriately advertised as "villas," along with all of the other services of a prosperous town—the Sampson and Wood meat market, the W. B. Jones Dry Goods and Grocery store, and the E.D. Newell Drugs. There were such necessities as the O.S. Gates Company (boat fleet and livery service), the Morse Ice Company, Mrs. Beers' restaurant, and a long list of physicians headed by old Doc Perkins, advertised as a "homeopathic physician."

Most of the activity of the little town took place along Water Street (the main street) from the M. and St. L. depot down two blocks to the shoreline and, then, spread east and west along the Excelsior waterfront. On the very shoreline at the foot of Water Street, visitors congregated to take boat trips around the lake or to neighboring Wayzata and back again. The shoreline was a maze of municipal docks for the steamers of all sizes—from the small private craft to the massive *Belle of Minnetonka*. Most popular spot in the area was the Blue Line—a combination restaurant, bar, gift shop, boat livery and general hangout for Pinky Wolfe and his gambling acquaintances.

Back from the Blue Line and the waterfront and across the lakeside road, the White House crowned a high bluff overlooking Excelsior Bay. The hotel was one of three fine hotels in Excelsior and simply derived its name from the fact that it was painted a gleaming white. Across the front of the hotel was a veranda topped by an open balcony porch which was outlined with an ornate latticework railing. From the veranda, guests could view all of Excelsior Bay, the steamers docking from their regular runs and departing again for other points on the lake, and the fishermen and their rowboats starting off for another catch in nearby St. Alban's Bay. Some fishermen headed around the point in what had now become

Gideon's Bay, named after Peter Gideon, another of the early pioneers who had been a community leader and a fruit-grower and who had developed the Wealthy Apple which he named after his beloved wife.

Along the shoreline running north from the docks was the green grass which spread out on to acres of flat ground called the Excelsior Commons. The Commons, supposedly the only one in the country outside of Boston, once was the home of Indian tepees and was known to everyone who visited Minnetonka. Young boys turned it into a baseball diamond during the day, and by night it became a favorite place to stroll for young lovers and older parents who were recapturing their own days of youth. From the White House, the view swung around to the northwest to catch a portion of main street and the LaPaul House—owned by Dr. LaPaul who was known as a gracious host and a particular favorite of visiting ladies from Memphis and St. Jo. To the south end of Excelsior Bay, the terrain rolled back from the shoreline to more hills and the Sampson House, the other leading hotel in Excelsior which boasted one hundred rooms and advertised such delights as "Heated By Hot Water," "Electric Call Bells in Every Room," and "Ventilated Chambers for the Tired Traveler." The popular hotel was owned by L.F. Sampson who had purchased a barn in nearby Wisconsin, had it dismantled, and shipped the lumber to Excelsior by rail to be used in the construction of the hotel. The Sampson House catered to visitors from St. Louis and Carleton, Missouri, and was eventually to serve its community halfway into the next century. Along the high bluffs to the west and overlooking most of the Excelsior shoreline were the boarding houses which had gained the more sophisticated title of villa. They included the Long View House, the Summer House, the Vineland Villa, the Slater House, Summit House and Pleasant Grove.

One of the most popular hotels on the lake was the Lake Park Hotel at nearby Tonka Bay, just three miles by rail and only a mile away from Excelsior by water. It was an impressive wood-frame building which sprawled out across wooded lawns and was capped by three large towers and a bright orange-colored roof. The hotel was leased by the M. and St. L. Railway which brought a spur line from Excelsior almost to its doors. It was one of the largest hotels anywhere on the lake and could accomodate nearly a thousand guests.

The Lake Park, too, advertised electric lights, call bells, luxurious carpeting, draperies, and a spacious dining room that could seat 400 visitors. The hotel included a boat house, a number of adjoining villas, and a special theater for light comedy and summer opera. Guests could further enjoy riding, biking, tennis and fishing and the management maintained a full corps of teachers and nurses to help visiting families and to relieve mothers and dads of some of their daily chores and parental responsibilities.

Although Excelsior was the largest community on the lake and was the hub of resort activity, it was not the only resort town with the good fortune to have Lake Minnetonka on its boundaries. Wayzata could be seen from the Excelsior Commons across the main body of water of the Lower Lake. It, too, had its share of hotels, general stores and business houses. And it also just happened to be located on the route of the St. Paul, Minneapolis and Manitoba Railway and the Great Northern. As a result, steamers from Excelsior made connections with the busy schedule of daily trains to carry passengers to all points on the lake.

Minnetonka Beach found itself on the same railroad line and its one grand claim to fame was its magnificient Hotel Lafayette, known as the largest and finest summer hotel west of Saratoga. The hotel was conceived and built by James J. Hill, powerful and wealthy president of the Great Norther Railway. The summer place was located between Crystal Bay and Lafayette Bay and a canopied veranda ran nearly two hundred yards along the front of the five stories. Flags flew from the high peaks of the French-styled architecture and hotel guests enjoyed spacious grounds which sloped down to the docks where almost every steamer on the lake touched down at least once a day. Advertisements for the Lafayette boasted that "The Sewerage and Sanitary Arrangements were unexcelled" and "Forty electric lights illuminate the house and grounds!" The resort was most proud of its accomodations for 900 guests. It provided electric bells and gas in every room, and was in the enviable position of being the only hotel on the lake with an elevator.

Smallest business community on the lake was at Mound City which had a population of about one hundred. It had its own postoffice, two boat fleets, a general store and a sawmill, along with one prosperous hotel—the Chapman House.

Over on the south side of the Lower Lake and not too far from Excelsior, the M. and St. L. had build a depot to handle the passenger traffic coming to the Hotel St. Louis in the heart of the area known as Deephaven. The hotel, a four-story frame building, overlooked St. Louis Bay and Carson's Bay. Guests also came via the spur run of the Chicago-Milwaukee Road and more visitors moved into the other Deephaven hostelry, the Keewaydin Hotel at neighboring Cottagewood, a favorite place for Sunday diners.

The lake, the rolling landscape, green trees and heavy foliage, the warm days and cool evenings, the steamboats, and the hotels, all combined their efforts in bringing new popularity to Lake Minnetonka as a summer resort. From meager beginnings in the seventies, the lake had now become one of the top summer attractions in the eighties. Visitors not only from throughout the United States, but from all over the world, were making reservations at the Hotel Lafayette or the White House or the Lake Park. The hotel registers carried the names of J. Bissell, wife and child, Syracuse, New York; C.G. White, wife, daughter and grandson, Kansas City; the Dixon children and nurse, St. Louis; Mrs. J.M. Thornton and children, Austin Texas; M. de Cerkes and family, Paris, France; Edward Macauley and family, Washington, D.C.; L. E. Dorf, Holland; W.P. Shattuck, wife and family, London, England; Dr. John Wright, Boston; and F.W. Wyman and wife, Hannibal, Missouri. There were bankers and railroad presidents, judges and doctors, clergymen, widows, divorcees, nurses with children, congressmen, and visitors numbering into the thousands.

J.P. Morgan stepped off the M. and St. L. at the Excelsior depot for a visit to Lake Minnetonka. On the north shore of the lake, the greatest general of the Union Army and former president of the United States, Ulysses S. Grant, enjoyed the latest in hotel accomodations at the Hotel Lafayette.

Excelsior's newspaper described the excitement and the volume of business brought on by the summer visitors: "City people accuse Excelsiorites of working only four months in the year, but there are plenty of men in this village who work twelve weeks in each month while the summer rush business is on!"

Another edition in September of the previous year had reviewed the past few months: "The tourist season is about finished and the

streets of Excelsior do not present the bustling appearance that they
did during July and August. And it is well, for human flesh and blood
cannot stand the strain all the year round that our merchants and
others are subjected to during the summer months."

There were steamboat races and sailing regattas by day and
dancing and moonlight cruises by night, elegant dining and endless
catches of fish. Joseph Jefferson of Louisville, Kentucky, and his son,
John, kept a record of every fish they caught. He was quite deaf and a
most friendly gentleman and his accounting showed a total of 2,770
pounds of fish one year and 2,773 pounds the next. Another fisherman, William Eldred, held the record for the largest fish ever caught
in Lake Minnetonka, a pickerel weighing thirty-two pounds. The
report in the local press explained that Mr. Eldred was so excited and
so anxious to get back to Wayzata to display the big fish that he left
his coat and a wicker flask on the Excelsior beach.

William Burr, president of the St. Louis National Bank, was about
to depart for Europe when a friend urged him to visit Lake Minnetonka for a month or two before going abroad. The old gentleman
visited the Excelsior House and postponed his trip to Europe for
several years."

But prosperity also brought some problems to the community of
Excelsior, and the village fathers acted promptly. Such situations,
brought about by local residents and visitors alike, were to be con-
trolled by ordinances such as this:

Section 1. No person shall swim or bathe within the limits of the
Village of Excelsior in a state of nudity or except when decently and
properly attired; and it is hereby made the special duty of the keeper of
the public grounds to arrest any person in the act of violating this
section.
Section 2. No person shall make, aid or countenance any noise, riot or
disturbance or improper diversion to the annoyance of the residents or
travelers to said village.
Section 3. No person shall play or countenance, the playing of any
public game or diversion upon the Sabbath day within the limits of the
village of Excelsior.
Section 4. No person shall play with or throw a ball in the streets or
lanes of said village.
Section 5. Whoever shall violate or offend against any provision of this
ordinance shall, upon conviction before the Justice Court of this village

be punished by a fine not to exceed fifty dollars and costs of prosecution for each offence, and be imprisoned until such fine and costs be paid, not exceeding sixty days.

Section 6. This ordinance shall take effect and be in force from and after its publication.

A.W. Latham, Recorder
George Bertram, Mayor

Another ordinance stipulated that *Any person who shall be found in a state of intoxication on any street or other public place within the limits of the Village of Excelsior shall, upon conviction thereof before the Justice Court of said village, be punished by a fine not exceeding thirty dollars and costs of prosecution, and be imprisoned until such fine and costs are paid.*

And had this final ordinance been carried out to the full letter of the law, the Excelsior village government would have had to take over an entire hotel to accomodate the violators: *Any person found within the limits of the Village of Excelsior loitering about the streets either by day or by night, and not having any known place of residence or any visible means of support and not being able or willing to give a satisfactory account of himself, may be arrested and brought before the Justice of said village, and upon conviction, shall be liable to the same fine and penalties provided in Section 1 of this ordinance.*

44

4

THE TRAIN RIDE from St. Louis to Excelsior had always been a pleasant one for Hillary Blair and the return trip at the end of July each summer had always been lonesome and filled with sadness and nostalgia which could not be changed, even by the happy memories of the month with Emmett. The trips to Lake Minnetonka had become an annual event for the Blair family since Hillary's father had become a vice president of the M. and St. L. three years ago. Although Mr. Blair made frequent business trips to areas served by the railroad, the long trip to Excelsior was the only one on which his family accompanied him. It was, in fact, the only such trip in which they were

45

truly interested in making and it had long since become a combination business and vacation journey for T.J. Blair and the whole
Blair family.

On the first of July each year, the Blairs would embark from the
Union Station in St. Louis for the trip to Minnesota. For Mr. Blair, it
was mostly business—with a few days set aside for some good old
Lake Minnetonka fishing and some time to spend with his wife,
Frances. They would have a chance for a few uninterrupted lun-
cheons at the White House and some of the other hotels on the lake,
including the railroad's own Lake Park. And for the most part, there
would be no children under foot. Robert, the oldest of the Blair
children, had only made the trip once before he was graduated from
Grinnell College and had left for New York and a job with the New
York Central. Hillary was the second oldest in the family and until
her mother had hired Emily, the colored maid, she was somewhat in
charge of her two young brothers, Tom and David, who had now
reached the complicated ages of ten and thirteen.

Hillary adored her father and he was probably more proud of his
lovely daughter than any of the rest of the Blair children. Perhaps it
was because she was the only girl in the family. But whatever the
reason, she could not be capable of any wrong-doing in the eyes of her
father. And he had never been disappointed. When she met Emmett
that very first summer, Hillary was only sixteen and the thought that
her father might disapprove of her seeing so much of a man far older
than she—Emmett was all of twenty-one then—hadn't even entered
her mind. Oddly enough, both her father and mother took a warm
liking to the young newspaperman. She saw Emmett constantly
during the four weeks each July and yet, they seldom wrote to each
other during the other eleven months in the year. For Emmett, it
appeared to be four weeks of summer fun, but for Hillary, it was love
at first sight and she had loved him since that first day when she
stopped at the newspaper office to buy the weekly edition of *The
Minnetonka News*. Hillary had opened the screen door to the newspaper office and stepped inside and up to a high counter. She was
wearing a pink afternoon dress and carried a large straw purse. The
newspaper office and print shop were all combined in a large room.
The new linotype machine, the presses, type cases and paper stock
seemed to be spread throughout the shop without any central plan,

and off to the right of the counter was a large library table which served as a desk for Emmett Markham. Hillary was not sure whether she liked the smell of the hot metal and the ink as she waited for someone to help her. It was Emmett who finally emerged from the maze of equipment and paper stock.

"Can I help you, Miss a——," he hesitated. After he began to speak, he realized that he did not know the lovely blond girl who stood at the counter.

"Yes. I'd like to buy the latest edition of the *News*," Hillary replied.

"Of course." Emmett walked over to his library table-desk where a stack of newspapers were quarter-folded and neatly piled. Hillary did not take her eyes off the handsome young man with the dark hair and heavy eyebrows. "Here you are, Miss. It's this week's paper— came out yesterday"

"Thank you." She laid the paper down and opened her purse to find the two cents needed to pay for it. She reached across the counter and gave the pennies to Emmett. There was an awkward moment when the two young people just stood there and looked at each other. Then Hillary smiled and spoke again. "I'm Hillary Blair." As if to make sure there was no mistake, she added, "MISS Hillary Blair." There was another silence. "I'm staying at the White House with my family. My father's with the railroad."

"I'm so happy to meet you," Emmett said. Then, as an after-thought, he stepped around the counter and extended his hand. "I'm really very glad to meet you. I'm Emmett Markham. I'm the editor here." The two shook hands and then Hillary looked at the palm of her hand and saw that it was smeared with printer's ink. Emmett could see her hand, too, and then looked at his own to discover wet black ink spread across the palm and his fingers. "I'm sorry——," he stammered. "I. . . ." The two young people looked at their inky hands and began to laugh. "Come on, I'll get that ink off with some powdered soap we have here in the shop." He led Hillary back through the print shop and past the type cases and printers who were busy setting type by hand in metal type sticks. Emmett stopped in front of a small dry sink and reached into a barrel along side of the sink for a handful of the powdered soap. Then he poured a little water over his hand and took Hillary's hand in his and began to rub the soap into the soft, but inky, palm. The soap began to foam and the ink disappeared, but some of the soapy water squirted out of his hand and splashed across the skirt of her pink dress. He was embarrassed. "I'm sorry, Miss Blair. I guess I've just made matters worse."

"No, of course not. It's perfectly all right." She brushed at the streak of water and soap on her skirt. "It's hardly noticeable and besides, we did get the ink off my hand." They both laughed and he handed her a soiled towel. She paused again, obviously not sure whether she should use the towel or not. They both looked at the towel, then at each other, and again, they began to laugh. Hillary dried her hands on the dirty towel and the two walked back to the front counter again. She picked up her newspaper and turned to thank Emmett once more.

"I'm sorry about the ink and the mess I made," Emmett apologized.

"It's all right," she assured him. "I'll stop again another time for a paper."

"Please do. I'll try to be more careful next time."

"Well——." She turned to go. "Goodbye."

"Goodbye Miss Blair."

Hillary remembered that summer afternoon of four years ago— the ink, the pink dress, and her first meeting with Emmett. And she remembered that he had paid her a call at the White House that very night to apologize again for his clumsiness. It was the first of many calls that summer.

This year's trip to Excelsior was different for Hillary. It was not the beginning of another exciting vacation, filled with all of the memories of past trips and with the expectation of what would be forthcoming in the weeks ahead. All of the landmarks that had signalled the diminishing distance between Hillary and Excelsior now made the trip more emotionally painful for her. It was only after Hillary had been staring at the same clump of trees and the same desolate road crossing that she realized the train had been standing still for some time now. Turning away from the window, she was startled to find her mother standing in the doorway to her compartment.

Frances Blair was a tall, beautiful woman of forty-three, who placed her marriage and her family above all else in this world. She was the daughter of a college professor and had grown to woman-hood on the campus of Grinnell College at Grinnell, Iowa. It was while she was visiting the home of a college girlfriend in St. Louis that she first met Tom Blair, then a student at Washington University.

Where her daughter had been seeing the same young man for three summers in a row, Frances Remington and Tom Blair ended a six-month whirlwind courtship in marriage in the chapel at Grinnell. Since then, it had been the railroad business—first at Cedar Rapids, Iowa, where Bob had been born, then on to Peoria, Illinois, and Chicago. Finally, they had "come home" to St. Louis where Tom had accepted a position as second in command of the St. Louis operation and was then named a vice president of the M. and St. L. and head of the St. Louis office.

"The conductor says it is only a short delay, dear," Mrs. Blair said.

"It's all right, Mother. I really hadn't noticed the time."

Mrs. Blair moved into the compartment and sat down across from her daughter. "It isn't gong to be half as difficult as you imagine," she assured Hillary.

"Perhaps not for him, Mother, but it will be for me."

Mrs. Blair showed more concern. "I would be glad to talk to Emmett before you see him, dear."

"No—no," she replied. "It's just that I hope he isn't waiting at the depot when we get there. It's going to be difficult enough just arriving." She paused. "If it wasn't for Dad, I would never have made the trip. You know that. I had no intention of ever coming back to Excelsior. That's one reason I didn't answer his letters."

Mrs. Blair frowned. "If it wasn't for your father, none of this would be necessary"

"It isn't his fault, Mother. I know he was disappointed when you and I insisted on a small, quiet wedding at home. And he is so proud of the marriage and the baby that I just couldn't let him down when he asked Jim and me to come with you on this trip. It's really not his fault, Mother."

"Perhaps not." She was impatient. "But if he were just a little more aware. . . ."

Hillary closed her eyes, almost in desperation, and was about to speak when the two were interrupted by the appearance of a pretty black girl in the doorway of the compartment. She was wearing a maid's uniform—a long black dress with a high neckline, puffed sleeves and set off with a white apron and starched white cuffs and collar.

"Ma'am. Little Jamie is asleep now and if one of you ladies would like to watch him for awhile, I'll go and have my lunch now."

"Thank you, Emily," said Mrs. Blair. "I'll sit with him while you eat."

As she rose to leave, she turned back to her daughter. "By the time Dad and Jim arrive tomorrow, everything will be all settled. Believe me, dear—I know it will."

Then Emily and Mrs. Blair left the compartment.

Hillary looked back out the window and then caught her own reflection in the glass. It prompted her to straighten her pretty blond hair and then she settled back in the deep-cushioned seat once again. The car lurched and then slowly started forward. They were moving again and it would not be long before they would once again see Lake Minnetonka and cross the St. Alban's Bay drawbridge which separated Excelsior Bay and St. Alban's Bay. From the bridge, they would be able to look across the bay to the Excelsior shoreline and see the main street running down to the shore and to the White House. Then, it was only a matter of minutes until the train circled the bay and rattled to a stop at the Excelsior depot.

The thought sent a shudder through the lovely young woman. It was almost time. And somehow, she and Mother would have to go through the motions of arriving until Dad and Jim could get here tomorrow from their business appointments at the Minneapolis office.

Then, almost as though she was giving up before she ever began, Hillary became limp. How could she ever explain to Emmett that she was now Mrs. James Stockton and that little Jamie Stockton was her son!

5

THE MARINE DINING ROOM at the White House Hotel was one of the finest anywhere on the lake. The large, bright dining room was located off to the left of the lobby of the hotel and overlooked Excelsior's busy waterfront and the heavy boat traffic in Excelsior Bay. Tall windows across the front of the room gave diners a panoramic view of the Lower Lake, to Big Island, and north—almost to Wayzata. The walls of the room were spotless white and the wood trim, window casings and baseboards and doors were painted in a color which manager Andy Ross called "Minnetonka Blue." The walls were tastefully decorated with large photographs and sketches of Minnetonka steamboats, sailing regattas, and familiar scenes from throughout the lake area. All were carefully matted in the same shade of blue as the window drapes and edged in shiny black frames. The room could accomodate about 150 guests and all of the tables were draped with white linen cloths while the chair-backs had contrasting blue dust covers.

Just inside the main entrance to the dining room, a small alcove to the left led to the "Captain's Bar," a favorite gathering place for the male guests at the hotel along with Excelsior businessmen and, in keeping with the bar's name, boat captains and skippers. The barroom ran across the rear of the hotel and by contrast to the bright dining room, was dull and secluded. The cigar smoke from those seated at the two poker tables helped add a depressing note to the atmosphere. The dreariness seemed to vanish bit by bit as the day progressed—at first it was hotel guests and then the waterfront crowd and businessmen who filtered into the long, narrow room just before lunch. The poker games continued through the afternoon after the noontime rush had diminished, but the crowds and the clamor grew steadily through the late afternoon and early evening and on into the early-morning hours of each summer day.

Mayor George Bertram sat at a small table near a front window in the main dining room where he waited for the arrival of his luncheon guest, Emmett Markham. He knew that Emmett would have only one drink at the most before lunch, so he had purposely arrived early to get a headstart.

"Here's your whiskey and water, Mr. Bertram," said the waitress as she served the drink from a tray she carried.

"Thanks, Rose," the mayor smiled.

The attractive young brunette turned to leave just as the pudgy Bertram had an after-thought about the drink. "Rose," he called. "Bring me one more before Emmett gets here." She smiled, nodded, and left in the direction of the bar. George Bertram's eyes followed her as though the middle-aged mayor had known much more intimately the womanly charms hidden by the long blue uniform and the white apron. Surely no one in the dining room or the hotel—or the whole town of Excelsior for that matter—would have guessed that what was on the mind of mayor Bertram was true! Strange as it may have seemed, the slightly balding man at the table by the window had, in fact, tasted the inviting lips and warm, smooth body of the young Rose Fortier. Not just once, but a number of times over the past two years.

It had not started that way. The Fortiers had come to Excelsior three years ago when Rose's father had taken a job as a chef at the LaPaul House down the street. The French family had remained during the winter and the handsome father had died in the early spring from pneumonia. Rose's mother had never been in good health and the pretty daughter went to work that summer as a barmaid in the Blue Line Cafe. Her mother's health continued to deteriorate and Rose went on working, serving drinks in the local bars where she attracted the young men visiting the lake during the summer, and the young locals during the winter months. Yet it was George Bertram who befriended her, saw to it that her mother was cared for and comfortable to the last, and who showed a kindness and tenderness to the attractive French girl that she had not known from her younger and more ambitious suitors. Bertram had arranged for her job here at the White House where she met and fell in love with John Stark. But there was an unexplainable obedience to George Bertram which went far beyond the normal bounds of gratefulness, and to which Rose Fortier submitted without question.

"This is a busy weekend for me, Rose," the mayor said when she brought the second drink. "Between being official host for the Fourth and trying to keep my office going, I just don't have much time for myself." She exchanged the fresh drink for the empty glass on the table as he spoke. "Are you free?"

"I'm working 'till eight tonight and then I'm busy this evening," she replied in polite tones. She did not want to tell him that she was to meet John Stark at the waterfront.

"Of course. I'm busy with this damn Fourth-of-July Ball on the Belle tonight, too, honey. But I've got a big day tomorrow so I'll be turnin' in about midnight." He paused. "You go on out and have yourself a hell of a good time tonight, Rose. And as I said, about midnight." Rose smiled obediently but did not speak. "Come back again when Emmett gets here," Bertram added. She nodded once more and left the table.

George Bertram was a rarity. He was always well-dressed but always had a disheveled appearance. He was overweight, had become a little paunchy over the years in Excelsior, perspired freely and smoked cigars constantly, all of which added to his unsightliness. Yet he had a quality about him that made him both an attractive man and one to be frightened of, all at the same time. Perhaps it was that mystic something that had made him a successful lawyer and three-times elected mayor of Excelsior. He passed himself off as a nephew of George M. Bertram, one of the founders of the Excelsior Pioneer Association. But there was no relationship. He had won the race for mayor on his first try as a candidate for the "wets" and his party "caucused" regularly in Fred Hawkins' Saloon and Hotel in the middle of Excelsior's two-block-long main street. A bachelor, Bertram lived in quarters on the second floor of the Hawkins hotel. He was unknown when he first arrived in Excelsior and had never met a single soul here whom he had known before. That is, until four years ago when he recognized a fellow graduate of his alma mater, Grinnell College. She was standing in the lobby of the White House and he saw her as he crossed the room.

"Pardon me, ma'am, but aren't you Frances Remington?"

"Why, yes. But no one has called me by that name since my college days," she answered, somewhat surprised. "I've been Mrs. Thomas Blair for a long time, now."

"Of course, I should have remembered," said Bertram in an apologetic tone of voice.

"Your face looks so familiar but I can't seem to place . . . You're not George Bertram?" she asked, almost unbelievingly.

"Yes, Frances," he nodded. "And I haven't seen you since you used to turn me down for dates at college." He laughed. "I recovered from all your refusals," he said, "and after Grinnell and law school, and a few years of practice in Chicago, I came here on vacation and found the town so inviting that I opened my law office here. Now I'm mayor and I want you to know that I place all of my services at your disposal."

George Bertram recalled that meeting four years ago and remembered how uncomfortable Frances Blair had looked at the time. Yet she was no more uncomfortable than he had been as a fumbling pre-law student who kept asking the best-looking girl on the campus for a date. And a professor's daughter at that. There was always some kind of excuse, though, and George Bertram never did get his chance to court Frances Remington. After that unexpected reunion in Excelsior, George Bertram had found himself occasionally thinking of Frances Remington Blair. Older, yes. But just as attractive as ever. And she would be arriving today. Not only would the Blairs be arriving today, but according to a note from an old law school classmate in St. Louis, the Blairs would have some surprising news, especially for young Emmett Markham. Bertram's disciplined mind pondered the situation, searching for an advantage. Somewhere he had been wrong about that young Blair girl. He could have sworn that she would come back and marry Emmett. But the message in his coat pocket changed all of that. How could he have been so wrong? Something did not ring true!

The clock on the alcove wall leading to the Captain's Bar showed a quarter after eleven. Emmett would be along soon, he thought. Bertram tapped the empty glass on the table and gazed out the window.

6

THE WHITE HOUSE was the oldest, and the smallest, of the major hotels in Excelsior. But it also occupied the finest location in the community and it had become the center of activity during the summer season. Because of its vantage point on the bluff overlooking Excelsior Bay, it commanded a magnificent view of the lake. It's front entrance opened on to a green, sloping lawn which ran down to a narrow but busy Lake Street along the waterfront. Through the screen doors in the front of the hotel flowed a steady stream of guests, vacationing businessmen on their way to a morning of fishing, lovely ladies on an afternoon stroll to the beach, and youngsters heading for the inlet where they could fish for carp in the quiet green slime waters away from the main lake, and try their luck at smoking dried lily-pad stems behind the foliage which hid them from the view of vacationers parading to and from the nearby Excelsior Commons.

The White House was unique, however, in boasting two front entrances. The lake-front lobby extended through the building to a second "front" entrance at what would normally be called the rear of the building which faced the Excelsior business district. This second entrance opened on to a circular driveway which also led to the hotel's own livery stable. Most of the activity at this second entrance involved the arrival and departure of guests via horse and buggy, the delivery of baggage by the dray line, and more buggies leaving to make trips to nearby hotels and to catch trains at the Excelsior depot. Excelsior businessmen coming to lunch or dinner and guests walking to the business district to shop were responsible for the foot traffic on the circular drive which was edged with well-trimmed shrubs and a soft, green lawn.

The hotel was leased by the railway and opened its doors each May 15th for the annual summer resort trade which continued through September. A staff of forty-three provided all of the services of the day for White House guests. Six chambermaids kept the rooms sparkling clean and changed the linen daily. Old Minnie Jacobs and Madge Phelps were the senior members of the cleaning corps and they assigned the younger girls, mostly local teenagers, to the various daily chores. Minnie and Madge both kept a close watch on guests checking out of the hotel and knew from years of experience which ones would leave half-filled bottles of booze behind when they left for home. As a result, Minnie and her partner had almost as much whiskey stashed away in their tiny third-floor quarters as the hotel had on display in the Captain's Bar.

In addition to the gardener and handyman and chefs and bartenders and bellboys and other employees necessary to make the White House operation successful, the hotel offered "expert fishing guides" who would help row the visiting fishermen across the lake to fertile off-shore areas or favorite spots where bass or sunfish or pickerel were sure to be waiting.

Saturday mornings were just like any other busy summer morning at the White House's registration desk. But the Saturday before the Fourth of July was a particularly hectic time for Andrew Ross, the manager of the White House. Andy was a bright young man who had grown up in the hotel business. His father had been the owner of The Nicollet House in Minneapolis for many years until he sold the hotel and retired. Each spring, young Ross would come to Excelsior with his family for the summer and each fall the Ross family would move back to Minneapolis to the Nicollet House for the winter. During the winter, the youngster had an opportunity to learn every inch of the hotel business—from serving as a bellhop and carrying whiskey and glasses to bedrooms to peeling potatoes in the kitchen. Each June, however, Andy had a chance to forget about the hotel and settle down to the business of being a boy, a young boy in a setting that was a haven for young boys. There was fishing and boating and raft-making and chasing the ice wagon for just one small chunk of ice on a hot summer day.

Andy went back to Minneapolis each fall and before long he had taken on more hotel chores with more responsibility. First it was "assistant night clerk" and then "night clerk" at the Nicollet House. Later he served as catering manager and doubled as bartender. Then Andy's old summer stamping grounds began to attract summer visitors and it wasn't long before summer hotels were sprouting up all over the Lake Minnetonka area. When the White House was completed, Andy left the Nicollet House to become assistant manager and, a year later, he was named manager by the M. and St. L. Railway which had leased the hostelry. T.J. Blair had been put in charge of the hotel properties for the railroad and he hired Andy on the spot after visiting with the young man for five minutes. He had never been sorry for his quick decision and his only wish was that there were three or four more Andy Ross's to manage the other hotels owned or leased by the railroad.

It was evident to Mr. Blair that his good fortune was only a temporary stroke of luck. Andy Ross had too much ability to remain as manager of the summer hotel for more than three or four seasons and he was well aware of Andy's ambition to head for the east and the New York hotel business. Andy was already drawing the best hotel manager's salary in Excelsior and he had now accumulated $2,700 for his eventual farewell to Lake Minnetonka and his own personal assault on New York. His savings were only half of what he felt he

58

needed for his eastern journey and he could not see spending another three such summers here to acquire the necessary funds. It was because of this urgency that he would meet this afternoon with his long-time friend, John Stark, and one of his own hotel guests—the gambler, Pinky Wolfe. The time was ripe for doubling the pot and the Fourth-of-July race between the *City* and the *Belle* was the means through which this could all be accomplished in one short afternoon.

There wasn't time for such reflections or ambitious thoughts on this Saturday morning, however, and the White House manager was busy straightening out a minor reservation mix-up when Emmett Markham came through the "main street" door at the rear of the hotel and hurried up the steps and across the lobby to the registration desk and Andy Ross. Emmett was another summertime boyhood chum of Andy's and the hotel manager had been helpful with information from the White House more than once for the newspaper editor. Emmett waited at the desk for a moment until Andy had assured the young couple standing there that their room would be ready momentarily and would they like to have lunch first while their accomodations were being prepared? The visitors thanked him for his help and stepped off toward the Marine Dining Room.

"Andy—I'd like to check again on the arrival time for the Blairs," Emmett said anxiously.

"Sure, Emmett. But I'm certain that the letter from Mr. Blair said they would be here on the 10:25 this morning."

Emmett appeared impatient standing there at the desk, and Andy, too, had felt an uneasiness in talking to Emmett about the Blair's arrival. He hadn't said anything to Emmett, but the Blairs had requested a larger suite of rooms this year which included two additional adjoining rooms on the same floor. The Blairs had always reserved 212, 214 and 216 but this year they had also taken two more rooms across the hall. Andy started to tell Emmett about the additional reservations but then thought better of it. "That's all I can tell you, Emmett. They have their reservations for today and they're due here this morning."

"Well, they're going to be late," Emmett replied impatiently, "and I couldn't wait any longer for the damn train. I must have lunch with our illustrious mayor and get the final details of the program for the Fourth. Let me know if Hillary arrives while I'm in the dining room."

Andy nodded assuringly. "Of course I will, Emmett."

Emmett turned and started across the lobby to the entrance of the Marine Dining Room where he could see George Bertram looking out one of the front windows and fondling an empty glass. An elderly man in a white coat and black pants, a long-time employee of the White House, greeted him at the door.

"Mr. Bertram is waiting for you, Mr. Markham."

"Yes, I see him. Thanks."

As Emmett approached the table by the window, George Bertram turned, saw him, and rose to greet him. Emmett noticed a slight smile on the face of the unkempt mayor. It was a smile that made Emmett feel uneasy, a smile that let him know that George Bertram knew something that nobody else knew. Something unpleasant, perhaps. He was never more right.

7

THE *CITY OF SAINT LOUIS* was a magnificent steamboat which had been launched at Wayzata in 1881 by W.D. Washburn, president of the M. and St. L. Railway. The big side-wheeler had dwarfed every other boat on the lake when it was first placed in the waters of Lake Minnetonka. The first of the larger steamboats on the lake had been the *Hattie May*, built in 1879 by Charles May. The *Hattie May* was a hundred-foot sternwheeler with a capacity for 300 passengers, but it was no match for the *City of Saint Louis* which was 160 feet long with a forty-foot beam, and a capacity of 1500 passengers. The hull for the *City* was built at Jeffersonville, Indiana, and the super-structure was

61

designed and constructed at Wayzata where the big steamer was launched. The famous steamboat, which was built at a cost of $55,000, made her trial trip on Lake Minnetonka on July 9, 1881, with a twenty-one piece band aboard to add to the festivities. During that first season from July through September, her receipts for passenger service and meals had reached $40,000. Painted a glittering white, it was heralded as "The First Boat In America To Be Lighted by Electricity," and its railings along the second and third deck were so ornate that it looked like a floating hotel from New Orleans. One author described the big boat as looking like a wedding cake, all tiers dripping with the white scroll work.

Up front, two tall, slender smokestacks belched out black smoke from the coal furnace in her hold, and inside, passengers were treated to an interior of mahogany with the floors of the dining room, bar, main cabins and other cabins covered with luxurious carpeting. A crew of thirty served the big steamer and its passengers who swarmed over the main deck and on to the second deck. There were three smaller decks with the wheelhouse at the very top, but passengers were seldom allowed above the first two decks except on special occasions when the *City* was at its capacity. Because it had a flat-bottomed hull, it drew little water and could pull into shore almost anywhere on the lake. After it was purchased by the Lake Minnetonka Navigation Company, it began a regular schedule of stops and cruises, based at Excelsior, to both the Upper and Lower Lakes.

There had been steamboats on the lake almost since the first pioneers arrived at Excelsior. In 1855, the first steamboat was launched on Minnetonka. It was the *Governor Ramsey*, built by Captain Charles May and owned by the Rev. Charles Galpin of Excelsior. Later it was named the *Lady of the Lake* and then became the *Minnetonka* before it was finally dismantled in 1874. The first propeller boat on the lake was the *Sue Gardiner*, brought from Detroit in 1863 and taken to Lake Pepin in 1873. Captain May always had a fleet of boats on the lake although some met a tragic fate. The *May Queen* sank at Shady Isle when its boiler exploded on June 28, 1879, and the *Katie May* met its end during a trip from Excelsior to Wayzata when the boiler exploded, killing the Captain, Charles Stoddard, engineer Albert Seamans, and injuring the pilot, Howard

Trumbull. That same year, the remains of the *Katie May* went into the *Saucy Kate*, a slightly larger steamboat and the forerunner of the *Hattie May.*

Probably the fastest boat on the lake was a ninety-foot double-decked propeller-driven steamer, the *Lotus*, which carried 300 passengers and sailed the lake from 1882 until 1896 under the command of Captain R.T. Mann. A rival to the *Lotus* was the eighty-five-foot iron hulled *Clyde*, built in 1883 by Colonel McCrory who ran a motor line to Excelsior. Later in Minnetonka's glorious history, would come the fleet of Captain Johnson with the *Mayflower, Puritan, Plymouth, Priscilla*—and, of course, the *John Alden*. They, in turn, would eventually be replaced by another fleet of streetcar boats or express boats, owned and operated by the streetcar company, which carried such names as the *Hopkins, Stillwater, Minnehaha, Como, White Bear* and the *Harriet.*

Steamboat names came and went from year to year. There was the tug, *Seventy-Six*, which had its name changed to the *Hercules, Kattie Lillinger, Austin Middleton* and *Dagmar*. Then there was the *Detective*, the *Fresco* which became the *Why Not*, the *Twin City* and the *Pilgrim*. The *Vergie* was later called the *West Point*, and the *Nellie May* became the *Casino*. The *Hawkeye* was rebuilt as the *Reindeer* and later as the *Archie*. And there were others—the *June, Phoenix, Leon Cascade, Ralph, Caroline, Signal, Alert, Flying Dutchman*, the *Minnie Cook, Uliss, Ariel*, and the *Nina* later named the *Winfield, Detroit* and, then, the *Fannie L.* There was the *Maplewood*, the *Topsy*, the *Frolic*, the *Tribune, Lula, Chicago, Patrol, Three Friends, Zulu, Nygoda*, the *Dot, Mable Lane, Geneva, Golden Grain Belt, Ypsilanti* and the *Kenosha.*

And the largest of them all was the *Belle of Minnetonka.*

The *City of Saint Louis*, however, was resting quietly in the afternoon sun on this Saturday along with the other big sidewheelers and sternwheelers at Excelsior's Municipal docks, and was only two piers away from its sister ship, the *Belle of Minnetonka*. On the second deck of the *City*, amidship on the starboard side, was the Captain's private cabin where two men were talking to the gambler, Pinky Wolfe. Pinky was seated in a heavy leather chair with Andy Ross seated, facing him, at his left. The skipper, John Stark, was standing with his back to the other two as he fixed the gambling man a drink from a small commode. "I knew you liked Scotch, Pinky, so I had some sent up from the bar," John said. He added two small, uneven chunks of ice to the glass of beer and John also poured a glass from a large pitcher for himself.

"I could never see why anyone would want to drink that stuff," said Pinky. "At least not while there was any booze around to drink." John turned to speak when there was a knock at the cabin door.

"Come in," he said. The door opened and a young deck hand stood in the doorway.

"Sorry, sir, but we're not quite sure how to re-string those bow guy-wires to the boiler deck and——"

"I can show you from up here," said the captain who excused himself and left the cabin door half open as he stepped outside to issue instructions to the deck hand.

Pinky Wolfe sat quite still, holding the glass of Scotch in his left hand. His right hand drummed restlessly on the arm of the leather chair and Andy could not help but notice the large star sapphire ring on his third finger. Pinky surveyed the small cabin while Andy sat quietly and watched the actions of the gambler. This was Pinky's fifth summer at Excelsior and he was, by far, the most prosperous gambler of the summer corps of card sharks and professional poker players who migrated to Lake Minnetonka each spring. He did not look like a gambler. Of medium height, he had a fine physique and a ruddy complexion and looked more like an athlete than a man who made his living at the card table. Most men did not regard him as very good-looking, but women found him attractive. His large eyes were surrounded by large dark shadows. His nose was strong and pointed, and he nearly always had a slight smile on his face, even when losing in a hot poker game. Pinky had made the White House his headquarters these past two years. Andy wasn't quite sure whether they called him "Pinky" because of his reddish complexion or because the gambler's hands were immaculate with nails trimmed and groomed perfectly and skin scrubbed clean, almost pink. The truth of the matter was that his family had called him Pinky since the day he was born because he was such a pink baby.

Before the two men could speak, John Stark had stepped back into his quarters and picked up his glass of beer. "I suppose you know why we've asked you to come here," John said to the gambler.

"Of course," said Pinky. "But I must warn you before you go any further, that I have no qualms about taking Andy's money here, but I cannot accept a bet from you, John." Both John and Andy were astonished by the gambler's remark but before either could speak, Pinky shrugged his shoulders and went on. "Like I say, in all good conscience, I could not accept money from the captain of the *City* to be put down on the *Belle* in Monday's race. You'll have to take your money somewhere else."

Still standing, John Stark held out his hand as to hold off the gambler from any further comment. "Just a minute, Pinky. You don't understand."

"No," Andy added. "We've pooled our money all right, and we want to make a bet with you on the Fourth-of-July race. But—"

"But we want to bet on the *City*!" John interrupted.

There was a moment of silence and then Pinky spoke. "I guess I DON'T understand." He paused again. "What makes you think this boat can win? It's only won a single race against the *Belle* in the last eight tries. Why should this race be any different than the rest?"

Andy edged almost out of his seat as he replied. "Because the *City* has never had John Stark as captain during a race before."

Both men turned to John who stood standing in the middle of the cramped quarters. "That's right, Pinky. I've been on the crew during four races and I know where old Jess made some mistakes. You'd be surprised what one or two errors in judgment will do to you when you're heading for home with a full head of steam. And remember that we'll have a sober captain here. I understand that Loos has been hitting the bottle pretty good these past few weeks. Yes, sir. We just think we can win it and we're ready to put our money on the line. If you don't want to take the bet, we'll find someone else."

Andy chimed in. "We have $5,700 between us, Pinky, and we're ready to bet it all! We'd rather make the bet with you than anyone else because we know you'll give us a fair shake. And you know our word is good. If you want, you can hold the stakes."

"Hold on, hold on!" Pinky raised his hand as if he had had enough. "I'll take the bet. Don't worry about somebody holding the stakes. Your word is good enough for me."

"Then it's a deal," John agreed. Both he and Andy extended their hands to the gambler and shook Pinky's hand. John offered to fix

65

another drink but Pinky declined, thanked them both, and left.

The two young men stood in the middle of the small cabin and looked at each other. Now that the bet was made, neither appeared to have the confidence they had displayed just minutes earlier. "Well, we're in for it now, John. Let's hope we can win it," Andy said, as he finished his beer.

John stepped to the small window and looked on the waterfront. He could see the superstructure of the *Belle of Minnetonka* docked less than half a block down the shoreline. "We've just got to win that race Monday, Andy, and by God, we will!" Almost as an afterthought, he added, "Even if I have to take out a little insurance."

"What do you mean by that?" Andy asked.

"Both boats are owned by the same company so the owner wouldn't get hurt no matter who wins. And Pinky wouldn't miss the money. Hell, he wins and loses that much money in a matter of hours two or three times a week. But this is all we have, Andy, and it would be so easy—just to make sure that we would win on Monday."

Now Andy looked worried. "John! You wouldn't do anything croo————"

"If it meant the difference between winning and losing—I don't know. Christ, we've got everything we own wrapped up in this deal. And besides, no one would ever know. I got the idea the other day when I overheard a couple of crewmen talking about how easy it would be. I could slip into the water and swim over there tomorrow night and loosen the rocker-arm bolts on a paddlewheel just enough to give it some play, and by the time they headed back from Wayzata Monday, the whole damn thing would come apart."

"But they'll check that wheel along with everything else before the race, John!"

"Yes, but they'll do their checking tomorrow afternoon after their last Sunday run. Then they won't fire up again until the Fourth."

Andy paced back and forth in the tiny cabin and then sat down on the arm of the leather chair where the gambler had been sitting. "Please, John, don't do anything rash, please. If they caught you monkeying with the *Belle* you couldn't get a job on this lake as a fireman. You'd be through—and so would I!" He was almost pleading with him now. "Promise me you won't do anything until you've talked to me about it again? Please."

66

John hesitated—then nodded in agreement. "All right, all right."
He stood at the window again and looked out toward the *Belle*. Andy
rose and moved to the window, too, and then both men noticed
George Wolfe standing on the shore, looking back at the *City*. Pinky
had left the big boat immediately but once ashore, he turned and took
another good look at the *City of Saint Louis*. He was sure he could
trust the two young men he had just made the bet with. Yet he felt a
tinge of suspicion. They were almost too sure of themselves. Perhaps
they knew something he didn't know. He would have to think about
that. Then he turned and headed for the White House on the bluff
above. It was just about time to start the afternoon poker game.

8

A KNOCK on the door had awakened Frances Blair from a much-needed afternoon nap after her arrival in Excelsior. It had been a long ride from St. Louis and upon checking into the White House earlier in the afternoon, she had taken a warm bath in her private bathroom, one of three such private baths in the entire hotel. Then she covered herself in a linen wrap and lay down for a short rest. She had dropped off to sleep almost immediately and it wasn't until the porter had arrived and knocked at the door to the hallway with the rest of the Blair baggage that she had opened her eyes and went to the door.

Now she was combing out her silken chestnut-colored hair and glanced at the clothes that Emily had laid out for her to wear to dinner and to the Fourth-of-July party to be held on the *Belle of Minnetonka* cruise later in the evening. She thought of her husband and hoped that perhaps he would finish his business conferences in Minneapolis early and might arrive on a late afternoon train. She would attend the party tonight, of course, but she would enjoy it so much more if only Tom would arrive. The room was quiet, almost too quiet, and the absence of noise quickly brought to mind her two boys, Tom and Dave. They had withstood the formalities of arriving at the depot and had helped their mother and sister and Emily catch a buggy to the hotel and check into their rooms. But they had not wasted any time after that, disappearing across the road, past the Blue Line and Red Line buildings, down to the waterfront and off toward the Commons. Emily would have no trouble with them at bedtime. They would be absolutely exhausted.

As Frances put the final touches to her hair, there was another knock on the door and she simply turned halfway toward the door and still sitting at the vanity, said, "Come in, please."

There was a still moment and then the door opened and a good-looking and smartly-dressed bellboy in a spanking new White House uniform stood in the doorway carrying a wooden tray with a bottle of wine and two wine glasses. "Compliments of the White House, Ma'am. Mr. Ross sent this up to you."

"Come in, come in." Frances motioned to the young bellboy.

He left the door open and marched into the room and set the tray down on a small table near the front window. "It's a Rosé from the Rhone Valley, Ma'am." He wanted to make sure she understood. "From the Rhone Valley in France, Ma'am! Mr. Ross says this is your favorite."

"And he's right."

"May I open it for you, Ma'am? It's chilled."

"Of course."

The bellboy held the wine bottle in a large white napkin with one hand and with the other, applied a corkscrew with all of the magnificance he could muster. There were not too many opportunities for such gracious service in the hotel and he was going to take full advantage of the occasion. When he had opened the bottle, he nodded toward the empty glasses and Frances motioned him to go ahead. He poured the wine into the glass, replaced the cork, set the bottle back on the tray, bowed gracefully to Frances, and then headed toward the door.

"Young man," Frances called out. "I'd like to give you something for being so helpful." She began to look around for her purse.

"No thank you, Ma'am," the boy replied. "Mr. Ross has already seen to that. And besides, it was my pleasure." With that, he closed the door and stepped off down the hall.

Frances smiled and picked up the wine glass and turned to the window to look out on the waterfront. She sipped the wine—yes, it was her favorite—and then recalled the events of the day and their arrival at the hotel. She thought of Andy Ross and how kind and understanding he had been when she and Hillary had checked in earlier in the afternoon.

"Hello, Mrs. Blair. Welcome back to Excelsior and to the White House. We've been expecting you and your rooms are all ready."

"Thank you, Andy. It's nice to be back," Frances replied.

"I'm anxious to see Mr. Blair. Did he stop somewhere along the main street?" Andy asked.

"No—he's in Minneapolis and will join us tomorrow," she answered.

"Fine. Fine. We've been preparing reports and have arranged some meetings for him." Then Andy turned to Hillary. "Hello, Miss Blair. Emmett Markham was asking about you earlier in the day but he had an appointment and couldn't wait for the train to arrive." Hillary looked embarrassed and turned to her mother. Andy noticed a sympathetic glance from Mrs. Blair and before Hillary could speak, Frances Blair broke into the conversation.

"I think it best that we register right away, Andy. We're all tired from the long journey."

"Of course, Mrs. Blair." He turned the registration book around so that Frances could sign the register, dipped the pen in the inkwell to the left of the desk, and handed her the pen. Andy watched as she signed, "Mr. and Mrs. T.J. Blair and family," but before he could reach out for the pen, Frances had turned and handed it to Hillary who hesitated and then stepped to the registration desk herself and proceeded to register, "Mr. and Mrs. James Stockton and family."

Andy blinked, started to speak, and then caught himself and

70

simply retrieved the pen from Hillary. He felt awkward and tried not to look surprised. He began speaking but for no other reason than to fill the void in the conversation.

"Thank you," he said. "We have your same suite of rooms overlooking the lake, Mrs. Blair." He turned to Hillary, "And your rooms are directly across the hall. I'm sure you'll find them very comfortable."

At that moment, the two younger Blair boys came up the steps to the desk accompanied by a negro maid carrying a tiny infant. Andy blinked again, turned to Hillary and, then, to Mrs. Blair. He quickly regained his composure and said something about looking forward to seeing Mr. Blair again. Without waiting for a reply, he called for a bellboy and dispatched him off with some of the Blair baggage and the keys to their quarters. Both Mrs. Blair and Hillary thanked Andy and said that they would see him later in the day and then turned to follow the bellboy up the stairs to their rooms along with the two boys and the girl carrying the baby.

Mrs. Blair gazed out the window of her room as she remembered the episode at the registration desk just a few short hours ago. Yes, Andy had been most understanding. Then she realized that this was the first time since she had taken her nap that she had thought about Hillary. She had survived the first announcement of her marriage here in Excelsior and before the day was over, she would undoubtedly complete the ordeal and meet Emmett. Frances sipped her wine again and continued to stare out the window. "My dear Hillary," she thought.

Hillary had just finished feeding her baby boy and set him back down in the crib which Andy Ross had sent to the room immediately after their arrival. Like her mother, Hillary had also been reviewing the happenings of the day and was thinking of the White House manager and his embarrassment when she had signed the register. As Hillary rebuttoned her blouse after the feeding, Emily entered the bedroom from the adjoining room. "I'll change little Jamie," she said, "and see that he gets to sleep now."

"Thank you, Emily," Hillary replied. "I really haven't had time to sit down since we arrived and I would like to just relax for a little while before dinner."

"You jus' go on in the other room, Miss Hillary, an' I'll take care of things." She motioned Hillary out of the room as though she were shooing chickens. "Go on, now!"

Hillary stepped into the adjoining room, a sitting room, which had just been re-decorated with a large black and white print wallpaper, white curtains and red drapes. The black floor was covered with a grey figured rug and a closed gateleg table was set against one wall. Across the room was a large settee upholstered with red velvet which matched other obviously new chairs spaced around the room. The windows looked out on the village side of the White House and as Hillary stood at the window, she could see Excelsior's main street off to the right. The street was crowded with the summer holiday traffic—buggies, couples and families out for an afternoon walk, and wagons carrying baggage and supplies between the docks and railroad depot and local hotels. Hillary could not see down the entire length of main street, but she knew that further down the block was the newspaper office and that Emmett was there. The late afternoon sun was beginning to slip behind the green trees on the other side of main street and the storefronts on the west side of the street cast ever-larger jagged shadows across the road and wooden boardwalk.

The shadows brought a feeling of melancholy to the lovely Mrs. Stockton as she turned from the window and went to the settee where she sat for a moment and then turned slightly and buried her face in the red velvet. She had never known such sadness as now, not even her parting from Emmett almost a year ago. That parting had been made more difficult because of the previous day, the day before the Blairs had left for home. Hillary remembered how she and Emmett had taken a rowboat out on the lake in the afternoon and then pulled ashore on little Gale's Island next to Big Island, where they climbed to a grassy knoll overlooking the lake to enjoy their picnic supper. Afterwards they had just relaxed there, hidden from the lake by the tall branches and leaves of the basswood trees climbing up from the shoreline below.

"This is wonderful up here," Hillary said. "I think this is the most beautiful view there is of the lake. No—it's the most beautiful view of anywhere—anywhere in the whole world."

Emmett laughed. "You're right, Hillary—at least for the moment. But it's partly because the sun is setting over there behind Sunrise Point. Tomorrow morning the most beautiful view in the world will be from over there on that high bluff near the Excelsior Commons and beach." He pointed through the trees and across the lake just a mile to the Excelsior mainland. "When that old sun comes up and hits Sunrise Point for the first time, then **THAT** will be the most beautiful view in the world."

Hillary had spread the blue woolen blanket out on the ground and the two had swung around so that they lay there on their stomachs, looking out over the lake.

"What makes it all worthwhile, of course, is having you here to enjoy all of this with me," Emmett said as he pulled out long blades of grass, one by one. He didn't look up but continued. "And all of this will change tomorrow when you go home."

"I know." She paused. "I don't want to leave. But there is no way I can stay."

Emmett continued picking at the grass and looked out over the lake. "I love you, Hillary." He did not look at her but kept on talking. "I guess you've known that all along. But somehow, just saying it to you doesn't seem to be enough. Maybe I ought to shout it—tell everybody in Excelsior that I love you." With that, he stood up, cupped his hands to his mouth and at the top of his voice, he shouted, "I love you, Hillary! I love you!" But the last words were drowned out by the heavy drone of the steamwhistle from the *Belle of Minnetonka*. The big steamboat had just churned around the west side of Big Island and was heading home toward Excelsior. Its decks were crowded with afternoon sightseers but they could not have heard Emmett shouting even if he had been standing there on the deck with them.

Hillary laughed and tugged at Emmet's sleeve. Emmett, too, was laughing now, and he fell back to the blanket and into the arms of his lovely girl. He kissed her tenderly and then held her close and whispered, "I don't want you to go home, Hillary."

"I love you, too, my darling—more than you will ever know." She clung to him as she spoke in a soft, low voice. "I've loved you ever since we first met, Emmett."

"I'm afraid I haven't always shown how much I really care for you."

73

"I've known, I've known!" She held his face in her hands, kissed him gently and then slipped her arms tightly around his neck.

"I love you. I love you." They were holding each other tightly now as Emmett spoke again. "What more can I say—what more can I do?"

Hillary's eyes were closed and she spoke softly into Emmet's ear. "Just be with me here." And the two sank slowly back on to the picnic blanket. In the distance, the familiar whistle of the *Belle* sounded again.

The sound of a distant steamboat whistle brought Hillary back to reality and she lifted her head from the velvet settee. "I must stop this," she thought. "If only Jim and Dad would finish their business and come out to the lake tonight." Hillary wiped her eyes and cheeks with a small handkerchief. Yes, it would help if her husband were only here. He was always so understanding. Why was she crying, anyway? A lovely hotel, with her own baby, her family, and her husband about to arrive. Yes, dearest Jim had always loved her, long before she even knew there was an Emmett Markham. If he wasn't the boy next door, he was, at least, the boy down the block—her playmate as a youngster, her silent admirer as a young teenager, a member of her confirmation class and her first date. He had proposed to her at least four times, Hillary remembered. And in the end, he had agreed to marry her, knowing she was pregnant and, yet, without question. It was mid-September as the two sat on a bench in Forest Park on a lovely autumn afternoon.

"Jim?"

"Yes, Hillary."

"Do you remember the last time you proposed to me?"

"I think it was yesterday."

"No. I mean really. Do you remember?"

"I remember that you turned me down again." He paused. "I think it was just before you left on vacation."

"Do you still love me?"

74

"Of course, Hillary. That's a silly question for you to ask."

"If I were to say 'Yes,' would you marry me?"

Jim stopped kicking at the fallen leaves on the ground and turned quickly to Hillary. "You know I would, Hillary." She stared at the ground. "You're not smiling. You're not kidding, either!" "What's wrong," he asked.

"I can't lie to you, Jim. I saw Doctor Babcock this morning and I'm going to have a baby." Jim sat rigid. He did not move and he did not speak. But he looked at Hillary in disbelief. He could hear her speaking but he could not make his own mind believe that this was Hillary Blair's voice.

". . . and I haven't told anyone yet, not even Mother. I'm going to have to tell her but I cannot tell Dad." She went on. "And that's why I'm not only degrading myself but insulting you—which is even worse, and . . ."

"Hillary." Jim spoke softly as she continued, almost crying and stumbling over the words. "Hillary!" He had raised his voice just enough to make her stop talking and she looked at him, tears streaming down her smooth cheeks.

"I'm so ashamed," she said. "And I'm frightened. Not for myself—but for Mom—and for Dad. I just can't do this to him—and the Blair name."

"Hillary," he said again. "Of course I'll marry you. I love you. You know that." He put his arm around her and could feel her sobbing. "Your Dad won't have to know. No one will ever know."

"But you'll know."

"So I know. It's all right. I love you."

The thoughts of Jim had stopped Hillary's crying. She rose from the settee and moved to the window again. She had not loved him when they were married. Yet, her affection for him had grown. And now she found herself longing for her husband. She had been so unfair to Jim. She had been so unfair to so many people. Perhaps she had been most unfair to Emmett, she thought, as she gazed out of the window once again at the little town. She had deprived him of her love. And she had deprived him of one of God's greatest gifts—of knowing his own son—of being a father to a child that was rightfully his—James Thomas Stockton, Jr.

9

The longer we run a newspaper and write about people and events, the more we realize how utterly impossible it is to scratch every man on the spot where he itches the most.
—*The Minnetonka News, 1886*

THAT EXCELSIOR had a thriving newspaper in 1887 was not unusual. Newspapers had been part of the little village almost since its beginning. The first of the chain-reaction publications was *The Excelsior Enterprise* which began publication in April of 1858, just five years after the area had been settled. It was edited by Frederick W. Crosby and was the first of a long line of weekly editions which would come and go down through the years. There was *The Enterprise, The Excelsior Cottager, The Northwestern Tourist, The Excelsior Weekly, The Minnetonka Mirror, The Minnetonka News,* and later—*The Minnetonka Record.* Associated with the various publications were such names as Harry B. Wakefield, A.S. Dimond and son, Charles E. Stratton, W.H. Mitchell, G.W. Hummel and Willard Dillman."

Emmett's father, William B. Markham, had been the publisher of *The Minnetonka News* since 1872 as a summer sideline, a diversion from his successful publishing business in the east. But the *News* had done so well that the summer publication had been extended to a year-around operation when Emmett became editor. Most of the inside pages of the eight-page tabloid newspaper were pre-printed but some carried local news and advertising as did the front and back pages. Advertisements varied from Harter's Iron Tonic to a 260-page Marriage Guide. The Cullom Brothers, Minneapolis dentists, advertised "vitalized air" and "no pain" with their best false teeth with a "rubber plate" for only $8. Excelsior advertisers included the sales messages of E.F. Seamans, "House, Sign and Carriage Painter," and the local hotels and boarding houses. Front pages also carried advertisements from The White House and the Sampson House along with ads for groceries—"staple and fancy"—and for flour and feed."

Most news stories on the front page were one sentence long. "F.J. Harrison drove to Anoka Wednesday with a load of clover seed." "Mr. Ferris, who has had a very severe attack of pneumonia, is better." "J.L. Dickinson has accepted a position with the Nicollet Clothing House in Minneapolis where he will be pleased to see all his friends." "Stove wood taken in exchange for subscriptions to the *News*."

Occasionally there would be a special item—"A child is born; the doctor in attendance gets $10, the editor notes the birth and gets 0. It is christened; the minister gets $4, the editor writes it up and gets 00. If it marries, the minister gets another fee; the editor gets a piece of cake or 000. In the course of time it dies; the doctor gets $1 to $10, the minister gets another $4, the undertaker gets from $25 to $100, the editor publishes the obituary and receives all the way from 000 to 0,000 and the privilege of running a card of thanks."

Sprinkled in with the news stories were the "reader" advertisements led by a product called Rocky Mountain Tea. The ads promised:

"Girls, if you wish to be a June bride with red lips, laughing eyes, a lovely complexion, take Rocky Mountain Tea this month. 35 cents. Ask your Druggist."

Another explained that "Taken this month keeps you well all summer. Rocky Mountain Tea made by Madison Medicine Co. 35 cents." And still another pointed out: "You'll never get tired, fagged out, disappointed, unhappy or make mistakes in marriage if you use Rocky Mountain Tea," and one such reader simply stated that "it takes a severe matromonial frost to kill the orange blossoms used in making Rocky Mountain Tea."

Rocky Mountain Tea—was a laxative!

The special Fourth-of-July programs had finally gone to press late Saturday afternoon and Emmett Markham stepped on to the main street boardwalk and started down toward the waterfront. He had taken only a few steps when he saw Andy Ross approaching from down the block. And when Andy recognized Emmett in the crowd of afternoon strollers, he stepped up his pace and reached Emmett quickly.

"Emmett," he gasped, trying to catch his treath. "I've—I've got to talk to you!"

"All right, Andy. What can I do for you?"

Andy seemed hesitant to talk there on the street. "Well, there are a couple of things, Emmett, and they are very important. Can we go some place and talk?"

"Sure. How about over there?" Emmett nodded toward the Fred Hawkins Cafe and Saloon across the street.

"Let's go."

The two men stepped off the boardwalk and started across the busy street in the middle of the block. They waited for a drayline wagon to pass and then had to hurry to escape being run down by a fast team drawing a surrey with the Bennett Livery Stable insignia painted on the side. They stepped on to the boardwalk on the other side of the street, side-stepped through the crowd, and walked from the bright sunlight into the darkness of Fred Hawkins' Saloon.

EXCELSIOR

The combination bar, restaurant and pool hall, was long and narrow. At the front of the building were tables and chairs where some visitors and a number of local businessmen ate their meals throughout the day. The long mahogany bar was located on the right about halfway back and separated the eating area from the booths and pool tables at the rear of the building. Along the left-hand side of the room was a long line of booths. The front ones were used by diners and the rest by drinkers at all hours of the day and from all walks of life. It was not unusual to find a roustabout from the dock area or an employee from the livery barn stopping for a beer and rubbing elbows with a successful businessman from Kansas City on vacation. The walls were also paneled in mahogany with delicate little mirrors inset in each booth. Gas lamps were mounted along the walls at intervals and the place was capped with a high metal ceiling with intricate designs and painted white. As Andy and Emmett passed the bar, they ordered two beers from old Fred Hawkins, himself, and the two men proceeded to a back booth and sat down.

"Now, what's this all about, Andy? What's so dammed important, and why all the secrecy?"

"I'll get on with the least important, first, Emmett. It's about the race on the Fourth."

"Don't tell me you've taken to bettin'." Emmett laughed. "I suppose next you'll tell me you've bet your money on the *City*."

Andy forced a faint smile. "That's right, Emmett. John Stark and I have put our money on the *City*—and I think we can win!"

"What makes you think so? It's only won once in the last half-dozen races, Andy. You know that."

"Yes, but John Stark is going to be the captain this time and he thinks he can win it. And I think he can, too. That's why I've got to talk to you."

Emmett now sensed that Andy was serious and leaned across the booth. "Then what's wrong?"

"I'm worr. . ." Andy stopped talking as Fred Hawkins brought two mugs of beer, slapped them on the table-top and turned and left without saying a word. "I'm worried because I'm afraid that John might try to fix the race. He's got some crazy idea about swimming over to the *Belle* tomorrow night and loosening something on the paddlewheel, just to make sure there's a breakdown on the Fourth. I

80

don't like it, Emmett. It's dishonest, and it's unfair to Pinky Wolfe who's been good enough to take our bet. Pinky's always been fair to me, Emmett, and I don't know what to do. That's one reason why I wanted to talk to you. John has a lot of respect for your judgement, and maybe he'd listen to you if you'd just talk to him. We'd both have to leave town if they ever caught him tampering with the *Belle*."

Emmett listened intently to Andy's story and could see the hotel man become more worried as he went on with the details of John's plan.

"I'll talk to him, Andy. If you both think the *City* can win, then take your chances on winning on the lake. I'll see him before tomorrow night, I promise you."

"Now, what else is on your mind?" Emmett continued. "You said there were a couple of things you wanted to talk about."

Andy took a sip of his beer and answered hesitatingly. "Yes, there is something else, and I'm not quite sure how to tell you—or even if I should tell you."

"Well, come on, man, out with it. What's on your mind?"

"This is not very pleasant for me, Emmett, but somebody has to break the news to you before you walk into this thing cold. And I guess I'm the one."

"Break what news," Emmett pressed him. "What the hell's going on around here that everyone else knows about but me?"

Now Andy took a full gulp of beer, swallowed it and then took a deep breath. "You're not going to like this at all, Emmett, but here goes."

"Come on, come on," urged Emmett. He was amused, but impatient"

"Well, you know that the Blairs arrived today," Andy started.

"Of course I know that. You know that I knew that."

"Well, they arrived after lunch today and checked in and—"

"Come on Andy, I'm aware of all that. What's the matter, has something happened to Hillary?" Emmett was more concerned now over Andy's difficulty in getting to the point.

"I thought it was kind of funny when the Blairs made their reservations last month," Andy continued. "They asked for an additional suite of rooms, and I figured that maybe they were going to bring another family with them."

There was a pause but Emmett did not speak. He just kept his eyes on Andy who seemed to be having trouble choosing his words.

"Well—they brought another family all right. It's Hillary's! She's married, Emmett!"

The words cut through the dingy air and created an absolute silence for the two men facing each other in the back booth of the saloon. "What the hell do you mean, she's married?" Emmett asked angrily.

"She's married. And what's more, she has a—she has a baby!"

Emmett simply stared at his friend and could not speak. He had heard the words but he could not believe that they were being spoken. Somehow it was some kind of dream or nightmare and he really wasn't here in Fred Hawkins' place at all. It just wasn't possible that Andy Ross could sit there across from him and tell him that the girl he was in love with, the girl he had waited a whole year to see, the girl he was going to ask to marry him, was already married! And had a baby!"

Emmett finally blinked his eyes a couple of times, shook his head, and demanded, "This is a lousy joke, Andy. It's not one damn bit funny. And if you weren't such a good frie————"

"It's not a joke, Emmett," Andy interrupted. "It's the truth. She signed in this afternoon as Mrs. James Stockton and family, and a colored gal was right there, holding the little baby."

Now it was Emmett who gulped down his beer. "James Stockton," Emmett repeated. "Of course, she's mentioned his name a number of times. She grew up with him, sort of the boy-next-door. But married to him—"

"I'm sorry, Emmett. But I thought you ought to know before you walked into this whole mess on the *Belle's* cruise tonight. I just thought you should know."

"Goddam you, Andy." Emmett knew that what Andy said was the truth. But he was angry, not for what Andy was saying, but for what he had heard. They were unpleasant words, unwanted words and he wanted to strike back at their source. He reached across the booth and grabbed Andy's shirt front. "Damn you, damn you! What the hell did you have to tell me this for? A helluva friend you are. Just get the hell out of here! Go on—leave me alone! Go on before I poke you one!"

Andy knew that his friend did not mean all of the things he was now saying. But he knew that the words had to be said and that, later, Emmett would be sorry for them and be grateful that Andy had told him. The hotel manager simply slid out of the booth and said, "See you later, Emmett." Then he turned and left. As he passed the bar, he reached into his pocket, pulled out a quarter and flipped it on the bar counter. "There's for the beers, Fred. Send another one back to Emmett and see that he's left alone for awhile." Fred nodded and Andy continued on, out the front door and back on to the main street. It was getting late and it was time to get back to the hotel anyway to see that the night crew was on duty. As he started down the boardwalk toward the waterfront, he shook his head and thought, "As a newsman, I'd make a damn good innkeeper."

10

ONE OF THE WEEKLY HIGHLIGHTS of the resort season on Lake Minnetonka was the Saturday night cruise of the *Belle of Minnetonka*. Visitors and guests from hotels everywhere on the lake looked forward all week long to the Saturday night festivities aboard the *Belle* which left the Excelsior municipal docks in the early evening and returned at midnight. The gala affair included a complete dinner featuring French cuisine, a full orchestra furnishing music during the dinner hour and for dancing, and moonlight strolls on any one of the five decks of the old riverboat. The evening cruise on the Fourth-of-July weekend was a particularly exciting event and

84

the couples and parties from the hotels, the wealthy husbands and their wives, the young lovers, the gamblers, the card sharks, and the local townspeople began crowding the gangplank at the bow of the steamer very early in the evening.

The *Belle*, docked at the foot of Excelsior's Water Street, was an impressive sight as it awaited its full load of passengers for the evening cruise. Originally named the *Phil Sheridan*, it had sailed the Mississippi and Ohio Rivers for years before being moved to Lake Minnetonka. But after the *City of Saint Louis* was launched in 1881 by W.D. Washburn, president of the M. and St. L. Railway, it was inevitable that James J. Hill, powerful president of the Great Northern Railroad which served the north shore of Lake Minnetonka, would launch his own steamboat. It was not long in coming—just a year later. In 1882, the *Phil Sheridan* was dismantled at LaCrosse, Wisconsin, and hauled overland to Lake Minnetonka where it was reassembled again and completely refurbished and rebuilt for lake use. And Jim Hill had his day. When the *Belle* was launched and ready for use, it dwarfed the *City*.

Where the *City* was forty feet wide, the *Belle* was sixty. Where the *City* was 160 feet long, the *Belle* was 300 feet in length—the length of a football field. The *City* could carry 1500 passengers. The *Belle* boasted a capacity of 2,500 and sometimes listed as many as 3,000 on its purser's reports.

The paddle-boxes on the big sidewheeler rose eighteen feet out of the water and the bright red twin smokestacks poured out black coal smoke that could be seen the full distance between Excelsior and Wayzata. Painted a glistening white, the lattice-work rail framed the large open deck stretching from amidships forward to the very bow of the ship. Two more smaller decks were located behind the twin smokestacks with the wheelhouse perched on the very top. Special quarters and cabins were located on the boiler deck between the paddlewheel boxes and extended on to the stern of the big steamer along with an ornate barroom and game room. On the second deck, the main cabin space had been remodeled into a huge dining room resplendent with heavy walnut and mahogony woodwork and scrollwork and magnificent chandeliers and sidelight fixtures.

Up on the Texas deck, an open belfry housed a grand bell—a gift of wealthy southern women who had enjoyed trips on the old *Phil*

Sheridan when it sailed the dark waters of the Mississippi. In appreciation of the good times aboard the steamer, the women, mostly from New Orleans, had contributed some $650 worth of their own silverware to be melted into the casting of the giant bell which was presented to the old steamer. The bell was cast in Cincinnati and installed aboard the *Sheridan*. When the riverboat was brought to Lake Minnetonka, the bell came along. Later, it would be moved to the *City* when the *Belle* was dismantled, and by the end of the century, the old bell would be retrieved from an obscure end in an Minneapolis junkyard by an Excelsior businessman and town official, Herbert Morse, and placed in the belfry of a new Excelsior school to ring youngsters to classes for more than half a century.

Captain Lamont Loos' table was located almost in the center of the main dining room aboard the *Belle*, and his guests for Saturday evening had all arrived early, all except one. Seated at the Captain's left was Frances Blair and next to her, already nursing his second drink of the evening was Mayor Bertram. Across the round table from the captain was Mrs. Loos, a small, slight woman with graying hair who was nervously twisting her napkin in her lap. Seated to the right of the captain was Hillary Stockton and between Hillary and the captain's wife was the empty chair reserved for the editor of *The Minnetonka News*, Emmett Markham.

Captain Loos was in his early sixties and he looked like what most visitors and tourists expected a captain of a steamboat to look. He was a tall man with a physique that belied his age, and in his dress blues, he appeared much younger. His grey hair was slightly curly, combed straight back, and quite long. And his grey mustache was heavy and curled up to little points at the ends. His blue eyes could be described as almost bulging. His strong features, commanding voice and coarse laugh caused most people to be so attentive to what he was saying that a slight limp from a crippled left leg went almost unnoticed. The captain, too, had kept pace with the drinking habits of George Bertram, and he was delighted to have such lovely women as Frances Blair and Hillary as his guests for this Saturday evening cruise. The captain and the Blairs were old friends and when Tom Blair and the captain played cards together, Tom often detected chewing tobacco on the old captain's mustache or chin and would chide him for it. The captain, however, would deny that he could ever acquire such a dirty habit as chewing tobacco and quickly change the subject to drinking.

"I'm sorry that Tom got stuck in Minneapolis, Frances. I had hoped that he would be able to make tonight's party," said the captain.

"I'm sorry, too," replied Frances. "He so enjoys these evening cruises and his visits with you."

The captain turned to Hillary, "And when is your young man arriving?"

"He's with Dad," Hillary explained. "But I'm hoping that they will both be here in the morning."

"I'm anxious to see your new baby," Mrs. Loos joined in. "I'll bet that you and your husband are so proud—"

"Now let's not get started talking about babies and dirty diapers," the captain broke in. "You women can talk about that some other time. Tonight we celebrate the weekend and the Fourth! Right, Mayor?"

Hillary realized that Mrs. Loos was trying to be friendly and she noticed that she had obediently accepted her husband's interruption without question and now sat quietly across the table. Hillary had a feeling that Mrs. Loos had been sitting quietly for years.

Mayor Bertram nodded his approval of the captain's celebration plans and took another gulp of his whiskey and turned to Frances. "You look wonderful tonight, Frances. I'm glad that husband of yours hasn't arrived. Now, we'll have you all to ourselves here at this table." Frances appeared uneasy as the cigar-smoking mayor continued with a wry smile. "And of course, you're all anxious to see Emmett Markham. It'll be like old times."

Hillary had been talking to Mrs. Loos but the name of Emmett Markham had brought the conversation to an abrupt halt. The mayor was gloating. Frances knew it and was about to speak when a blast from the steamwhistle of the *Belle* blotted out conversations throughout the dining room.

"Excuse me, good people," said Captain Loos. "I must be off to get our cruise underway. But I'll be back. In the meantime, go right ahead and start your dinner. I'll catch up." Then he looked at his watch and added, "I hope that Emmett gets aboard in time."

EXCELSIOR

Andy Ross had been right. After sitting alone with two more beers, Emmett Markham had faced up to the fact that Hillary was married and was here, in Excelsior, with her husband and baby. And he was sorry for the things he must have said to his friend in the Fred Hawkins Cafe and Saloon. He had left Fred's place for his boarding house, shaved, bathed and dressed in his finest grey flannel suit with the black edging. Now he realized that he was late and might possibly miss the *Belle's* cruise if he did not hurry. Emmett ran the last block down Water Street to the lakeshore after hearing the whistle from the steamboat. He was the last to step on to the gangplank before two husky crewmen pulled the boarding ramp on to the deck of the steamer.

He hardly had time to think about what he would say or do when he came face to face with Hillary. But he was more grateful now than ever that Andy had broke the news to him in the back booth of the saloon and he was as ready as he would ever be to face the one person whom he loved—but could not have. Emmett slid past the crowds in the narrow passageway leading from the bar, up the stairs to the dining room into the main cabin of the steamboat. He stood at the edge of the crowded room, looking for the captain's table, and Hillary. There she was, her glistening blond hair, her long, slender neck—she was beautiful—dressed in a white satin gown. Emmett made his way past the other tables to Hillary and she caught her first glimpse of him as he approached her table.

She spoke first. "Hello, Emmett."

"Hillary." He paused. "You look lovely. I'm so glad to see you." There was another awkward pause and Emmett suddenly noticed the others at the table. His eyes met the smile and the hard stare of Mayor Bertram across the table, and Emmett remembered that same look on the mayor's face when they had met at lunch time. Of course, he thought, he knew all along.

Rose Fortier set the last clip into her hairdo and made a final survey of herself in the mirror before leaving to meet John Stark. She was wearing a black lace gown, sleeveless and with a low, square back. The skirt had a cinch top which was accented by a tightly-laced corset underneath. Corsets had become the favorite subject for idle conversation and social arguments at teas, in the newspapers, the ice cream parlor and across the evening poker table. Those denouncing the frightening looking undergarment maintained that by compressing the solar plexus, the corset affected a woman's mind and lowered her moral character. The "supporters" of the "latest style to a womanly figure and curves" pointed out that by supporting the internal organs favoring thoracic breathing and preventing consumption, the corset had proved itself to be woman's best friend. But Rose was neither worried about her character nor her health.

Satisfied with her appearance, Rose whirled away from the mirror and made sure that her room was in order before she left. The little room was one of the third-floor cubicles on the rear side of the White House where the summer help lived. But most of the time, the small living quarters were so warm that the employees spent as little time as possible there. Rose skipped past her cot, closed the door behind her and started down the hall toward the back stairs. She passed the open door of the room next to hers where Minnie Jacobs and her partner, Madge Phelps, were enjoying a cool drink from their latest haul of left-over booze. The two were the only employees on the third floor who didn't seem to mind the heat and they would sit there into the early hours of the morning, still dressed in their hotel uniforms, barefooted, drinking and telling stories of their younger days and hotel experiences. Their voices drifted out into the hall as Rose passed.

"And then I told that old son-of-a-bitch that I didn't mind cleanin' his room and makin' his bed. Or even havin' a drink with 'em, but my services for the hotel didn't include what he had in mind!" With that, both Madge and Minnie broke into uncontrollable laughter which Rose could still hear as she neared the second landing of the back stairs. In a matter of minutes, she was out the main-street entrance of the hotel, had crossed the back lawn and continued down the boardwalk toward the lakefront. She crossed Lake Street, which ran parallel to the shoreline, and then cut across a wide, grassy area near the waterfront, past the Excelsior town bandstand, and went on along the shore toward the *City of Saint Louis* just a half-block away.

John Stark was waiting for Rose at the gangplank and helped her step across the runway to the deck of the steamer which lay quietly docked for the night, almost completely dark except for a dim light in the wheel house and a faint glow of light rising out of the passageway which led to the boiler room in the hold. He led her along the main deck and then up the stairs, two flights, to the hurricane deck where the young captian had already arranged for a pony of cold beer, glasses, sandwiches, and potato salad, all spread neatly on a small table in front of a deck lounge.

"Oh, Johnny," Rose exclaimed. "What a wonderful surprise! I'd prefer this to dinner on the *Belle* anytime."

"I was hopin' it would all right, Rose." John was apologetic. "I haven't seen you all week and I guess I just wanted us to be alone tonight."

"I know, John, I've missed you, too."

The two stood face to face without speaking and then he put his arm around her small waist and drew her to him. "I love you, Rose," he whispered. "And I want to marry you. But I can't ask you to marry me—at least not yet—at least not until—well, I'm hopin' that I won't have to put this off any longer—longer than this weekend. He kissed her softly and she responded by sliding her arms around his neck. They didn't even notice the gay lights of the *Belle* as it passed the stern of the *City* on its way out to the main lake. And the music from the *Belle's* main deck drifted into the growing darkness—leaving the two lovers alone with only the sounds of the constant ripple of waves lapping at the siding of the docked steamer.

It was near midnight when the *Belle of Minnetonka* steamed into Excelsior Bay with its deck and cabin lights reflecting on the dark waters. Emmett and Hillary had left the captain's table to take a stroll along the top deck, leaving Frances and Mrs. Loos to cope with the captain and the mayor, both of whom had had more than their share of liquor for the evening. It had been an awkward night for both Hillary and Emmett. She had made no attempt to explain what had happened, and Emmett had not pressed the matter. As they strolled along the rail toward the bow of the boat, Hillary finally spoke of her marriage for the first time to Emmett.

"He's a fine man, you know."

"Yes, I know. You mentioned him so many times over the past few years."

"I meant to write, Emmett. But neither of us has ever been very good at writing. And a letter seemed so inadequate."

"I still don't understand." Emmett shook his head. "I—"

"Please, Emmett. I've known Jim a long, long time—long before I ever met you." She paused. "When he asked me to marry him, I guess I realized then that I had loved him all these years and hadn't even known it. I'm Mrs. James Stockton now, Emmett. And I'm a mother, too. All the explanations in the world won't change anything!"

"I know that, Hillary. But I also know that I still—"

Again Emmett was interrupted. This time by the familiar and almost deafening noise of the steamwhistle which sounded the arrival at Excelsior and the end of the evening cruise.

Mayor Bertram was the first to rise from the captain's table and say his goodbyes for the evening. After shaking hands with Captain Loos, he bid goodnight to Mrs. Loos and turned to Frances Blair. "I've enjoyed our visit tonight, Frances. It's always a pleasure to talk over old times with a schoolmate and, as I said before, perhaps we will have an opportunity to visit again while you're here. We may even have more things in common besides Grinnell."

The squinting, smiling little man in the rumpled suit shifted the cigar in his mouth, nodded to everyone, and was lost in the crowd which was now making its way toward the outer doors of the spacious dining room. Frances was uneasy. She did not like the little man and she liked him even less after tonight. She would be happy when Tom arrived tomorrow. She did not hear the captain ask her if he and Mrs. Loos could escort her to the hotel and he had to ask a second time before her thoughts turned away from the unpleasant Mr. Bertram.

"Oh yes, of course," Frances answered, "but, if you'll just see me to the dock, I'm sure that Emmett will walk both Hillary and me back to the hotel."

"We'll find those two on deck, I'm sure," replied the captain. "Come."

There was a surprising number of people standing along the shoreline near the Excelsior municipal docks as the big steamer churned into its home base at the foot of Water Street, lights bristling on all decks and the sounds from the two giant paddlewheels almost drowning out the music on the main deck. Gas lights along the dock area added enough glow to make the hour appear as festive on shore as it was on the *Belle*.

Standing in the crowd, awaiting the docking of the giant steamboat, was a brown-haired young man, dressed in a dark business suit and carrying his hat. He was Jim Stockton and he had arrived at the Excelsior depot only a hour-and-a-half ago. He and his father-in-law had completed their business in Minneapolis and the two of them had decided to join their families as quickly as possible. The last train to Excelsior arrived at 9:25 p.m. and the two men had gone directly to the White House. Tom Blair was still there, relaxing with a drink in the suite of rooms occupied by him and Frances and the two boys. Jim was more anxious to see Hillary, however, and after checking with Emily and making sure that the baby was fine, he had stopped by the Blue Line Cafe for a drink and then walked down the steps to the dock area as the steamwhistle sounded the arrival of the *Belle* from its Saturday night cruise.

In a way, Jim Stockton was glad that he was standing on the shore-line instead of on the deck of the steamboat. He didn't know how to swim and he was uncomfortable around water—especially lakes. Now he scanned the decks and the rails, looking for his wife as deck hands flipped bowline knots around the large dock pilings, pulling the dock ropes tight from the steamboat. The passengers were pouring off now, crowding the gangplanks and shuffling on to solid ground again. Jim began to move forward, still looking for Hillary and being bumped and shoved by the crowd moving away from the gangplank and starting toward the Blue Line, the White House, and the main street. Then he saw her—standing on the second deck, talking to a man. They were face to face and he was holding one of her hands with both of his. They were talking, paying no attention to the passengers pushing by them toward the stairways leading to the main deck. Jim stopped and watched. He knew who the man was. Emmett Markham. He was younger than he had imagined him to be. And—Hillary reached up, kissed him on the cheek and quickly turned and left Emmett standing at the rail. Jim watched until she disappeared into the crowd and he began to move forward again when he heard his name.

"Jim, Jim—over here," called Frances. Jim saw his mother-in-law as she turned to say goodnight to Captain and Mrs. Loos. Then she made her way toward Jim and the two met along the shoreline and embraced. "Hello Jim—it's so good to see you. Where's Tom?" she asked.

"He's back at the hotel. He was tired and said he'd fix himself a drink and wait for you there. I thought I'd come down and meet you and Hillary."

"I'm glad you did, Jim. Hillary will be right along," Frances explained. "She's been on deck with Emm—" Frances caught herself, but it was too late. She realized at once that there was nothing to hide, but at the same time, she knew how obvious she had been. "Hillary's been on deck with Emmett Markham." There was silence. "He was a guest at the captain's table, too," she added in explanation.

Jim Stockton simply smiled and nodded understandingly.

EXCELSIOR

On the deck of the *Belle*, Emmett had tried to explain his feelings to Hillary and perhaps learn how all of this could happen to the girl he loved. But Hillary had not wanted to listen, nor did she want to explain anything to him. She had simply thanked him for a nice evening, kissed him on the cheek, and was gone—leaving the newspaperman standing at the rail. He watched the gangplank and, in a minute or so, he could see Hillary emerge from the lower deck, cross to the shore and go into the crowd. Then she was running, pushing, shoving and finally ran into the arms of a well-dressed young man in a dark suit. The two of them embraced and Emmett could now see Frances standing along side of the couple. Emmett watched as the two spoke to each other, embraced again, and then headed for the street and the hotel up the hill. As they turned to leave, Hillary's husband took one last look over his shoulder at the upper deck and the eyes of the two men met for the first time. It would not be the last.

The pocket watch showed 12:28 when George Bertram lifted it out of his vest pocket and set it on the night stand beside his bed. The pudgy mayor sat, barefooted, on the edge of his bed in the darkness of his room and proceeded to disrobe. He dropped his shirt on the floor beside his bed and then sat quietly there in his undershirt and pants, chewing on his cigar and causing on occasional warm glow to spread across the room with each puff. The mayor reviewed the happenings of the day as he sat there in the darkness, his thoughts wandering from his letter with the information about Hillary Blair, his meeting with Emmett Markham at noon, and the evening cruise with Frances Blair. His thoughts returned to the present, however, with a light knock on the door. "Come on in, the door's always open," he called out.

94

The door to his apartment opened slightly and a slice of light from the outer hall knifed across the room. Then the door opened wider and Rose Fortier stepped inside and closed the door behind her, shutting out the hall light. She stood there for a moment with her back against the door and her hands behind her, holding the door knob.

"Hello, Rose," said the mayor in a quiet, friendly voice. "You're right on time."

"Yes," came the answer from the pretty brunette. She moved away from the door and into the darkness of the room. As she moved toward the bed, the glow from another puff of Bertram's cigar gave enough light so that Rose could see the mayor sitting on the edge of his bed in his underwear, his clothes lying on the floor next to his reddish feet. She stopped at the foot of the bed and stood there for a moment. Then she unbuttoned the bodice of her black lace dress and let it drop to the floor.

Sunday, July 3

> *O God, our help in ages past,*
> *Our hope for years to come,*
> *Our shelter from the stormy blast,*
> *And our eternal home.*

ALL THREE CHURCHES in Excelsior found their pews filled to the very last row each Sunday morning during the summer tourist season. Largest of the church buildings was the Excelsior Congregational Church, and almost as big was the new Methodist Church. It was easiest to fill Trinity Episcopal Chapel which was located across from the Excelsior town hall. Trinity was the smallest of the houses of worship.

The parish of Trinity had been organized the very year that the Excelsior Pioneer Association arrived at Lake Minnetonka in 1853. Two years later, a log church building was built on neighboring St.

Alban's Bay. The Rt. Rev. Jackson Kemper, Missionary Bishop of the Northwest, consecrated the little log building, and the parish continued to worship there for the next five years. The settlement's sawmill burned down, however, in 1857 and, by 1860, the community of St. Alban's had begun to dwindle. The Civil War took most of the young men away from the south side of the lake and yet the neighboring town of Excelsior seemed to be thriving and growing. So it was decided to move Trinity parish across the bay to Excelsior where a new building was started in 1862. The walls of the new little chapel were made of lakeshore stones, Shakopee lime, and sand from the shore of Lake Minnetonka. A year later, the church had been completed at a cost of about $1,500. Because of the Indian uprisings in southern Minnesota, a stockade was constructed around the little church to protect citizens from the possibility of attack, an attack which fortunately never came. The stockade had since been dismantled.

The little church building had been fashioned after a typical English chapel with a high-pitched roof and four tall, narrow cathedral windows on each side. At the front entrance there was a small vestibule and atop the high peak roof at the church front was a gold wooden cross. A small sacristy had been added near the back of the church on the right hand side of the equally small chancel.

Inside, the pioneers of twenty-five years ago had done their job well. Trees were felled on the hillside and hewn into beams with axe and adz. Pews were carpentered from boards sawed from basswood trees, and the ceiling above the cross-beams was paneled and colored with a dark stain. Because the chancel was so small, the choir stalls were located in the nave of the church building and church-goers sitting in the front pews on Sunday morning could easily get the feeling that they were members of the tenor section. At the right of the chancel was the half-circle pulpit and on the left was a smaller lectern from where the lessons were read each Sunday morning. Extending across the little chancel was a small, dark-stained altar rail which could accomodate about eight people kneeling at one time when the common cup was administered for Holy Communion. Behind the rail was a small altar table bearing two sets of candelabra and a small gold cross. A stained glass window behind the altar table was set off with these words on the wall, curved across the top of the window, *Worship the Lord in the Beauty of Holiness.* A second sentence was found on the high wall over the entrance to the chancel, *Surely the Lord is in this Place.*

And surely He was. There was a stamp of honesty here and those who came to Trinity also came to feel that trowel and plane were plied with a spirit of reverence, that the builders were attended by a sense of permanence, and although they would soon pass, their work would long endure.

Emmett Markham had been an Episcopalian all his life and he and his father had attended Trinity services each summer through his boyhood days. The past few summers had found Emmett attending church at Trinity with the Blairs, who were members of the Cathedral Church in St. Louis. But this Sunday morning, Emmett had arrived at Trinity Chapel earlier than usual and sat near the front of the church on the left side of the center aisle. By the time the Blairs and Hillary and Jim Stockton had arrived, the church was so crowded that they could not all sit together. Mr. and Mrs. Blair and their two boys squeezed into one pew on the left while Hillary and her husband sat across the aisle and back a row or two. In the very last row of the church sat mayor George Bertram. He wasn't an Episcopalian. But then he wasn't a Methodist or a Congregationalist, either. Yet he moved around from church to church to make sure that he had been seen on each Sunday morning, especially by those of voting age. He had not been seen by the Blairs as they entered, found their place to sit, and knelt on the small wood kneeling benches to say a personal prayer. He actually preferred either of the other two churches in town, mostly because he preferred to sit. There was too much work to being a member of Trinity's congregation on a Sunday morning what with all of that singing and kneeling and standing. But George Bertram had been drawn to Trinity on this holiday weekend for one reason—Frances Blair!

He was thinking about her when the three acolytes, a young boy carrying the cross and two more boys carrying the American Flag and the Church Flag, entered the church with the small choir and the vicar of Trinity Chapel, the Rev. Henry Horton. The serving boys wore bright red cassocks and white cottas and the choir was robed in black cassocks and white surplices. The Rev. Mr. Horton also wore the black robe and white surplice and he promptly began the service

with an opening prayer. Then came the sound of a small pump organ
from the front of the church and the choir followed the acolytes down
the narrow aisle toward the chancel, singing the opening hymn—*Oh
God, our help in ages past*. Then the priest knelt in the small chancel
and the congregation knelt on the hard kneeling benches.

"Let us humbly confess our sins unto Almighty God," said the
priest. Then the whole congregation joined in.

> *Almighty and most merciful Father; We have erred,
> and strayed from thy ways like lost sheep. We have
> followed too much the devices and desires of our own
> hearts. We have offended against thy holy laws. We have
> left undone those things which we ought to have done;
> And we have done those things which we ought not to
> have done; And there is no health in us. But thou, O Lord,
> have mercy upon us, miserable offenders. Spare thou
> those, O God, who confess their faults. Restore thou those
> who are penitent; According to thy promises declared
> unto mankind in Christ Jesus our Lord. And grant, O most
> merciful Father, for his sake; That we may hereafter live a
> godly, righteous, and sober life, To the glory of thy holy
> Name. Amen.*

The priest arose and made the sign of the cross as he spoke the
Absolution. The congregation remained kneeling and then followed
by reciting the Lord's Prayer. Now the congregation stood to sing the
Venite.

> *O Come, let us sing unto the Lord; let us heartily
> rejoice in the strength of our salvation.......*

An unexpected, but welcome calm had come over Hillary Blair as
she stood there in little Trinity Chapel. Although she knew the
chants by heart, she did not sing. Her thoughts carried her back to
yesterday. The journey on the train had been a very unpleasant
experience for her, and she thought of her embarrassment at the
hotel and on the steamboat last evening. Her inevitable meeting with
Emmett was even worse than she had expected, at least for her. Now,
she realized, for the first time since she had left St. Louis, she felt
comfortable, here in Trinity. But she was still unhappy, even with her
husband here, standing next to her. She had hoped that was all she
needed and she had believed that yesterday in her room. But seeing
Emmett last evening changed all of that again. I still love him, she

admitted to herself. No matter what has happened, I still love him—and he loves me. I have made such a mess of things, and there's no one to turn to. No one can help me. My husband? No, that was out of the question. Mother? No. Dear, understanding Mother. She has already had more than her rightful share of this grief. Hillary thought of her father, and for the first time, the pangs of resentment began to swell inside her. Dear Father, the one whom we all adore, the one whom we would do anything for, the one who is responsible for me being here now. Yes, dear Father, dear stupid Father! So hopelessly unaware of other people's problems, even his own family's. I should have told him right at the beginning, she thought. Why didn't I tell him? Why didn't I tell him! She was sinking in the depths of her own desperation now and as the singing around her neared its end, she whispered ever so softly, "God help me! God help me? Oh please, God, help me!"

The priest announced, "The Psalm for today, the Fourth Sunday in Trinity, is Psalm number seventy-five found on page four hundred and eighteen of the Prayer Book. Psalm number seventy-five." There was a pause while those crowded into the church thumbed through the pages to page 418. Then the priest and congregation alternated in reading the Psalm.

The reading was followed by a second canticle and the Rev. Mr. Horton moved to the lectern and asked the congregation to be seated.

Here beginneth the twenty-second verse of the third chapter of the Book of Lamentations. It is of the Lord's mercies that we are not consumed, because his compassions fail not. They are new every morning; great is thy faithfulness. The Lord is my portion, saith my soul; therefore will I hope in him. The Lord is good unto them that wait for him, to the soul that seeketh him. It is good that a man should both hope and quietly wait for the salvation of the Lord. It is good for a man that he bear the yoke in his youth. He sitteth alone and keepeth silence, because he hath borne it upon him. He putteth his mouth in the dust; if so there may be hope. He giveth his cheek to him that smiteth him; he is filled full with reproach. For the Lord will not cast off for ever: But though he cause grief, yet will he have compassion according to the multitude of his mercies. For he doth not afflict willingly nor grieve the children of men. Here endeth the First Lesson.

The congregation stood again to sing the Jubilate Deo.

O be joyful in the Lord all ye lands.....

Tom Blair was particularly happy this Sunday morning. Except for his oldest son, he had all of his family surrounding him at his favorite place, Excelsior. He was pleased with himself. He had shown Jim how to complete their business in town yesterday with a minimum of effort on his part. Now he was free, or almost free, for the next few weeks. Yes, there would be conferences with Andy at the White House and with Roger Bingham out at the Lake Park Hotel. But they were so competent and eager to satisfy him and the M. and St. L., that their reports would be unquestionable. It would simply be a formality, going through the motions of the business meetings. Perhaps he would take a quick run up to the Lake Park this afternoon to let Bingham know he was here. But enough of business, now it was his family. The boys would certainly like it here and little Emily would keep an eye on them, and his grandson. My, he was proud of that little Jamie. Of course it was a little early to travel so far with such a little one. But he was a true Blair, that little fella, and Hillary would perk up some after a few days rest. She's just tired, that's all. Yes, sir. It was mighty pleasant to have everyone together here. And wasn't it nice that Hillary had a chance to see that young Markham last night. Mighty fine young man. Bet he was surprised to hear about Hillary and Jim. Tom Blair's thoughts went rambling on and he did not even hear the words being read by the Rev. Mr. Horton.

Here beginneth the twenty-fourth verse of the tenth chapter of the Book of Matthew. The disciple is not above his master, nor the servant above his Lord. It is enough for the disciple that he be as his master, and the servant as his Lord. If they have called the master of the house Beelzebub, how much more shall they call them of his household? Fear them not therefore; for there is nothing covered, that shall not be revealed; and hid, that shall not be known. What I tell you in darkness, that speak ye in light: and what ye hear in the ear, that preach ye upon the housetops. And fear not them which kill the body, but are not able to kill the soul: but rather fear him which is able to destroy both soul and body in hell. Are not two sparrows sold for a farthing? and one of them shall not fall on the ground without your Father. But the very hairs of your head are all numbered. Fear ye not therefore, ye are of more value than many sparrows. Whosoever therefore shall confess me before men, him will I confess also before my father which is in heaven. But whosoever shall deny me before men, him will I also deny before my father which is in heaven. Think not that I am come to send peace on earth: I came not to send peace, but a sword. For I am come to set a man at variance against his father, and the daughter against her mother, and the daughter in law against her mother in law. And a man's foes shall be they of his own household. He that loveth father or mother more than me is not worthy of me; and he that loveth son or daughter more than me is not worthy of me. And he that taketh not his cross, and followeth after me, is not worthy of me. He that findeth his life shall lose it: and he that loseth his life for my sake shall find it. Here endeth the Second Lesson.

When Emmett had entered the small Church this Sunday morning, he had knelt to say the usual prayer. He had continued to kneel and ask for God's help in understanding what had happened to him since yesterday. The girl whom he loved had come back, but not to him. She was married, she was a mother, and she did not want to offer any explanations to him. The sharp, keen senses of this young newspaperman had suddenly gone dull. He was confused. He could not get any answers from Hillary, even after spending four or five hours with her last evening aboard the *Belle* And in the bargain, Emmett had not been particularly friendly to a truly good friend, Andy Ross. I'll not shrug this thing off, he thought. Someone has to put me straight and, if not Hillary, then who? Frances Blair. Yes, of course. She had always been kind to Emmett and understanding about his relationship with her daughter. Yes, he would find Frances later today and talk to her. She would clear this whole thing up. Maybe then he could make some sense out of this weekend, a weekend he had so looked forward to, one which had turned into a nightmare.

There followed more chanting and the recitation of the Apostles' Creed and appropriate prayers for the day. The Rev. Mr. Horton, kneeling in the chancel, continued:

> *O God, the protector of all that trust in thee, without whom nothing is strong, nothing is holy; Increase and multiply upon us thy mercy; That, thou being our ruler and guide, we may so pass through things temporal, that we finally lose not the things eternal. Grant this, O heavenly Father, for the sake of Jesus Christ our Lord. Amen.*

The priest again asked the congregation to sit and he then made the usual Sunday morning announcements, welcoming the visitors, and reminding them of next Sunday's services. The Rev. Mr. Horton had originally served Trinity only in the sumer months from his post as an assistant in a Minneapolis parish. But for the past two years, he had become a full-time, year-around priest at Trinity and had been so successful that he was now to be called on to leave Trinity—and Minnesota. Although his parishioners were not yet aware of it, he had been asked to become chaplain at West Point Military Academy in the fall. He had already accepted, but he had not made a public announcement. He was a handsome man with a receding hairline and slightly graying. He was about fifty years old but the glasses he wore made him look older. He was loved by his own parishioners and the rest of the community as well, and it was going to be difficult to tell his parish of his plans. A scholarly man, he would do well at West Point, but both he and his attractive wife, Martha, would be missed in Excelsior.

Mayor Bertram was relieved just to sit down and listen to the announcements. My God, he thought. I'd forgotten how much damn gettin' up and sittin' down and kneelin' and standin' these Episcopals do! The mayor had been so busy keeping up with everyone around him that he had little time to watch Frances Blair or think much about her. But he was thinking about her now. And his were not the

104

thoughts to be found within the house of God. Just why Hillary Blair had married someone other than Emmett Markham was still nagging George Bertram. But right now he was staring at Frances Blair. She was a beautiful woman and somehow, someway, he would arrange to see her. There had to be a way, and George Bertram would surely find it. As he sat there, listening to the words of the vicar, he was unaware of just how close he was to finding the key. When he did, he would get more than he had bargained for. He was just getting settled when he found it was time to stand up again and sing another hymn, "Dammit!"

"The sermon hymn for today is number 309 in the Hymnal," said the parish priest.

God bless our native land;
Firm may she ever stand
Thro' storm and night:
When the wild tempests rave,
Ruler of wind and wave,
Do thou our country save
By thy great might.

For her our prayers shall rise
To God, above the skies;
On Him we wait;
Thou who art ever nigh
Guarding with watchful eye,
To Thee aloud we cry
God save the state. Amen.

It would have been better for Hillary and the baby if we hadn't come. That was what Jim Stockton was thinking as he and his wife sat down after the hymn. Jim was glad that he and his father-in-law had left Minneapolis last night and came directly to Excelsior. He had missed Hillary and he was concerned about her. He knew she didn't want to make the trip and he had tried to talk Tom Blair out of insisting that the whole famly come along to Lake Minnetonka. But, in the end, everyone packed up and did what Mr. Blair wanted. Even

Jim found himself doing what the head of the Blair household wished. It bothered him.He had married Hillary knowing exactly what the situation was. But he had not bargained for all of this obedience to her father, regardless of the consequences. As he sat down, Jim glanced at his wife and knew how upset she had become. If everyone would just leave her alone for a few days, perhaps she'd find herself again. If not, Jim had decided that he would talk to Frances. Maybe it would be best if Hillary and Jim and little Jamie left Excelsior early and headed back for St. Louis. Whatever was best for Hillary, that's what they should do. That's what they should all do. He hoped that Emmett Markham felt that way, too.

Two elderly men passed the collection plate following the Rev. Mr. Horton's sermon, and the congregation knelt once again for the concluding prayers offered by the clergyman from the altar. He announced the recessional hymn and everyone stood to sing as the organist began to play. Then the choir filed out of the choir stalls, bowed toward the altar and came down the aisle followed by the clergyman.

Frances Blair had found solace in the Morning Prayer service at Trinity.She had dutifully participated in the service, she had listened to the reading of the lessons, and she had hoped that others in her family had gained as much as she had from the words of the liturgy and the sermon of the vicar. She had been so concerned about her family, especially Hillary, that she was mentally and emotionally exhausted when she arrived at Trinity on Sunday morning. But in this hour, Frances Blair's failing drive and vitality had been replenished. She had prayed to God that she and her whole family would be able to live from day to day in the glorification of God and that, in doing so, He would have mercy and forgiveness for all of those who had a part in the unhappiness and sadness which had been dormant these many months, the unhappiness which had once again emerged since arriving in Excelsior. The choir came by and Frances nudged her two boys to remind them to bow their heads as the Crucifer marched past them. It was a new day, now, and she once again had the strength and the will to do almost anything necessary for the welfare of her family, and especially for her daughter. Hillary had already suffered enough, Frances thought. It must end—and soon.

The Son of God goes forth to war,
*   A kingly crown to gain;*
His blood-red banner streams afar:
*   Who follows in his train?*
Who best can drink his cup of woe,
*   Triumphant over pain;*
Who patient bears his cross below,
*   He follows in his train. Amen.*

12

WHEN JOHN STARK was growing up, he was unaware of how poor his family was or how much money some of his neighbors had. John's dad had worked as a driver for a dray line in Excelsior and, when John was very small, he had dreamed of becoming a driver of a dray line team. When he was six or seven years old, he asked his dad for a job.

"Not this year, John," said his bearded father. "You come around to the barn next spring and we'll see."

Well, John came around the following spring but he was still too small. So he began to hang around the docks where he could at least tie and untie the mooring lines for some of the boats that pulled into

Excelsior. By the time he was twelve, he was one of the best fishing guides on the south shore and probably knew the lake better than some of the old hands who had been around for years.

Young Stark didn't seem to mind, or even notice, that his family didn't have very much money. His mother did a little sewing for a few of the ladies who lived over on West Lake Street on the bluff. And his father always made enough to feed and clothe his small family and still have money left over at the end of the week to bring home a pail of beer on Saturday night. The three of them used to go for a buggy ride on Sunday afternoon with a rig from the livery barn that also owned the dray line. His dad could get the horse and buggy free and it was always a pleasant way to spend a Sunday afternoon. But when John started rowing boats and pointing out good fishing spots to lake visitors, his Sunday buggy rides were numbered. The family rides stopped, of course, when his dad keeled over one day from a heart attack and died before Doc Perkins arrived. John used to take his mother for a boat ride occasionally after that, but she preferred to stay pretty close to home and continued to take in sewing. It was something she enjoyed and did well.

The folks of some of John's boyhood chums were a lot better off than the Stark family, but it didn't seem to matter to John. He could run faster than most of the other kids, could swim better and further than all of them, and knew the lake better than anybody. It wasn't until John was 17 and thinking about buying a small boat that he realized how poor he really was. Up until then, he had no idea how much a boat was worth. But when he found that his savings, nineteen dollars and twenty-six cents, were simply not enough to get into the boat business, John made up his mind to do something about it. It didn't take long for some of the captains of the large steamers and the excursion boats to recognize John's knowledge of the lake, and each new job brought John Stark a better financial offer and a chance to salt more money away for the day when he could buy his own boat, regardless of cost. When the young boat skipper found himself in love with Rose Fortier, the urgency of his goal to become his own boss became even greater.

The Fourth-of-July race now took on additional importance with the bet that John and Andy Ross had made with Pinky Wolfe the day before. This Sunday morning John was busy gettin the *City* ready for its Sunday cruise into the Upper Lake. It would make a stop at the Lake Park Hotel for passengers who wanted to take the short trip to Tonka Bay to enjoy Sunday dinner at the plush hotel, and then continue on to the Hotel Lafayette and other stops along the way. John stood on the dock along-side of his boat, dispatching orders to crewmen who were preparing for the Sunday visitors already beginning to gather on the green lawn along the shoreline.

"After we leave the Lake Park, I want every inch of this boat checked while we're moving to make sure that everything is ship-shape for tomorrow," the acting captain told two of his crewmen. "This is an easy run today, so we'll have plenty of time to go over everything, from the stacks to the boilers." The two husky members of the crew nodded in agreement and jumped the short distance from the dock to the main deck of the steamer as it awaited the start of the Sunday trip. John had his back to the shore and did not see the first passenger walk out on the dock and approach him. It was Pinky Wolfe.

"Good morning, John," said the gambler. "Looks like we have another sunny day for our Sunday cruise." He looked at the sky, squinted his eyes a little, and added, "Hope it's like this tomorrow. Like I say, it would be a shame to have to race in the rain."

Recognizing the voice, John turned. "Hello, Pinky." John looked up at the sky, too. "Naw—it's going to be nice again tomorrow, Pinky, and besides, it wouldn't make any difference. My boat can win it, rain or shine."

Both men laughed."

"You're a little early today, Pinky. You usually don't get down here for your Sunday trip until sailing time."

"This weekend is a little something special, John. I've got a lot of money riding on that race tomorrow and I thought I'd just take a look around today."

"Go ahead and look. We're not adding extra engines or gearing up the paddlewheels," said the young captain. "Look all you want."

"I will," Pinky replied with a wink and a slight nod.

"I'd stay and talk," said John, "but we're going to take our boat check today while we're making our trip up to Arcola, so I'd getter get goin'."

"It's all right. Guess I'll go aboard myself.""

110

The two turned back toward shore and boarded the glistening white steamboat near its bow. The Sunday trip aboard the boat was a ritual with George Wolfe. The gambling man would sleep late on Sunday morning after a long evening at the card table the night before. Then he would rise, bathe and shave and eat a light breakfast before strolling down to the waterfront for the late-morning departure of the *City of Saint Louis* for the Upper Lake. This was Pinky's day off, at least while the sun was up, and he would not sit down at a poker table until after sundown when he had returned from his Sunday excursion. He enjoyed seeing the same scenery each Sunday noon as the big steamboat paddled its way across Minnetonka. But the boat trip and the never-changing scenery were only the means to an end for George Wolfe. Upon his arrival at the Hotel Lafayette early in the afternoon, he would be met on shore by an elegant woman—Mrs. Walter Chase. A widow, the beautiful Mrs. Chase was a frequent visitor to the Hotel Lafayette even though she owned her own mansion on nearby Brown's Bay. Her husband had been a milling executive and, after his death, she spent each summer at the lake but seldom left her estate. She had broken her regular routine one weekend, however, by dining at the Lafayette on a Sunday evening and was introduced to George Wolfe by a business associate of her late husband. She was attracted to Pinky's easy, but always correct, manner and it wasn't long before she was visiting the Lafayette each Sunday. At first, the two simply talked and enjoyed dinner together in the main dining room overlooking the lake in the late evening. But their meeting time kept getting earlier until the striking Genevieve Chase, dressed in the latest fashions, would meet the early steamboat from the Lower Lake and they would board her carriage for the short ride to her own lake home, Fairmount, for a more private Sunday afternoon.

The gambler strolled along the main deck of the *City* which was still moored at the Excelsior pier. As he turned to step inside at the main passageway, he saw two crewmen climb down from the giant paddlewheel box, dragging lines and carrying tools.

"Getting her in shape for the race tomorrow?" he inquired.

"Yessir," the two young men answered in unison.

"Think the *City* can win it?"

One of the sailors looked down the waterfront toward the

magnificient *Belle of Minnetonka* and then turned back to Pinky again. "Well, sir. Everybody thinks the *Belle* is going to win. But don't bet on it." Then the two crewmen hurried off, leaving Pinky Wolfe standing there alone, mulling over what might be painfully accurate advice.

Rose Fortier had reported for work in the dining room of the White House as usual at 10 o'clock in the morning and had been told by Thelma Wright, another waitress on the morning shift, that Andy Ross wanted to see her in his office. Rose proceeded to tie on a fresh white apron as she left the dining room and crossed the lobby to Andy's office which was next to the registration desk. She stopped at the door and politely knocked.

"Come in," came Andy's voice from inside the office.

Rose opened the door, paused, and then asked, "You wanted to see me, Mr. Ross?"

"Yes, Rose. Come in, come in."

She closed the door behind her and stood there. Andy Ross was busy at his desk which was covered with small piles of papers, receipts, reports and other busy work. The office was small—with room for a good-sized desk, chair, a filing cabinet, and two upholstered chairs crowded in front of Andy's desk. The lower walls were wainscoted with a narrow, inexpensive lathing which had been stained and varnished. The upper walls were painted white and were decorated with photos of other lake hotels and trains and steam engines, undoubtedly those of the M. and St. L.

Andy looked up from his work, stood up and greeted the pretty waitress. He motioned to one of the chairs in front of his desk. She thanked him and sat down. Then Andy sat down and leaned back in his swivel chair. "How long have you been here at the hotel, now, Rose?"

"This is my second summer here," she replied.

"Do you like it here?"

"Yes, sir."

"Well——I want you to know that I am more than satisfied with your work here."

"Thank you, Mr. Ross."

There was a short, awkward silence. Rose wasn't quite sure why she was in the manager's office if he was pleased with her. Andy fidgeted with a pencil on his desk, seeming to know what he wanted to say but somewhat hesitant to say it.

"I'd like to talk to you about another matter this morning, Rose. Partly because it affects me, but mostly because I like you, and I'm speaking now as a friend, not your boss."

"Yes, sir." Rose sat still, her hands in her lap, waiting.

"There've been some rumors about you, Rose, but I didn't believe them. I just couldn't. That is, until last night. When I came down the back alley last night behind the Hawkins Hotel and Saloon and saw you come down those back stairs, I knew that the rumors were true. Am I right?"

"I've never denied them," she answered calmly.

"John's told me how he feels about you."

"I feel the same way about him."

"Then what the hell are you doing playing footsie with that goddamn George Bertram for?" Andy had jumped up from his chair and pounded his desk as he stared at the waitress.

Rose was startled. Then she looked down at her hands which she held in her lap. "I know it's hard to understand, Mr. Ross. I know I should be ashamed. Perhaps I am—a little." She looked up at Andy standing across the desk. "But if you only knew how kind he was to my mother when she was alive. And to me. While every young man in this town was propositioning me and taking it for granted that with every order of beer they were entitled to a pinch or a grab or a feel, George Bertram was the kindest, the most tender man I have ever known. He didn't so much as touch me while mother was alive."

"But he damn well has since, hasn't he?" asked Andy.

"Yes! Yes he has!" Rose's voice was rising now. "But it's not like you think. The first time it was my idea. I was—I am grateful for all he has done for me, and all he did for my mother!"

"But you didn't owe him that much! You don't have to obey his every whim. You don't——" Andy could see her trembling. He stopped shouting, moved around the desk and lowered his voice.

"What about John? What if he finds out? He loves you. You know that. What do you think he'll do when he finds out? He'll kill the bastard, Rose. That's what he'll do. And he damn well might kill you, too! Did you ever think about that?"

She put her face in her hands. She was crying and trying to speak at the same time. "I know, I know. And I don't know what to do about it."

"I'll tell you what to do about it. And for a goddamn selfish reason, too. It's important to me that John wins that race tomorrow. And if John were to find out about the mayor, he'd blow sky high! All of our savings, John's and mine, are on that race, and I don't want John to have to think about anything, or worry about anything— except beating the *Belle* on the Fourth of July. Do you understand that?"

Andy was standing over her now, not quite sure whether he was angry with her or pitied her. Perhaps it was a little of both. "If you love him, you'll promise me right here and now that this thing with Bertram is over. Right here and now!"

Rose looked up. There were tears streaking across her cheeks. "I do love John, I do."

Andy spoke more softly. "It's not just what John might do, or the money or the race. It's for your sake that I'm talking to you, too." Andy felt awkward again and paced back and forth across the small room. "You're just too nice a girl to have this happen to you. You're young, you're pretty, and you have someone who loves you and wants to marry you. That should be more than enough reason for you to promise me now that this other thing will never happen again. You don't owe him your future."

Her white apron was soiled with tears and wrinkled as Rose tried to dry her eyes. She finally stopped sobbing and looked up at Andy again, and nodded before she spoke. "You're right. Of course you're right. I've known all along, but I guess I had to have someone make me listen while they told me what I already knew." She paused a moment. "It won't happen again, Mr. Ross. It won't. I love John, and I'm going to marry him. And I'll not see Mr. Bertram again."

Andy looked relieved. He sat back on the edge of his desk and forced a faint smile. "Good. I'm glad." His voice became more business-like once more. "Now take time off to go wash your face and freshen up before you go back to the dining room. The Sunday dinner crowd will be along in another hour."

Rose, too, smiled slightly as she thanked Andy again and left. When she had closed the door, Andy stood there, looking at the empty chair where she had been sitting. Yes, he thought, she was very pretty, indeed. Pretty enough to fall in love with very easily. Perhaps another time, a different place, under different circumstances, he could have loved a woman like Rose Fortier.

Mayor George Bertram had intended to visit with Frances Blair on the lawn in front of Trinity Chapel following the Sunday morning service, but Frances, Hillary and Jim Stockton were busy meeting with townspeople whom the Blairs had not seen in the past year. As a result, Mayor Bertram had to settle for small chit chat with Tom Blair. On any other Sunday he would have been looking at attractive women he could single out. But he decided to bide his time with Mr. Blair, however, in the hopes of exchanging a few words with Frances.

Tom Blair, on the other hand, was impressed with the fact that the village mayor would seek him out to speak to after church, and the elder Blair was delighted.

"Yes, Mayor, it has been a whole year since we were here and we're so happy to be back again. All of us."

"I'm sure you are Mr. Blair. I talked to your wife and daughter last evening and I understand that you are a grandfather now."

"That's right. A grandfather. And we're so proud of that little Jamie."

"I'm sure you are," added Mayor Bertram. "To tell you the truth, Mr. Blair, I didn't even know your daughter was married, let alone being a mother, until she arrived yesterday. Yessir, it was quite a surprise to some of us."

Tom Blair seemed to be the center of attention, at least to himself, and he loved it. "Well, Mayor, you weren't anymore surprised than we were last fall when Hillary and Jim just off and eloped. We were disappointed, of course, that we couldn't give

Hillary a big church wedding, but you know how young people are. There's just no stopping them sometimes."

"Last fall?" The question came in an off-hand manner from the mayor.

"In September," replied Tom dutifully. They just up and left one weekend and the next thing I knew, I had a new son-in-law. Of course, I wasn't disappointed in Hillary's choice. Jim has lived down the block from us for years, and has always been close to Hillary."

"I always thought your daughter had a likin' for young Emmett Markham," the mayor asked.

"Oh, that. Just a little summer fun," said Mr. Blair. "Hasn't seemed to bother Hillary since she returned. No, it was Jim Stockton all along. And of course, we were so happy when the baby was born. It came early, you know—about seven weeks. But it was big and healthy and got along right fine." Tom Blair was obviously pleased with himself and with his family. But the mayor suddenly became more interested in Hillary and the baby.

"When was the little tyke's birthday, did you say?" he inquired.

"May ninth," said the proud grandfather. "I think Hillary has done remarkable well to make the trip up here after only being out of the hospital since early June.

Bertram's mind was counting months and days rapidly now as he continued his conversation—remembering when the Blairs had left Excelsior last summer and recalling the conversation he had had with one of his political henchmen, Will Bates, who had seen Hillary and Emmett Markham together in the long grass on Gale's Island the day before the Blairs left for home.

"How long are you staying this year," probed the mayor, seemingly changing the subject.

"Same as always," replied Tom Blair. "We'll be here until the first of August. A little business with the hotels, you understand, and a little time to spend with my family. I always like to have my family around me, you know. Nothing like a family!"

"Yes, of course," the mayor agreed. But he had other things on his mind. An elopement by Hillary Blair. The baby coming so early. And the two summer lovers. He remembered that the note he had received from St. Louis with the news of Hillary's marriage hadn't made sense to him. There was something strange in the whole affair

116

last night aboard the *Belle of Minnetonka*, and by God what if Emmett Markham **WAS** the father and didn't even know it? Christ, this stupid Blair doesn't even know it, thought Bertram. His mind was whizzing now, methodically putting everything in place and thinking of how he could test his case on Frances Blair.

Tom Blair kept right on talking and then was interrupted by other church-goers who wanted to welcome him back. As others crowded in to shake his hand and talk, George Bertram backed off until he was alone. If he was wrong, Frances Blair would ignore him. But if he had accidentally fallen on a family secret, she could be had, and he would waste no time in trying to rattle the skeleton in the Blair family closet. He would try this afternoon.

13

THE FOURTH-OF JULY RACE between the *Belle of Minnetonka* and the *City of Saint Louis* was not the only race on Lake Minnetonka over the holiday weekend. Thousands of visitors were arriving by train and the motor line from Minneapolis this Sunday to witness a variety of sports attractions including sailboat races, shell races, and some local events on the waterfront. At least three different classes of sailing were underway before noon with the Excelsior and Deephaven Yacht Clubs racing for Indepencence Day honors. The shell races took on more of a national flavor. Some of the annual visitors from the east were entered in the races which included singles, fours and eights. The afternoon races would be highlighted by the eight-man shells because of the crew from Darmouth College which would compete against a local crew from Excelsior and two shells manned by athletes from Minneapolis. The races would start across the lake at Wayzata and the finish line would be at Excelsior.

More popular with spectators would be the local contests, and the program published by Emmett Markham's print shop listed the matches:

—*EXCELSIOR HOLIDAY PROGRAM*—

ROWING MATCH for a purse of $20 by H.H. Porter, champion oarsman of Lake Minnetonka, against any opponent except professionals. Distance will be one-half mile. Boats used to be the Harrison half-clinker. Entrance fee $1. Takes place at 1 p.m.

ROWING MATCH for ladies, purse $5.

ROWING MATCH with flat-bottom boats. Purse is $5. Entrance fee is 25 cents.

ROWING MATCH for boys 15 and under. Purse, $2.50. Entrance fee, 25 cents.

PRIVATE MATCH between L.F. Sampson and O.S. Gates for the scrub championship and a pound of peanuts. Also one between G.B. Halsted and A.S. Dimond for heavy steaks, rare done, and served without sauce.

A SWIMMING MATCH for dogs.

On the Excelsior Commons, the Gun Club would hold its weekly shoot with a new gold badge for the holiday winner. The firing would precede the baseball game which boasted a purse of $10 to the winning team. Excelsior's nine was favored to win the afternoon contest even though the visiting team from Spring Park had a "society slicker" from Wayzata pitching for them. Excelsior would be led by Willie Munn and Billy Taylor. Munn was the smallest man on the team but he could easily throw a runner out at the plate from centerfield. Taylor was missing two fingers from his left hand but never muffed a ball in his career.

None of the athletic contests nor the afternoon band concert held any interest at the moment, however, for the two youngest members of the Blair family. Tom and Dave had hurried off from the church service on Sunday morning and headed straight for the small inlet near the Commons. The little cove was half-hidden by heavy brush and foliage, and the quiet, murky water there was covered with green slime and lily pads. It was a haven for boys, the best spot anywhere for catching frogs, playing hid 'n seek, and keepin' away from your folks. It was almost noon when the two Blair boys crept back into the brush near the inlet and found the lily-pad stems which they had set out to dry the day before. Hunched down near the ground with their heads between their knees, the two boys each stuck a dried stem in his mouth and Dave struck a kitchen match on a stone to light the straws. Holding the stems between their fingers, the two youngsters crouched there in the brush, puffing away on the dried stems.

"Yessir," drawled Tom, "there's nothin' like a good smoke!"

Tom Blair sipped his coffee as he finished Sunday dinner with his family in the Marine Dining room at the White House. "Emily will just have to see that those kids get something to eat when they get back to the hotel," he said. "In the meantime, I'd like Jim to come along with me for a short boat-ride over to the Lake Park right after dinner. We won't be gone long, but I'd like to show him our other hotel."

"I'm not much for riding boats," Jim replied. He looked uncomfortable, and he kept glancing across the table at Hillary. She knew that her husband was uneasy about going out on the lake but there just wasn't anyone else to go along with her father this afternoon. Hillary was still tired from the long trip, and her mother was not eager for another cruise so soon after the one last night.

"Go ahead, Jim," Frances urged. "It really is a short trip and you'll both be back before the band concert is over."

"Sure! Come on, boy, we'll go over on the *City* and catch Captain Mann's *Lotus* on the way back. It's the fastest boat on the lake and we'll be back in no time." Tom Blair was already standing, waiting for his son-in-law.

Jim nodded. "All right. Let's go so we can get back." He laughed. He knew he was stuck and, if someone had to go along with the old man, he'd rather it be himself than Hillary or Frances.

120

"Good, good! Tom bent down and kissed Frances on the cheek. "We won't be gone too long. I just want to say hello to everyone up there and let 'em know I've arrived. I'll go up there again next week and get my work out of the way."

Jim took Hillary's hand for a moment. "You rest this afternoon. D'you hear? I'll be back as soon as I can." He turned to Frances. "You make sure she takes it easy, even if she has to miss something this afternoon."

"I'll watch her, Jim. You go along before you miss your boat."

The two men left quickly, leaving Frances and Hillary seated at the table. They both sat quietly for a moment, watching Tom and Jim disappear through the doorway.

"What are we going to do with him?" she asked her mother.

"I don't know, my dear."

"He just seems to always get his own way. I know that Jim didn't want to go up to Tonka Bay with Dad this afternoon. But he's gone."

"Be thankful your father didn't insist on you going along," added Frances.

"I know, Mother. But it's getting worse. We're all living under one roof at home—because he wants it that way. We're all here now—because he insisted that we come, baby and all. He doesn't even hear us talking half the time. He just goes right on, doing exactly what he pleases, and we just let him keep doing it! It's not fair to any of us, Mother, and it's got to stop!"

Frances looked out the windows of the dining room where she could see her husband and Jim down below at the docks, heading for the *City of Saint Louis*. "I know, Hillary," she said. "I know."

14

MAYOR GEORGE BERTRAM won his first political race in Excelsior in 1881, if not by a landslide, at least a small cave-in. It was the first time that the little village had a lawyer as the head of its town council and, for the first two years, Mayor Bertram pretty much had his own way about governing the community. In March of 1883, however, he had developed opposition from some of the townspeople, and local politics broke out into open warfare on the Saturday night before the election, the traditional night for the caucus at the village hall. Mayor Bertram had set the time for the caucus at 7:30 p.m. but failed to realize that the bulk of his support came from Excelsior merchants and businessmen who did not get through with work until eight o'clock on Saturday. The mayor presided at the caucus and tried to hold off any voting until after eight, but the opposition clamored for a vote and finally got it, winning 47 to 45. A half-hour later, the Bertram backers assembled at the hall, but it was all over. They had lost their chance to win the caucus and decided to retire to the nearby S. and S. Grocery where they went ahead and nominated their own slate—exactly the same except for the mayor who was also president of the council. Harold Banner headed the official caucus ticket and George Bertram headed the businessmen's choice. All other candidates were exactly the same. Bill Morse, the iceman; C.B. Ice, the blacksmith; and groceryman Will Bates were the candidates for the three seats on the council. Perry Rachel was the lone candidate for treasurer, Fred Powers for constable, and Tippy Smith for the park board. Both Bertram and Banner were considered "wets" by the voters and the liquor issue was once again on the ballot. When the voting was all over, Bertram had won again and continued in office, winning again in 1885.

By the time the fourth election had come around in 1887, George Bertram's law practice had kept him so busy that he wasn't sure he could continue as mayor. In fact, the pudgy little lawyer had announced that he would not run again, even though he thoroughly enjoyed his role as Excelsior's number one citizen during the tourist season each summer. The office brought with it a long list of invitations to dinners and social gatherings, all particularly attractive to the middle-aged bachelor. But the press of business had swayed Bertram to decline to run for re-election again, even though he had enough support to win and had actually done a pretty good job as mayor of the bustling little resort town. So Harold Banner was elected in March and then declined to take the job because he was already the town marshall which paid him $100 a month, and the mayor's post was only worth $15 a month. Just about everybody liked Harold Banner but couldn't blame him for refusing the newly-won job. And everyone liked George Bertram, too, and urged him to stay on as mayor.

"I am not the mayor," said Bertram, "and as much as I appreciate the honor and glad as I would be to keep the office, my resignation is in the hands of the village council. I just don't have the time," he asserted. But while he was making all of these statements, Excelsior merchants were meeting at a nearby dry goods store with legal plans to keep George Bertram in office. Will Bates explained that the law "says that when an officer of the village of Excelsior is elected, he shall hold office until his successor is elected and qualified. Harold Banner was elected, but he didn't qualify, and, therefore, the incumbent must keep right on being mayor. We're simply going to put a 'nolens volens' on Bertram and there won't be no way for him to get away from it."

Well, the "nolens volens" worked, and Bertram agreed to stay on as mayor of Excelsior for another term. Besides, it was getting on toward spring and the prospects of another "interesting" summer as chief host for Excelsior helped Geroge Bertram decide on a fourth term.

Introducing the visiting concert band from the Minneapolis Park Board at the sunday afternoon concert on the long Fourth-of-July weekend was just one of the many official duties of the mayor, and he took time for a short, but eloquent, speech to townspeople, tourists and visitors for the day, before turning the program over to the musicians. George Bertram stepped down from the open bandstand which was decorated with red, white and blue bunting especially for the holiday occasion, and headed for the concession stand and a cold glass of beer. He had seen Frances Blair arrive with her two boys while he spoke to the crowd and he would find her quickly now before the rest of her family arrived on the scene.

It was a lovely afternoon thought Frances Blair as she arrived with young David and Tom at the Commons for the afternoon band concert. She was dressed in a summer material known as Rajah and the jumper frock was extremely pretty and far more fashionable than the so-called "jumpers" or pinafore dresses worn by the young women. The long afternoon gown was set off by a narrow belt which drooped distinctly in front and which was held in place by a buckle at the back.

The Excelsior Commons was a colorful scene this day. Women wore their finest strolling fashions and hung on the arms of their escorts who were dressed in fashionable suits and top-hats despite the heat. Some of the husbands dared take their coats off to stay cool during the heat of the afternoon. The hot July sun beat down on the races and ballgames and sailboats alike. Yet Frances was right. It was a lovely sight and an exciting afternoon, and she hoped that Jim and her husband would get back to enjoy at least part of the band concert. She had left strict orders with Emily to keep Hillary and the baby in their rooms for a rest, and decided that her two youngest children could escort her to the afternoon festivities.

She had no more than found a vacant park bench near the shore and still within earshot of the band, than the boys were off to the refreshment stand and the inlet near the Commons. She was not alone for very long. When she looked up, George Bertram was standing there. "Hello Frances," greeted the mayor. "I saw you arrive just as I finished my speech. You missed it."

"I'm sorry, George," replied Frances. "I didn't realize you were on the program. But then, I should have known."

"Perfectly understandable," he answered as he stood there, smiling. "It's just that I didn't get a chance to visit with you after church this morning and I wanted to talk to you for a moment—privately."

"I wouldn't exactly call this privately." Frances looked around at the crowded scene.

"No. You're right about that," said Bertram. "But no one is close enough to hear what I'm saying, and for your sake, I hope they don't." He smiled again and his smile seemed to broaden as Frances looked up inquiringly and frowned.

"I don't know what you mean."

"It's about your daughter," he continued.

"What about my daughter?" she asked.

"And Emmett Markham!"

Frances shook her head and an ever-so-slight smile crept across her face. "If you mean that they were together on that cruise last night, Mayor, it's perfectly proper. Her husband knows. He was waiting for her on shore when we docked last night."

"I'm afraid you don't understand," replied the mayor. "I know about your daughter—and Emmett—and the baby!" He watched Frances like a tomcat stalking an unsuspecting sparrow. The faint smile was gone from Frances Blair's face now and Bertram's words had made her as sick to her stomach as a boxer who had just been dealt a carefully-aimed low blow. She tried desperately to keep her composure, to keep from going under without a fight, and as she fumbled at the ruffles on her blouse, she swallowed hard.

"I don't know what you're talking about, George."

"Oh yes you do, Frances." He pressed on. "I know about Emmett and Hillary on Gale's Island last summer, about the elopement last fall, and about the baby." Now he mixed a little Bertram finesse with the truth and added, "I also knew all of this even before you arrived yesterday."

Frances had time to recover slightly and stood to meet her aggressor face to face. "You're wrong, George Bertram. You're wrong. How could you even think such a thing?" Her voice was calm but Bertram could detect a slight waver as she spoke. "This is really not like you, George," she continued. "You're a lawyer and you ought to know better than this. I could have you in court for such lies!" She was catching her breath now, and was counter-punching bravely.

The pudgy lawyer puffed on his cigar, smiled at Frances and spoke again. "You don't mean that, Frances. You know it and I know it. As a matter of fact, I'd just as soon not tell anyone else about it at all. And I'm sure that we can work this thing out so's no one will have to know, not even Emmett, or your husband."

The voice was calm, but the words had struck the knockout blow. Frances Blair began to wilt. "I don't know what you're talking about." She looked down at the ground.

"Oh, come on, Frances. Of course you know what I'm talking about. But I tell you, there's no problem. Everyone makes a mistake now and then. I've made a few myself over the years. I'm sure you have, too. And I'm not anxious to spread your secret. I just know we can work something out." He sat down beside her on the bench.

"What do you mean—work something out?" She tried to be non-committal, but it was obvious that she had lost. Now George Bertram was ready for the terms—for the clincher. And suspicious as she was of Bertram, Frances was not prepared for what followed.

"You know how I feel about you Frances Remington Blair," the mayor asked. "I've admired you for years and to me you're more attractive now than ever. In fact, if you and I were to get together, alone, for awhile, I'm sure that I could forget all about this whole unpleasant incident."

Frances could not believe what she was hearing. It was

126

inconceivable—but it was happening. George Bertram was propositioning her. He was blackmailing her. And unless she agreed. . . . The whole idea was repugnant to her, and yet she knew that the sloppy little man was persistent, that he would finally have his way.

"How do I know that this won't simply be the beginning?"

"You have my word."

"Your word?" she asked, unbelievingly.

"I know you won't believe this but you really haven't much choice. I've done a lot of shady things in my time, Frances, and I admit that I'm a bastard. But I do have one admirable quality. In my own twisted way, I have a set of ethics. And if I tell you that you'll only have to see me once, then it will be so."

It was incredible, Frances thought. She and fat little George Bertram. He simply sat there beside her on the park bench in the middle of a Sunday afternoon and in matter-of-fact tones, did not ask her—but told her that she must go to bed with him. To anyone watching, it would appear that two old college friends were talking about their children, or the weather, or tomorrow's race. Yet, here he was, telling her there would only be one such episode. And for some strange reason, she believed what he was saying. Just as she had always given what was needed for her family, she could see no other way to protect Hillary and her grandson. And so she was ready to succumb.

"When?"

"Tonight."

"But what about my husband, my fami———"

"I don't care what you tell them. Just come to my rooms tonight. Let's say ten o-clock."

Frances answered in a whisper. "I'll be there."

The lobby of the White House was a busy place this Sunday afternoon. Emmett Markham pushed his way through the crowded hotel lobby toward the registration desk just in time to meet Andy Ross coming out of his office

"Andy," he called. "Andy—I'd like to see Frances Blair. What room is she in?"

"She's in 212, Emmett, but she has gone out for the afternoon. I saw her leave with her two boys about forty-five minutes ago."

"What about Mr. Blair? Is he in this afternoon?"

"No. He and his son-in-law left earlier to take a trip up to the Lake Park. They stopped in just after lunch and then headed for the docks." Andy paused, then spoke again, reluctantly. "Hillary's in her room, though."

"I see."

"It's two-fifteen."

"Thanks, Andy." Emmett started to move away from the desk and then turned back to Andy once more. "Andy." he hesitated. "I'm sorry about yesterday. Really, I am. You know I didn't mean what I said. And I do appreciate what you did for me. I hope you'll accept my apology."

Andy smiled. "Forget it, Emmett. I knew how you felt and I knew you had to say those things to someone. I'm just as glad it was me."

Emmett turned to leave again and Andy called out to him. "By the way, Emmett. You won't forget to talk with John, will you?"

"No, I won't forget. I plan on visiting with him later this afternoon or early evening—before it gets dark and before he can do anything he'll be sorry for. I'll talk to him, I promise." He turned once again and picked his way through the groups of visitors and tourists filling the lobby until he finally reached the stairway. As he started up the stairs, he looked back to see Andy Ross watching him from behind the registration desk.

Hillary Stockton was resting on the red velvet sofa in her room She had promised the rest of her family that she would take a nap but she had been unable to sleep. The knock on the door brought her upright. She waited. There was another knock. "Who is it?"

"It's me, Emmett," came the voice from the hallway.

Hillary arose and moved to the door quickly. Then she unlocked the latch and opened the door. Emmett stood there in the doorway.

"Hello, Hillary."

"Hello, Emmett."

"May I come in?"

"Yes, of course."

128

Emmett stepped inside. He felt awkward and he seemed to search the room with his eyes, looking for someplace or something where he would feel more comfortable. He moved toward the windows overlooking the town. "It's a nice view you have from here."

"Yes, it is." Hillary closed the door and stood motionless.

"I don't believe I've ever looked out on this side of the hotel before." Emmett looked down on the main street. "You can see all the way down to our newspaper office."

"Yes, I know."

"I must confess," he continued as he looked out the window, "I really came to see your mother, but she's not here."

"She has gone to the band concert with the boys," Hillary replied. Why did you want to see her?"

Emmett turned away from the window and looked squarely at Hillary. "Because I need some answers about you, Hillary, and I haven't been able to get them." He took a step or two towards her. "You haven't been much help—and I must know what's happened."

The young woman looked down at the floor and bit her lip as Emmett continued. "I believe I'm entitled to some answers, Hillary, and I didn't get them last night on the boat. I thought perhaps your mother would set me straight." He paused. "I'm sure this is not easy for you under the circumstances. But it has not been easy for me, either. You see, regardless of what has happened, I still love you!"

"Please, Emmett! Please!" She moved past him to the window. "I'm married, I have a son, and there's nothing more to say. Mother can't tell you anymore than that." Her voice lost some of its strength and began to fade.

Emmett turned and stood behind her now. "Hillary, there has to be more to it than that," he pleaded. I know you're married. I know you're a mother. I've seen your husband. But that doesn't change how I feel about you. I love you, Hillary, and so help me God, I cannot imagine going through the rest of my life without you. I had waited at the depot yesterday to meet you and ask you to marry me, and even now, knowing what has happened, just seeing you makes me know there could be no other one for me, except you."

Emmett's voice had suddenly become soft and quiet and as he spoke, he took Hillary gently by the shoulders and turned her around to face him. As he did so, she began to shake and as she looked up at him, she began to cry.

"Oh Emmett, I've tried not to, but I still love you!" She fell into his arms and he kissed her gently. Then he simply held her as she sobbed. "I'm so ashamed, I'm so ashamed." The two lovers stood there in the middle of the room and held each other close.

The door to the adjoining bedroom was ajar and quietly standing back from the opening was Emily. Her hands were trembling as she reached up to wipe away the tears streaming down her brown-skinned cheek.

15

DOC PERKINS was very deliberate in checking over the two young boys who were lying on a blanket near the shoreline. Frances Blair leaned over the doctor to watch as he pinched the skin down on their cheekbones with his thumb to look at their eyes. He asked both David and Tom to stick out their tongues. Then he pulled their shirts out and pushed his hand around on their bare stomachs. A small crowd had gathered to watch what was happening to the two boys.

Frances was concerned, but relieved that Doc Perkins had been nearby, watching the baseball game when the boys took sick. They had come back from the refreshment stand to find their mother visiting with the mayor, and complained of stomach pains. They not only didn't feel very good, they didn't look good either. Their faces had turned a pale green and while their mother began to question them about what they had eaten, they both turned and made a dash for the lake. They didn't make it, however, and both had vomited before they reached the shoreline. That's when Frances made them both lie down on the blanket and asked someone to call a doctor.

Doc Perkins was not only a good general practioner, he was a good businessman as well. He owned a number of parcels of property in Excelsior village including a most valuable lot and building at the main intersection of town in the heart of the business area. He was surely old enough so that he should be slowing down in his daily work, but there just didn't seem to be enough medical men to go around and, as a result, he was working longer hours now than thirty years ago when he first came to Excelsior. He knew more people, had delivered more babies, treated more families, and knew the intimate problems of more husbands and wives than anyone in town. Yet, he had never violated a confidence, had never turned down a request, and had helped a number of young men and young couples financially without so much as a signature.

Baseball, though, was his one weakness and if there was an emergency on a Sunday, it was common knowledge to look for Doc Perkins at the Commons where he would surely be watching the locals take on a visiting team. And although it miffed him that he was going to miss an inning or two of the ball game, he hurried through the crowd along the shoreline to treat the two sick Blair boys.

The doctor now patted both boys on the forehead and stood up to face Frances with his diagnosis.

"Well, doctor?"

"Don't worry, Mrs. Blair. They're going to be all right. It's true they're sick right now, but I'd suggest you just leave them here for awhile and then take them back to the hotel. They won't want to eat much the rest of the day but they'll be fine by this evening so they can see the fireworks."

The two youngsters still looked deathly sick to Frances as they lay quietly on the blanket, eyes closed, holding their stomachs.

"But what's the matter, Doctor?" inquired Frances. "Is it some kind of food poisoning? I'm sure they didn't have enought to eat or drink here to make them THAT sick."

A smile crept across Doc Perkins' face as he listened to Frances. "No, Mrs. Blair, it's not any kind of food poisoning. And, you're right, it has nothing to do with what they might have consumed here." He scratched his head as he spoke. "I'd say they're suffering from a common boyhood disease called—lily-pad-stem fever!"

The boys heard the doctor's report to their mother, but they were still so sick that they didn't even seem to care.

The mid-afternoon sun was hot on the skin of George Wolfe who was stretched out on the sandy beach along Smith's Bay. He lay there on his stomach, in a grey swimsuit with short sleeves and three black stripes ringing the chest, waist and bottom of the suit. He was all alone, with the sandy shore stretching out almost a quarter-mile on either side. The sand ran from the water's edge inland about twenty yards to a rock wall. A well-trimmed lawn sprawled out beyond the sand, back to the mansion called Fairmount, the home of Mrs. Walter Chase.

The house could not be seen from the small road which wound along the north shore of the lake. Heavy foliage and giant cottonwood trees kept the estate hidden like some magic fantasyland amidst the wooded and almost uninhabited area around it. Only from the lake could the tall slate roof, the gables, the shuttered windows, and the beautiful lawn, which rolled down to the sandy beach like a green carpet, be seen.

Pinky Wolfe dozed for awhile and then awoke, still too comfortable to move. The lake was quiet and most of the commercial steamboats did not come near this stretch of shoreline which was not on the regularly travelled routes around the lake. An occasional private boat would pass by, but for the most part, Fairmount stood like a castle with a commanding view of the magnificent blue waters of Lake Minnetonka.

Pinky really hadn't been thinking about anything in particular until his mind wandered back to yesterday's wager with the hotel manager and the young Captain Stark. He mused at their insistence that the *City* could beat the *Belle* in the race tomorrow. Yet, he remembered the hesitancy he had felt when he had left the steamboat, how he stood on the shoreline and searched the super-structure for some tell-tale sign that obviously was not there. He thought of his short conversation with the *City's* crew on the trip up here today. Even they communicated that same sureness, the same confidence that the race would not be another pushover for the larger ship. Both Stark and Ross were reputable and honest young men. Surely there would be no trickery involved. Still, there was something they knew that he didn't know. Perhaps it would be wise to simply cover his bet with another wager before the race tomorrow. He didn't need the money anyway. Business had been better than usual during the first month of the summer and there was no need to take a chance on tomorrow's race. He'd nose around a little tonight in the Captain's Bar at the White House and perhaps across the street at the Blue Line Cafe. He would have no trouble finding someone to bet on the *Belle* while he took the *City*. He might even get odds—something that his young friends could have easily bargained for yesterday afternoon.

A door slammed shut in the distance and Pinky looked up from his sandy bed to see Genevieve Chase hurrying across the grass toward the boathouse some twenty yards off to the right. She was wearing a long white linen housecoat with large ruffles down the front and it flowed out behind her like a wedding train as she moved across the lawn. She was carrying a large tray filled with dishes, silverware, a teapot, and two or three other covered dishes.

With all of the servants at Fairmount, Jenny Chase didn't have much chance to carry a tray of food anymore. But Sunday was a special day. Most of the staff were given the day off on Sunday and only the two oldest members of the household staff remained on duty, mostly because they wanted to. Louis and Mattie preferred to spend Sundays at home and after preparing a late breakfast and attending to a minimum number of household chores, Mattie would fix cold chicken and fresh fruit for the late afternoon picnic for the Missus and that Mistah Wolfe. Louis had only to walk down the narrow entrance road to the foot of the hill at the back of the mansion to the small livery barn and hitch up the team to the Sunday carriage for the weekly trip to the Lafayette Hotel. Later in the day, Louis would drive "the Missus and her gentleman friend back to the Lafayette so's he cud ketch the steamer back to Excelsior at sundown."

134

Jenny enjoyed this part of the day. It was the only time in the whole week that she served herself to a meal, and the informality of the Sunday afternoon picnic suppers in the boathouse or on the lawn with Pinky Wolfe reminded her of her childhood when she would help her four sisters prepare meals for the farming crews on her dad's farm in North Dakota. She had met her husband when he came through the little town of Fairmount to purchase land alongside of the Soo Line Railroad right-of-way for a new grain elevator. After they were married, they came to Minneapolis and within five years, the milling business had been so successful that Walter Chase had "Fairmount" built here on Lake Minnetonka.

Jenny loved the lake and Fairmount, luxuries she had never even dreamed about as a farm girl in North Dakota. She had learned to swim and sail here. Everything had been so wonderful. Her husband had been a handsome man—and wealthy. He found her to be strikingly beautiful and they were very much in love. However, there were two telling disappointments in her life. Her marriage was marred by one void, the absence of children. It was disappointing to them both, but as long as they were busy with their social responsibilities and obligations and frequent business trips and vacation journeys, they remained reasonably happy. It was only on peaceful Sunday afternoons like today that they would sit out on the lawn, quietly admitting inwardly to themselves alone, that each longed for the sounds of youngsters splashing in the water, running along the sand, whacking away at striped croquet balls with colorful mallets, the crying, the laughter, and the special kind of tranquility that comes when youngsters have ended their busy day and have gone to sleep, utterly exhausted.

The second blow to the young life of Genevieve Chase was the most cruel of all, the death of her husband. After twelve years of marriage, she had found herself a widow at thirty-one. A wealthy widow, to be sure, who had carried on through the next few years, courted occasionally by an eligible bachelor—usually another grain executive—and, once, harassed by a married man, the vice president of another large Minneapolis firm. But it was only her meeting with George Wolfe that had brought back the enjoyment of life, the charm and grace of this lovely young matron. The only trouble now was that she was really living only one day a week. Through the rest of the week, she would try to keep busy, but found herself re-living the past Sunday and looking forward to the next. Why, oh why wouldn't Pinky let her visit him in Excelsior? It was a delightful little town and she liked going there. But that gambling man would not hear of it. Right now she didn't care. Pinky was here, and she didn't have to abide by all of the formalities of entertaining as she did with other guests. She could dress as she pleased, in a housecoat if she liked, and go barefooted, just as she did as a young farm girl.

"You've got time for a short swim before we eat," she called out as she crossed the lawn to the boathouse door.

Pinky rolled over on his back. "Good. I'm hungry, but I'll take one more swim before I call it a day." He sat up and thought for a moment. "How about going skinny-dippin' with me?"

He could hear her laughing at his invitation from inside the boathouse.

"You go ahead," she answered. "I'll get the food ready."

"Aw, come on," he called out as he stood and brushed the sand from his swim suit.

He walked across the sand toward the water and out on a narrow, but quite long dock. When he had reached the far end of the dock, he looked back toward the boathouse and decided that he would have to swim alone. He turned toward the lake again, thought for a minute, then slipped his swimsuit off, down around his ankles, and carefully hung it on the last dock post. Then he dove into the deep blue water.

Jenny had watched from the upper floor of the boathouse as Pinky disrobed on the dock, and after setting the small wicker table near the screened front windows of the boathouse, she made her way down the small steps to the water level inside the boathouse. From beyond the dock Pinky heard a splash in toward shore. When he looked up, Jenny was swimming out to him. He treaded water while he waited for her to reach him and as she approached, he could see she was nude. She swam directly to him and the two embraced and kissed gently. Then they both laughed, turned and began to swim away from the shore. When they had finished their swim, the two slowly swam back through the open door of the boathouse, and climbed on to the wood planking running along both sides at the water-level. Their wet bodies dripped water up the narrow stairs and when they had reached the upper floor, they turned and embraced.

They stood there for a moment, holding each other closely. Then Pinky lifted her off the floor, carried her across the room and gently laid her down on the daybed.

Later, the two would have a quiet supper, Jenny would ask once more about coming to Excelsior tomorrow, and Pinky would check his watch to make sure of the time. As the brightness of the day began to fade, Louis would once again hitch up the team and drive Jenny and Pinky back to the Lafayette in time to meet the steamer, *Hattie May*, on its return trip to Excelsior.

On the lonesome trip back to Fairmount, she thought some more about Pinky. Perhaps tomorrow she would celebrate the Fourth with a visit to Excelsior. Yes, tomorrow.

Back on the waterfront of Fairmount, a grey swimsuit with three black stripes still hung from the last dock post.

16

"I'M DAMN GLAD you came along with me, boy," said Tom Blair as he patted his son-in-law on the back. The two sat in the crowded first-deck bar of the *City of Saint Louis* on the afternoon return trip from the Lake Park Hotel and drank their beer. The blond-haired Jim Stockton had been quiet and just nodded his head in agreement. He was uneasy. Mostly because he did not like the water or boats. He was not completely at ease with his father-in-law, either, even after living with the Blairs as a member of the family since last fall. He was uncomfortable now and had been all afternoon. He was worried about Hillary and the baby and he had no desire to see the Lake Park

138

today. He recalled the scene at lunchtime, however, and realized once again that T.J. Blair was going to have someone go with him to Tonka Bay this afternoon and, if it hadn't been Jim, it would probably have been Hillary. He smiled and shook his head in disbelief. They had made the trip up on this same steamer, certainly a formidable and safe-looking boat, even to Jim. Still he was glad when they had landed at Tonka Bay and moved back on to dry ground. He would have preferred coming back by horse and buggy, but as usual, Hillary's father was insistent that they return by boat.

The brief visit to the company-owned hotel had been interesting enough, even to Jim. Mr. Blair spent perhaps a half-hour with Roger Bingham, the manager of the Lake Park. Tom Blair was the only connection between the hotel ownership and the management, so his arrival took on the appearance of the president of the railroad visiting the Lake Park. When Bingham discovered T.J. Blair had stepped on the Lake Park's docks he swung into action immediately. He sent word to pull two housemaids off their present duties to come back down on the first floor and straighten and clean the manager's office and living quarters. There had been a sort of party the night before at the hotel and Bingham had entertained some of the hotel's guests into the morning hours. In fact, Mr. and Mrs. Baker, the visitors from Memphis, never did get back to their own quarters until breakfast time. Lester Baker had passed out on the leather couch in the office, and his wife, Josie, had spent half of the night in Mr. Bingham's bedroom and the other half of the night either tending to Lester or making sure that he had not revived.

The hotel manager sent two busboys to the front porch of the spacious hotel to set a special table for Mr. Blair, and a waitress rushed off to the kitchen to make sure that whatever was ordered from the porch would be fitting for the railroad's hotel representative. Bingham himself did not look in the best of shape this afternoon, but he brushed himself off, straightened his clothing, and shined his shoes by rubbing one foot at a time on the back of the other pants leg. Then he headed for the boat landing to welcome Mr. Blair.

Jim Stockton had enjoyed coffee and a piece of fresh raspberry pie while sitting on the veranda, waiting for his father-in-law to finish his short business conversation in the manager's office. When Tom Blair emerged from the hotel and returned to the veranda, he was

139

beaming with pleasure. Bingham's quick house-cleaning had apparently been accomplished in time, and the preliminary report of the hotel's first month of operation for the summer was encouraging. Tom Blair joined Jim for coffee and pie and then proceeded to take his son-in-law on a quick tour of the hotel and its grounds.

Someone had written that there were two classes of summer resort hotels. The first was the old and time-honored hostelries which commanded large patronage from times long past, from wealthy families and their families before them and their families before them. But these long-time favorites were giving way to the second type of summer resort—the palatial hotel which had been erected seemingly overnight to attract and service patrons in new and mushrooming summer resort areas. Such was the Lake Park Hotel, leased by the railroad and the last stop on the M. and St. L's spur-line out of Excelsior. It was acknowledged to be one of the largest and one of the most modern summer resort hotels in the northwest with a capacity of a thousand guests.

The huge, three-story structure rose from high elevated land with a commanding view of the entire lower lake. Four pointed towers capped the frame construction and their flags could be seen flying from the spires by steamboat passengers far out on the lake. The ornate exterior of the building only hinted what would be found inside—carpets, draperies, luxurious furniture and beds, electric lights—all of the conveniences to which guests of the leading public houses of the country were accustomed. The ground floor included the office of Roger Bingham, a beautifully appointed parlor and reception room, a reading room, private parlors, guest chambers, a kitchen, and a dining room which would comfortably seat 400—with one of the finest menus on the lake. The hotel also boasted a kindergarten for the youngsters with teachers and nurses to take care of the little ones. One section of the pavilion adjacent to the hotel contained a cool, light and airy billiard parlor. The pavilion also housed the Lake Park Theater where summer opera, light comedy and other theatricals were provided for the benefit of hotel guests and visitors. Tennis courts and baseball grounds were included in the hotel's park and one of the finest stables on the lake arranged for the proper care of horses. There were walks and drives through the picturesque grounds, bicycle trails, an excellent swimming beach, and landing facilities for steamboats making regular runs as well as the special charter boats.

Flags and bunting were draped over portions of the two-story-high porches facing the lake during this holiday weekend and more flags were used to decorate the lobby and the dining room. Out on the front lawn which led down to the boat landing, the Iowa State Band was tuning up for a short concert this afternoon. They would play a complete formal concert in the Lake Park Theater tonight to a packed house.

"It was a great afternoon, Jim. A great afternoon." Tom Blair was still beaming. He was obviously pleased with himself and his trip to the Lake Park. He had not even noticed that from his arrival at the hotel in Tonka Bay until his departure, there had been staff members waiting on him, ready to answer any request and eager to fulfill any need that the railroad executive might wish for. Jim Stockton had noticed it, however, and had also realized that not once, not one single time from the moment they put their feet on the Lake Park dock until they waved goodbye on the *City*, had Tom Blair ever once uttered a "thank you" to anyone. He just went on his merry way, expecting, and getting, the same obedience he received in all of his business contacts, and from his family at home. Jim just shook his head and sipped his beer as Tom Blair went on.

"Lucky thing how we ran into that gamblin' fellow, what's his name?"

"Wolfe, I believe," answered Jim.

"Yes, that's right. Pinky Wolfe, they call him. Quite a fella, yessir, quite a fella. Imagine making your living with a deck of cards and a poker hand? Might nice fella, though. I remember playing with him last year while we were here. He's honest. Yessir, he's honest. Funny how he was all alone on the trip up here. But he did say he'd be back tonight in time for a game or two. Yessir, Jim, I think you ought to join us for a friendly game of poker tonight. We'll play a little and then watch the fireworks with Frances and Hillary. Yessir, I'm sure glad you came along, Jim."

Life for a young Negro in Minnesota during the summer was not as lonesome as one might suspect, particularly at Excelsior and other resorts on Lake Minnetonka. Mose Daniel White had spent three summers at Excelsior as a member of the crew of the *Belle of Minnetonka* and, although the hours were reasonably long each day, he found that he still had too much time on his hands during the week so he hired out as a fishing guide. When he first came to the lake as an eighteen-year-old fireman to work in the boiler-room of the *Belle of Minnetonka*, he found very few friends along the waterfront. First to say a kind word to him was John Stark on the *City of Saint Louis*, and his first real friend in Excelsior was Emmett Markham. He had met Emmett when he went to the newspaper office one June morning to see if there were any rooms advertised for rent in the local paper. Emmett not only helped him find a room but personally took him over to Mrs. Smith's to see that he would get a fair shake with the landlady. From that time on, Mose Daniel White and Emmett Markham had become good friends. When Emmett and John Stark would go fishing, as they often did, they would take Mose along and show him all of the best, and secret, fishing spots on the lake.

Afterwards, the three of them would sit on the deck of the *City* and drink a half-pony of beer in the later afternoon sun and talk about women. Mose was a farm boy from Missouri who lived close enough to the Mississippi river to be attracted to steamboats, and, eventually, he hooked a ride and a job on a riverboat named the *Charleston* which commuted between St. Louis and St. Paul. He was the youngest of a family of eight children and his brothers and sisters all remained close to home near Hannibal, Missouri.

At first it was a lonely world at Minnetonka for Mose, but then there was the fishing with John and Emmett. His second summer at Excelsior was even more fruitful. Besides moving out of the boiler-room of the *Belle*, Mose also discovered that there were a number of wealthy southern families who brought their entire household staff with them to Excelsior for their summer vacation. And most entourages included a number of young Negro-women to mind the youngsters and to look after the household. With his new-found role as a special host to visiting servants, Mose White was in great demand. The fact that he could strum chords on a guitar and sing a few of the currently popular songs along with the folk tunes he had

142

learned as a child back in Missouri, made him almost as popular with the whitefolk as it did with their hired help.

The success of Mose White was one of the reasons that the handsome young Negro was not getting along so well with Captain Loos on the *Belle*. Not only was Mose much wiser now, in his third summer at Excelsior, but he resented the obscenities and the rudeness extended daily by Lamont Loos. The indignities had become worse this summer, partly because of Mose's growing popularity, partly because of his mounting knowledge of the lake, and partly because the captain was particularly unkind to him when the captain had been drinking. Loos had started to celebrate he Fourth of July not long after he had docked Saturday night and was still going at it this Sunday afternoon. Mose had finally finished his chores aboard the giant steamer, but not before he had received Loos' usual tongue-lashing along with two or three deadly whacks across the back and shoulders with a longpole, ordinarily used in shallow water to help push off the boat from shore. Loos was still half drunk and apparently unhappy with the amount of time his crew had spent in making the final day-check of the boat before the race on Monday.

Now Mose White hurried up Excelsior's main street, looking for Emmett Markham. He had already checked the bars at the Blue Line Cafe and the White House and had asked for Emmett at Fred Hawkins' Saloon. He was headed for the office of the *News* now, and, if Emmett couldn't be found there, Mose planned to hike up the hill overlooking Excelsior Bay to the Palmer House villa to see if Emmett was at home. The newspaper plant was locked up and dark, so Mose started back in the direction of the waterfront again and stopped just out in front of the boarding house to look down on the docks and off toward the Commons at the left where the Sunday crowd was still gathered, watching the final innings of the baseball game. His back hurt like hell.

Inside the Palmer House villa, Emmett Markham was soaking in a large copper boiler which had been placed in the middle of the kitchen floor. His clothes were scattered across the floor. The house was empty, except for Emmett and Mrs. Palmer's dog, Boo, who stayed his distance from the portable tub and the soapy water on the kitchen floor. The water had been heated on a large, black, wood-burning range which occupied almost one whole end of the kitchen.

143

Cord-wood was stacked along one side of the stove and a square kitchen table had been pushed from the center of the room to make way for the tub.

Emmett had come down the back stairs of the White House when he had finally left Hillary in her room, walked across the street to the Blue Line Cafe and ordered a drink while he sat there, watching for the *City* to come in from its Sunday run. He was still as confused as ever about Hillary, her husband, and the baby, and he had no more in the way of answers now that he did yesterday when Andy Ross had let him have the bad news right between the eyes. He knew one thing for sure. Hillary still loved him. How could she love him and yet marry Jim Stockton? He would still see Frances Blair this evening. But he had promised Andy to talk to John Stark about the race and John's boat would not be in for another hour. So Emmett hiked up the hill to his boarding house room and decided to bathe and change clothes. It was too damn hot, anyway, and he would dry off by sitting out on the balcony of his room and look down over the sights of Excelsior Bay.

He was about to get out of the tub when there was a knock at the back door. "Who is it?" he called from the kitchen. Then he heard the screen door slam on the back porch and Mose White stuck his head through the doorway into the kitchen.

"What the hell are you doing here, Mose?" chided Emmett.

"Hello, Emmett."

"Come on in, Mose." Emmett motioned him in with a wet, soapy arm. "I'm just getting out, but you're welcome to heat some more water and take a bath if you like." Then he laughed. Mose did not join in his laughter, however, and Emmett quickly sensed that the fellow had something more serious to say. "What can I do for you, Mose?" Emmett asked as he stepped from the tub and reached for a large white towel. "If you're looking for a fishing partner, this is just not the day for it." But Mose White did not smile, and Emmett changed his tone as he began to dry himself. "All right, Mose, what's the matter?"

Emmett started to leave the kitchen and headed for the back stairs up to his room. As he moved toward the stairs, he motioned to Mose to follow.

Mose climbed the stairs behind Emmett and then followed him

144

down the long hall past four rooms and out an open door on to a second-floor balcony overlooking a front yard, the busy street below, and the lakefront some two hundred yards beyond. Emmett wrapped the towel around his waist and sat down at one end of the small balcony. Mose stood by the door for a moment and then spoke.

"Emmett, you and I have been good friends for a long time."

"Yes, that's right."

"And as long as you've known me, I've never done anythin' dishonest." He did not ask a question but merely stated a fact.

"That's right, Mose. I don't think that either one of us has ever done anything that was downright dishonest."

"Well, I'm about to—and I've come to you for advice."

Emmett sat up a little straighter. "What do you mean, Mose?"

"Well—" He hesitated.

"Well—?" Emmett urged him on.

"Ya see . . . I know something no one else knows. And I'm not sure what to do about it."

"Well, what do you know, Mose?"

"See these marks on my back and shoulders," he asked of Emmett. And as he did so, he turned and pulled his white shirt up to his neck. Emmett could see the ugly welts made by the longpole and Captain Loos.

"They came from Cap'n Loos this afternoon. He was half-canned and he didn't like the way I was making the check of the ship for tomorrow's race."

Emmett had been cooled off by the bath and the fresh air on the balcony, but the sight of the welts and the words of Mose White made him start to sweat. He was a peaceful man, a man who did not like violence and who had no time for anyone who would inflict pain on anyone else, human being or animal.

"Is that how you got that?" he asked angrily as he motioned to Mose's back.

"Yassir," Mose nodded. "But that's not why I'm here."

"It's reason enough for me," Emmett replied.

Mose continued. "I found sumpin' out this afternoon while I was checkin the *Belle*, Emmett, but before I could say anything to the Cap'n, he hauled off and started swinging at me with a longpole. So I just took my lumps and didn't say a word. That's why I'm here now. I know sumpin' and I don't know what to do about it."

"Well, what is it?"

Mose looked around as if someone might overhear, but there wasn't anyone in the house and the nearest people were down on the street, far from the sound of the two men's voices.

"It's the stack of the *Belle*."

"What about the stack?" Emmett was listening carefully, now.

"It's going to burn out. It's going to burn out before we can get to Wayzata and back tomorrow. It's the stack on the portside and I found it today when I made the check of the smokestacks. It's as thin as cigarette paper right now and it'll go tomorrow just as sure as hell."

Emmett sat up straight and pressed the matter. "Tell me, Mose, is it dangerous?"

"No sir, it's not dangerous. The stack is simply goin' to burn out tomorrow and ole Loos will have to cut back his power when it happens."

"You mean no one is likely to get injured or burned or anything?" Emmett asked.

"No sir. It'll jus' burn out while we're racin' and we'll have to slow down. And that smart-ass Cap'n's going to lose." Mose was smiling.

Emmett was standing now and his thoughts, his plans and the consequences of what he had just heard were whizzing through his head. It would serve that son-of-a-bitch right if he did lose tomorrow. And the Navigation Company didn't have anything to lose. They own both boats anyway. He looked down at the waterfront and then grabbed Mose by the shoulder. It was as though a charge of electricity had been transmitted from Emmett through his arm to Mose, and he, rightly, sensed at once that the matter had taken on more importance than he could possibly imagine.

"Have you said anything to anybody, anybody at all?" Emmett asked hastily.

"No sir."

"Good. Then don't . Except for John Stark. I want you to hightail it down to the docks and when the *City* comes in, you find John Stark and tell him I sent you. Then go ahead and tell him exactly what you told me. Exactly. After that, you just go about your business the rest of the day just as though nothing has happened. Do you understand?"

146

Mose was grinning, now. "Yassir? I knows exactly what you mean!"

Emmett patted him on the arm and sent Mose back through the house, down the stairs and on his way to the waterfront. He looked back out over the balcony and could see the *City of Saint Louis* entering Excelsior Bay. This would solve Andy's problem with John Stark. He would have to tell Andy Ross. And there was one more person to be tipped off on what was going to happen tomorrow. He'd stop and see Pinky Wolfe after supper.

17

JOHN STARK was satisfied with the condition of the *City of Saint Louis*. The crew had been able to complete the on-board check of the giant flatbottom as it lazily made its way across Lake Minnetonka on its Sunday afternoon run to the Upper Lake and back again. Only two weak paddle-wheel cuplets could be found and they would be repaired or replaced after they had docked in Excelsior. It wasn't his own boat he was worried about. It was the *Belle of Minnetonka* that concerned the young captain. He had done a lot of thinking about her since he and Andy had made the bet with Pinky Wolfe yesterday and he had decided that the simplest, and surest, way of tinkering with the *Belle* would be to loosen the flange-pins at the paddle-wheel end of one of the connecting rods. By the time the big steamboat would reach Wayzata in the race, the pins would give way from the force of the boilers and the strain on the giant paddle-wheels. They could be replaced promptly, but she would lose valuable time, and if the race was close, as John knew it would be, the delay would mean the difference between winning and losing.

John's plans, however, just a day old, were already outdated. He was discarding his plan for a midnight swim under the docks to the *Belle* and his mind was somewhat relieved as he sat in his cabin this late Sunday afternoon, listening to Mose tell the same story he had told Emmett less than an hour ago. Mose stood in the center of the small cabin and completed the last detail of the story. He noticed John was now smiling. As far as John was concerned, there was no question about the validity of the condition of the smokestack. Mose was an experienced crewman, and a trusted friend. There was no reason to doubt him now.

"Thank you, Mose," John said quietly.

Mose did not speak but nodded understandingly.

"You did the right thing in going to Emmett. I'll thank Emmett, too, when I see him today or tomorrow. I know that you have no idea how much this means to me, Mose," John continued, "but I want you to know that it is very important."

Mose shook his head. "I don't want to know anymore than I do already."

John showed him out the door and then added. "One thing more, Mose."

"Yes?"

"We're going to beat that lousy captain of yours tomorrow!"

Both men laughed.

The Captain's Bar in the White House had been reasonably quiet on Sunday afternoon but it had taken on its familiar atmosphere again after sundown. Once more it was crowded with visitors and

149

tourists. Cigar smoke clouded one end of the bar and half-hid the poker table where Pinky Wolfe presided. His face was reddened from the afternoon sun and his hands were more tanned, setting off his sapphire ring as he dealt the cards to T.J. Blair and the two other men who were hotel guests at the White House. One chair was empty. It had been occupied by Mayor Bertram who had just left.

The clock on the alcove wall at the entrance to the Captain's Bar showed a quarter to ten when Emmett walked in, looking for Pinky Wolfe. He had stopped to see Andy Ross to tell him about Mose White's visit, but Andy had left for the evening and was not in the hotel. Emmett scribbled a short note to Andy about the *Belle* and its stack, folded it, and had it placed in Andy's own mail box behind the registration desk. Now he could see Pinky at the poker table and moved through the crowd to the end of the bar. When the hand was finished, Emmett waited to catch his eye and when Pinky looked up from the table and the chips, he saw Emmett standing there.

"Let's take a ten-minute break," the gambler said to the other men. They all agreed and called for a waitress as Pinky excused himself, pushed back his chair and stepped to the bar. The two men greeted each other, shook hands, and ordered drinks.

"What's on your mind, Emmett?" asked the gambler. "I don't see you around here very often unless you're on business."

"It's sort of business," Emmett replied. "It's your sort of business."

"If you want to get in the game, Emmett, there's an empty chair." He motioned toward the poker table. "George Bertram just left about five minutes ago."

"No, Pinky. But I'd like to talk to you for a minute about your bet with John and Andy on that race tomorrow."

The gambler became more alert to the conversation and was about to speak when the bartender slid the drinks across the counter. "Here, let me pay for them," Pinky offered. Before Emmett could reach in his pocket, Pinky had the money on the bar.

"What about the race, Emmett? Who do you think will win tomorrow?"

"I think the *City* is going to win." He paused. "And that's why I'm here."

"Oh?" Pinky watched Emmett carefully and waited for him to continue.

150

"It's not that I think the *City* will win, Pinky. I know it will, through no fault of John Stark or Andy Ross, believe me." Emmett watched for the gambler to become disturbed. There was a lot of money riding on this wager for him. But Pinky Wolfe sipped his drink calmly. "Believe me, Pinky, there's a flaw in the *Belle* and it's going to lose. And only a few of us know about it. We'd prefer to keep it that way, but I know how much money is involved and I don't want to see you get burned."

The gambler smiled. He seemed unruffled by Emmett's words and sipped his drink again.

"I'm not surprised," he told Emmett. "I had a feeling about this race and I couldn't put my finger on why I felt the way I do. I thought about it all day today and the more I thought about it, the more I began to believe my hunch. Like I say, no rhyme or reason, just a hunch. So I covered myself. I bet on the *City*, half with Captain Loos right after supper and the other half with the mayor—not more than a half-hour ago. With odds!" He looked at Emmett and smiled. 'I don't do that very often—but, like I say, I just had a feeling." He shrugged his shoulders. Then he added. "But thanks, anyway, Emmett. I appreciate your telling me."

"I want you to know that neither John or Andy knew about this when they made that bet with you," Emmett assured the gambler.

"I think I know them both pretty well, Emmett, and I believe you." The gambler nodded and started back to the poker table, leaving Emmett standing at the bar. When Emmett had finished his drink, he started to leave and as he passed through the door to the lobby he heard someone call out his name, ever so softly. The noise of the crowd both inside the barroom and in the lobby almost drowned out the voice, but he could hear it all the same.

"Mistah Emmett! Mistah Emmett! Over here."

Emmett turned toward the muffled sound. A small pretty black girl stood against the wall, holding her hands in front of her, her fingers fumbling nervously. She was dressed in a black and white uniform—obviously a member of the staff of one of the families staying at the hotel. Emmett stepped toward her.

"What is it, girl?" "How do you know my name."

"Excuse me, sir," she answered quietly. He strained to hear her speak. "I'm with the Blair family and I've got something to tell you."

151

She stammered. "At lea-lea-least you ought to know about it!"

"My God, but I've been let in on a lot of secrets these past two days," Emmett said mostly to himself. He smiled and asked her to go on. Perhaps it was word from Hillary.

"It's not FROM Miss Hillary," Mistah Emmett. "It's ABOUT her. I—I—I . . . ."

Emmett took her by the arm and moved with her toward the main-street entrance of the hotel and out on to the darkened lawn toward the livery stable. "What is it, girl?" he demanded. "Has something happened to Hillary?"

Emily looked frightened. She also looked determined to speak her piece. She drew a deep breath and went on. "I—I—I . . . I was in the other room today when you came to see HIllary."

"Oh, is that all." Emmett relaxed. "It's all right. Hillary and I are old friends."

"Yessir," she answered automatically, and then went on. "But I knows that you came to find out somethin' . . . an' you didn't."

"It's all right Miss——"

"Emily," she answered quickly. "It's Emily."

"Well, Emily, don't worry your head about it. I'll learn what I need to know," he assured her.

"But I knows what you wants to know, Mistah Emmett." She was more excited now. "An' no one else is goin' to tell you. It's about the baby, and Miss Hillary gettin' married, an' all . . . ."

Emmett quickly looked around to see if anyone was near, but they were alone in the dark shadows of the livery barn. And he had suddenly become a good listener. She went right on.

"Miss Hillary couldn't tell you this, Mistah Emmett, but Mistah Stockton is not little Jamie's father . . . and Mistah Stockton knowed that before he ever married Miss Hillary!" The soft little voice continued to ramble on but the words were seemingly shut out of Emmett's mind. The girl's words kept on repeating themselves in Emmett's ears—"Mistah Stockton is not little Jamie's father . . . and he knowed that when he married her!" Over and over came the words and in the background he could hear Emily going on and on and on.

"Wait a minute——" He stopped her and grabbed the pretty black girl by the arm. She looked frightened now but did not pull away from him. "Do you know what you're saying, girl?"

152

"Yessir," she answered promptly, and kept right on. "And that's not all. You might as well hear the rest from me 'cause you ain't goin' to hear it from anyone else. Mistah Emmett . . . what nobody wants to tell you is that Jamie's your baby!"

There was silence. Emily had stopped talking. Emmett stood there, stunned. Not believing what he had heard. Not believing that he could have even heard such words. Not believing that Hillary would keep such a thing from him if it were true. Not believing . . . .

"My God, girl. Do you know what you're saying?" he shouted at her. "Do you **KNOW** what you're talking about?"

The questions prompted Emily to begin again and she continued explaining to Emmett—how Miss Hillary discovered she was pregnant last fall and how she wanted to protect her family's name from the scandal and how she asked Mistah Stockton to marry her and . . . .

Emmett's world was crumbling around him. He thought he had heard the worst from Andy Ross yesterday in the Hawkins' Saloon. He remembered how he had felt—that what had happened was some kind of cruel dream, a hoax, some nightmare that would eventually right itself. Even in this short span of twenty-four hours, he had been able to accept the cold, hard and unalterable fact that Hillary **WAS** married and that her baby was here with her. But now the logical, although unanswered pieces of his puzzle were falling all around him. His son! Their son! My God! It could be true! Of course it could! "Oh, my God!" Emmett spoke quietly now and wrapped his arms around the frightened Emily. "Thank you, Emily. Thank you," he sighed.

In a moment, Emmett tried to come back to reality. He took Emily by the shoulders and held her back from him. "Who knows about this, Emily? Who knows?"

Emily had taken on new confidence, now. "Not many," she answered. "Even Mistah Blair don't know. But Miss Frances knows An' so does that old mayor. She told me so and told me what to say if'n Mistah Blair comes back from his card-playing before she gets back from seeing the Mayor."

Emmett's heart began to pound hard. Of course, Bertram knew all the time. He knew yesterday at lunch and he knew last night on the boat. And now he's blackmailing Frances into . . . . Emmett guessed the truth! He was breathing harder now. That lecherous old bastard was holding this whole thing over Frances' head and, by God, he was going to have her for it! Emmett almost shook Emily.

"Where is Mrs. Blair now?" He was shaking her before she could even answer.

"She's gone to see the mayor, I told you. Wherever he lives." Then she added. "She was to meet him at ten o'clock."

At that moment, there was a thunderous sound, a deafening explosion—the black sky was lighted by colorful stars breaking open over Excelsior Bay and lighting up the whole community. The annual fireworks had begun! But Emmett did not look up. He started to run—down the embankment and across the boardwalk towards main street. He shouted back to Emily to get the hell inside and not to tell Mr. Blair. There was no time to think about Hillary and the baby and himself now. Only Frances Blair was important at the moment. And, if he did not get to Frances in time, it would be his fault.

Inside the mayor's apartment, a faint light from the fireworks flickered through the windows and flashed across the almost darkened room. Frances Blair had arrived a short time ago. And Bertram had been waiting. When she knocked lightly on his door, she heard Bertram inside. "Come on in, the door's always open."

Frances slowly turned the door knob and reluctantly entered the room. As she stepped from the brighter light of the hallway into the darker apartment, she found it difficult to see. The furniture and walls seemed like dark, fuzzy objects hovering around the room. A small gas lamp was turned down low on Bertram's dresser near his bed and he stood in the middle of the room in his shirtsleeves, waiting to welcome Frances. He smiled.

"Come in my dear."

She closed the door behind her, then turned toward the mayor. He stepped forward and clasped her hand as he greeted her.

"I've waited a long time for this, Frances Remington Blair," he said quietly. "But it's worth waiting for." He let go of her hand and walked around her, eyeing her like an auctioneer looking over a head

154

of cattle before putting the animal on the auction block. "You're more beautiful now than ever." He paused, noticing that she was standing rigid and still. "Relax, Frances, I'm no stranger to you." He spoke with a tone of persuasion in his voice. "It won't be so bad. After all, we're old friends."

Frances spoke for the first time. "Let's get on with it, George." Her voice was strong, and it bothered Geroge Bertram. She should be trembling. Frightened. She should be willing to succumb. As he completed his circle around her and met her face to face once again, his soft eyes turned steel-hard and he reached up and ripped down hard on the white, frilly blouse she was wearing. Frances shuddered. The blouse was in shreds and he held it for a moment and then dropped it on the floor.

"Dammit, Frances," he shouted. "Don't be like this!""

She was still standing motionless in the middle of the darkened room, but she began to breathe more heavily now and Bertram could see her breasts rising under her chemise. The sight pleased him and excited him. He smiled again. And the tone of his voice became softer. "Come on, Frances," he pleaded. "Let's be cooperative. After all, I've promised to live up to my share of the——." He stopped speaking as she crossed her arms at the waist and pulled the white cotton chemise over her head. Now she stood there, bare to the waist, her long hair falling across her shoulders. Bertram stared at her, at her firm, round breasts swelling rhythmically with her frightened short breaths. He was gloating over the lovely white skin, the attractive waist. She was even more beautiful than he had imagined.

Emmett Markham was taking big strides now. It was as though he were racing down main street at midday. The brilliant light from the fireworks out on the bay lighted every nook and doorway along the deserted street. Everyone was at the shoreline watching the fireworks. Everyone except Bertram—and Frances. And Emmett knew what she would do—anything to protect her family! He was at the mainstreet door which led up the stairs over the Hawkins' Saloon and he stopped, looked up and down the street, and slipped inside where he stopped again to catch his breath. Then he quietly started to climb the stairs to the door to Bertram's rooms. Outside he could hear the pop and burst of the fireworks.

When he reached the top of the stairs he stood there in front of Bertram's closed door for a moment. He was still gasping slightly for his breath after the long run from the White House, and he was trying desperately to muffle the heavy breathing. He pressed his ear to the door, trying to hear. The door would not be locked, he hoped. He had been here before and had heard Bertram issue his usual announcement to "come on in, the door's always open." He hoped it was now.

At that moment, he heard Frances' voice pleading, "Please, George——" It was enough for Emmett. He stepped back and slammed his shoulder to the door as he turned the knob. The door swung open and Emmett came smashing across the small room. He could see Frances' bare back and the leering George Bertram standing close to her, facing towards him. There wasn't time for either of them to move before Emmett had charged on. As he passed Frances, she screamed, and his arm shot out and hooked Bertram around the neck.

"Oh God—don't!" Bertram cried.

But before he whirled around, Emmett reached back and smashed him across the face with his right fist. The blow crunched Bertram's jaw, jarring his teeth loose! Blood spewed from his mouth as he was sent reeling backwards, sprawling up against an overstuffed chair and nearby table! Before his body could slide down toward the floor, however, Emmett was on him, grabbing him up by the shirt-front and smashing his head back against the wall! Wild-eyed and befuddled, Bertram tried to speak, to protest, but his arms flayed helplessly from the first crushing blow. Blood poured out of his reddened nose.

It was as though a tornado had flashed across the upstairs apartment, taking with it the mayor and furniture and smashing them all against the wall, splinters and pieces flying in all directions,and, like a tornado, leaving something else untouched by it all—Frances Blair. She was standing in the middle of the room, holding her hands to her mouth in sheer fright as she watched the devastation. Emmett sunk his fist into the mayor's soft belly and then

156

grabbed Bertram by the shoulders and smashed him against the wall, over and over. He was half screaming, half crying as he shook the older man—frightened by his own violence. He wanted to hit Bertram again and again but he could only shake him hysterically as the mayor slid out of his grasp and down the wall to the floor. Emmett stood there over the mayor, gasping for breath, so angry, yet so weak that he shook—now incapable of inflicting any further punishment. His lungs were drawing in deep breaths now and he was crying as he looked down at the pitiful Bertram who lay crumpled on the floor, his balding head and grey hair matted with blood, his face a mass of welts, glassy-eyed, with blood trickling from his mouth on to his white shirt.

There was silence in the little room and only a distant explosion of the fireworks finale could be heard through the open window overlooking the main street. Frances stood frozen, horrified at what she had seen and frightened by what she had experienced. There was more silence and then Emmett looked up and realized that she was standing there. Instinctively she reached down to the floor, picked up the chemise and clutched it to her breast.

"I'm sorry, Frances. I know about the baby . . . I'm truly sorry."

Frances bit her lip. "Oh, Emmett. I'm so sorry . . . for Hillary and for you. I thought I could . . . ."

"Let's not talk about it now, Frances," he said. "Let's get you out of here." He looked around the room quickly. The mayor lay on the floor, still motionless, but groaning quietly. Emmett looked back at Frances and the two of them realized that she was still standing there, nearly half nude. Emmett couldn't find anything to cover her and quickly pulled off his own coat and draped it around her shoulders. Then he led her through the door to the hallway. It had been only minutes since she had come up those stairs and knocked on the door. Yet it had seemed like hours. Emmett put his arm around her and led her down the hall and down the back stairs. When they reached the bottom step, he pushed open a screen door and the two stepped outside into the cool night air. It was quiet. Only the faint noises of laughter and men's voices from inside the Fred Hawkins' Saloon broke the silence. Emmett looked around for a buggy. There were three or four rigs parked in the back alley and all but one were hitched to teams. The one single-horse buggy belonged to the White

House livery stable. Emmett recognized the rig and knew that it had been rented for the evening.

He helped Frances into the front seat of the buggy, untied the halter-hitch from the rail, climbed into the front seat along side of Frances, and started down the alley in the darkness toward the hotel. Frances sat quietly as the horse and buggy moved along the alley, across Second street, and up the hill toward the White House. Then she began to cry softly as Emmett pulled on the reins and guided the buggy toward the back entrance to the hotel's livery stable where he brought the brown mare up short in the shadow of the barn. There was more noise here, signalling that the holiday festivities on the night before the Fourth were still going strong, and Emmett put his arm around Frances to comfort her as he helped her from the buggy. The horse stood motionless and Emmett did not bother to tie the mare up. They were already on home grounds and the horse would not stray.

He and Frances started toward the back entrance of the hotel, staying in the shadows of the large shrubs along the fence until they reached the back door which led to the kitchen and to the back stairway used by the employees. Frances was crying now and Emmett was more worried about her as they walked through the door and along the back porch toward the stairway. He opened the door to the inside hallway, started up the narrow stairs and reached the first landing. When they turned to start up the second set of stairs, Emmett came face to face with Minnie Jacobs, the head chambermaid. Madge Phelps was not far behind. The two had been celebrating the Fourth with a few drinks in their room and were on their way out to watch the fireworks finale. Both had known Emmett Markham since he was a youngster hanging around the hotel with young Andy Ross. Even as tipsy as they were, both old women sensed the emergency when they stumbled on to Emmett and Frances coming up the stairs.

"My God, Emmett. What's happened?" Minnie asked as she stared at Frances who was still crying.

"Never mind that now," Emmett said quietly but firmly. Mrs. Blair needs help. I don't want anyone to see her like this. Can we take her up to your room Minnie?"

"Of course you can," she agreed. It was obvious that Minnie had been drinking, but the urgency of the situation had sobered her almost instantly. Quickly she dispatched Madge to see if the Blair quarters were empty and to bring Mrs. Blair some fresh clothing. Madge had a pass key so there would be no trouble getting into the room. Then Minnie led Emmett and Frances up the second flight of stairs to the third floor and down the hall to the room she shared with Madge. Quickly they laid Frances down on the bed and Minnie was at her side with a pitcher of water, a pan, and wash cloths, sponging Frances' face and trying to make her comfortable. Frances was still sobbing and occasionally her whole body shook. Emmett covered her with a light blanket and it was not long before Madge was back with fresh clothing.

"Here, Emmett," Minnie ordered. "You need a drink." She handed over a whiskey bottle to Emmett but not until she had taken a swig herself. Emmett sat down on the window ledge and gulped down the whiskey. She was right. He had needed a drink. He would need a few more before the evening was over, trying to forget the violent scene in Bertram's room and the terrible indignities which Frances had been subjected to.

"What the hell happened?" Madge inquired.

"It's too long a story to go into now, girls," Emmett replied. "I'll tell you all about it later. Right now we've got to get her calmed down a little and back to her own room before her husband or anyone else finds out what's happened to her.

"We'll take her back downstairs." The voice came from the doorway. It was Hillary's voice.

Emmett whirled to see Hillary and her husband standing in the doorway.

" Hillary! What are you doing here?"

"We saw the chambermaid leaving the room with mother's clothing and simply followed her up here," she said. "What's happened?"

"She's been through a terrible ordeal," Emmett spoke in firm tones. "And there was no need for it at all." He was starting to get angry as he spoke and he looked straight at Hillary and Jim Stockton. "She's been busy, paying off a debt to that lousy Bertram because of you and me, Hillary! He knows abut the baby. And so do I. And you had damn-well better tell your father about it in the morning—or I will."

He turned to Minnie and said, "Let her rest awhile and then get her into those other clothes and downstairs to her own room." Then he walked to the door of the tiny room, shouldered his way between Hillary and Jim, and hurried down the stairs.

Hillary and her husband and the two chambermaids stood still for a moment and then turned to Frances. She was sleeping.

Monday, July 4

18

THE EARLY-MORNING SUN edged over the tops of the trees and settled on the east bank of Excelsior Bay. It peeked through the green leaves and spreading branches, seemingly with the same anticipation that a small boy would enjoy with his first glimpse of Lake Minnetonka from the window of an M. and St. L. train breaking into view of the beautiful lake. As usual, Sunrise Point felt the first warm rays of the July sun as it cleared the trees, spreading its warmth across all of Excelsior Bay.

John Stark felt the comforting warmth as he slept on the top deck of the *City of Saint Louis* where he had spent the night. He often stretched out on the flat, hard deck near the stern of the giant steamer and fell asleep looking at the stars and hearing the maze of noises along the shoreline on a late summer's night. But his choice of sleeping quarters this past night had more purpose, to guard the boat on the night before the Fourth-of-July race with the *Belle of Minnetonka.* There had never been an attempt to tamper with the *City,* but he just felt better having slept aboard ship on the night before the race. He lay on the hard deck, stretched out on his back, barefooted, with wrinkled pants and shirt. And in the quiet and serenity of the early-morning stillness, he could unconsciously hear the water lapping at the side of the ship and smell the freshness of the lake. The silence was broken occasionally by the clip-clop sounds of a team of horses and a wagon coming down the lakeside road and fading out of hearing again. That would be the farmers bringing in fresh vegetables to the hotels and fresh chickens to the local meat markets who would dress the meat to be distributed to the hotels in the lake area later this morning.

The early-morning sounds brought thoughts of other early mornings for John Stark. He remembered sleeping on the front porch of his home as a boy, the brisk fall mornings, and the chilly wind at night which never seemed to be able to invade the warmth of the blankets and the old red and white quilted comforter his mother had made. He could remember snuggling under the massive pile of bed clothes, still able to hear the leaves falling from the cottonwoods in his front yard on fall nights as he drifted off to sleep. The front porch had been his bedroom each summer and into the fall until it became so cold that the fortress of blankets could no longer withstand the attack of the approaching winter. But John would be back on the porch for the first spring rain, crawling back under those covers and waking early each spring morning, hearing those same old cottonwoods shedding in the wind, and feeling the spray of rain as it blew through the screens and across the foot of his bed.

But the morning of each Fourth of July was something special to John. The memories of his younger days came back to him this holiday morning. Things hadn't changed much. He was awakened by the faint sounds of firecrackers. At first just a single explosion . . . sounding miles away. Then another . . . perhaps two . . . from far away. More silence. Then another barrage. Closer this time and

162

becoming more frequent. As a boy, John would pretend that the sounds were those of the Confederate artillery along Seminary Ridge at Gettysburg, firing their opening volleys of the day in preparation for the battle that was to follow. He wondered if that was the way it sounded to his Dad who had been one of the surviving members of the 1st Minnesota Regiment along Cemetary Ridge on another July morning some twenty-four years before.

There was an unfamiliar ring to this holiday morning, however, and John lay quietly, eyes still closed, listening to the early-morning noises and the distant fireworks. It was clearer now, but he heard the sounds again. Out of place on this morning, he thought. A sound of discord, out of step with the rhythm of the waves or the passing teams. It was a ringing . . . metal ringing . . . an uneven hammering . . . metal on metal . . . and not far away! Down the shoreline! The young captain suddenly opened his eyes and raised up on one elbow as he looked down the line of boats toward the pounding. His eyes opened wider as he stared. The sounds were coming from the deck of the *Belle of Minnetonka*. My God! They're replacing a smokestack!

Captain Lamont Loos was in good spirits this morning. The morning of a Fourth-of-July race was always an exciting morning, even for an experienced old hand like Loos. He had enjoyed the special races between the *Belle* and the *City* perhaps because his steamboat had won the last five races against its sister ship, but there was something more to it than the sixteen-mile course and another trophy presented by the Minnetonka Yacht Club. The captain had been a competitor all of his life and, even now, as he settled back to skipper the easy-going *Belle of Minnetonka* on its quiet tour of the lake each summer day, the aging Lamont Loos could feel the excitement in the competition . . . the chance to test his mental and physical capabilities, his skill and his determination against the opposition. And in this case, the challenge was far greater than usual. Against his old friend and drinking buddy, Jess Williams, Loos enjoyed the race and the victory. But it was a friendly victory, one that he and the loser could re-live over a bottle of booze or a game of cards. Today's race was different. Now the challenge took on more somber tones and there was a new excitement for the captain of the *Belle*. There was a slight trembling in his veins, a nervousness which he had not known since his days in the U.S. Navy during the War Between the States when he served as an executive officer and later a captain on the war sloop, *Cleveland*, in the Gulf of Mexico with Admiral Farragut's fleet. Later he served in Atlantic waters, before leaving the service at the end of the war.

The challenge, of course, was not the *City* itself, but John Stark, its young captain. Now at that age when nothing seemed so important that he could not go to sleep at night, or so urgent that the problem could not be solved tomorrow or the next day, Lamont Loos was again feeling that old zest, that tinge of anticipation.

He had good reason to feel particularly good this morning as he stood on the boiler deck of the *Belle* in the early-morning sun and watched a crew from the Navigation Company's boatworks replace the defective smokestack. The old section of chimney was about to be removed and the new chimney would be swung into place and secured by noon. The crew now working above the super-structure of the big steamboat had been on the job since before dawn. They had been notified last night about midnight that they would be needed very early in the morning to replace the smokestack on the *Belle*. H.W.Farnsworth had personally called at the home of each crew member to make sure they would be on the job early this morning. Farnsworth was the time-keeper and treasurer of the Navigation Company and had already dispatched another six workers just before midnight to find the replacement stack and haul it over to the Excelsior municipal docks during the night so it would be ready when the crews arrived in the morning. Farnsworth, in turn, had been located shortly before midnight by Captain Loos who was obviously upset when he called on the company time-keeper.

"Harold, I need a new smokestack for the *Belle*, and it has to be done right now!" There was no apologizing for the intrusion at the late hour. No explanation. Simply a demand. He had to have a new smokestack and it had better be at the municipal docks in the morning along with a work crew. With that, he turned and started back down the street, leaving Harold Farnsworth standing in the doorway of his modest home, clad only in a night shirt. While Farnsworth and workmen were notified and called to the job, Lamont Loos returned to his boat and to his captain's quarters. Three drinks and he was ready for a good night's sleep. The new stack would be here before morning and the crews would be at work before sunrise.

Lamont Loos was not a grateful man. Yet he had thanked his young nephew, Walter Rashel, for knocking on his cabin door earlier in the evening. He had gone to his cabin following the Sunday night fireworks and was fixing himself a drink when young Rashel appeared. He had never liked the boy, mostly because of the young man's appearance. Walter was twenty years old, and the son of Lamont Loos' sister. He was clean-shaven, neatly dressed and well-groomed. But he was pudgy. His face was puffy. Lamont Loos had often thought that if someone punched the kid, all the air would come rushing out of him. The boy was just effeminate enough to make Loos feel uneasy whenever he entered a room. He had made the captain feel that way again as he entered his cabin. Loos could not remember the last time Walter had been aboard his boat.

"I'm sorry to bother you, Uncle Lamont," the boy stammered.

"Not at all, boy. Come in. Come in."

"I know it's late, but I thought this was so important that I'd better see you right away. I came as soon as I could get off work."

Captain Loos saw the kid occasionally at night at the White House where Walter worked as a night clerk behind the desk. He did his job well, almost too well. In his second summer on the job, he had already made some "business friendships" with the bellhops and a couple of the younger housekeepers, and he had become a compulsive snooper. It was this probing quality that had led him to cautiously open the note left in Andy Ross' mailbox by Emmett Markham.

"I can't imagine anything so important that you would have to leave work at eleven o'clock at night to seek me out here on board," his uncle remarked. Walter could detect a faint sarcastic tone to the old man's voice, but he kept on.

"Sir. I couldn't bring the note with me, but there's a slip of paper in Mr. Ross' mailbox that says a smokestack will burn out on your boat tomorrow. And it's signed—'Emmett'."

Loos was up from his chair now and across the room to stand face

165

to face with his young nephew. "Are you sure about this?" he asked.

"I saw the note myself. It's still there in the mailbox at the registration desk."

The captain paced back across the state-room. "How the hell could Markham know that one of my stacks is about to blow? And why would Andy Ross be so interested in my boat? They couldn't be betting on the race tomorrow. Neither one of them has ever bet a dime in his whole life. If it was John Stark, I could believe it," the captain thought. But Emmett and Andy . . . .

He stopped pacing, thanked Walter for the information and promised him that he would be properly reimbursed tomorrow for his information.

"I know you'll make it right with me tomorrow, Uncle Lamont," the boy replied as he left. "I just wanted you to know."

Loos swung into action. He called his first mate to accompany him as he checked both smokestacks, and when the defective stack had been discovered, he immediately left the steamer and headed for Harold Farnsworth's house. As he hiked up the road, he got to thinking about that note and the smokestack and Emmett Markham. Then he remembered that gamblin' fella had made a wager with him on the race tomorrow. Maybe he was in on it too. Anyways, he'd show all of those bastards. There'd be a new smokestack on the *Belle* by race time.

Almost all of the hotel guests at the White House slept late on this Fourth-of-July morning with the exception of a half-dozen men and a few of their youngsters who just knew how good the fishing would be on Lake Minnetonka this holiday morning. They had risen, dressed and crossed the street to the docks of the Blue Line Cafe where thirty or forty other such early-risers waited for their rowboats and fishing guides. The lake was still, and the quiet of the holiday morning was broken only by some workmen on the deck of the *Bell of Minnetonka* who seemed to have work to do, holiday or no holiday.

While the fresh minnows were being placed on fish hooks by the small hands of a young fisherman, the well-kept hands of a vacationing businessman, or the sun-baked hands of a native guide, most White House guests slept on into the sunny morning with shades drawn, unconsciously delaying the start of the holiday until their minds and bodies could be replenished after the festivities of the night before.

There was plenty of activity at this hour, however. In the White House livery barn, stable boys were already at work, cleaning out stalls, feeding their stock of horses, shining up harnesses, and sweeping out buggies for the coming day. Business would be particularly heavy today as the one-day visitors started to arrive from Minneapolis and from other parts of the lake to spend the Fourth at Excelsior.

Kitchen help also began their day at an early hour, preparing for a holiday menu which would be served to nearly 1,000 guests and visitors during the day and into the evening which seemed so distant at six o'clock in the morning.

By seven o'clock, the dining room corps arrived and promptly sat down to enjoy a full breakfast in one corner of the kitchen which was still reasonably cool from the night air, but which would begin to steam as the breakfast orders started to come in.

Having eaten, most of the dining room staff carried fresh linen into the Marine Dining Room. Chairs were still piled upside down on the tables of the dining room and the floor had been scrubbed during the night. Its orderliness seemed like an almost magical transformation from the celebration there the night before which had left the room in a shambles. Now the chairs went back in place with fresh blue dust-covers attached, and fresh white cloths were placed over each of the tables.

Rose Fortier was the last of the dining room staff to eat her breakfast. She sat at the corner table in the kitchen, sipping her coffee and mulling over the events of the past evening. She had watched the fireworks from the deck of the *City of Saint Louis* with John and then remained on the very top deck of the big steamboat until after midnight, watching other boats come and go into the night. The fireworks had made her sad and it had been so comforting to her to feel the strong arms of John Stark around her as the sky-rockets shot into the dark sky and flooded the bay with bright colors and hundreds

of tiny stars which floated down to the water and disappeared. She
remembered the first two Fourth-of-July holidays here at Excelsior,
recalling how she watched the fireworks with her father and mother.
She had found the crowds almost as exciting as the fireworks display.
Thousands of visitors would crowd the shoreline and hundreds and
hundreds more would spread blankets on the bluffs stretching back
into the village and watch the display through the oaks and elms
which ran along the shoreline drive.

Rose's thoughts were interrupted by Andy Ross who carried a
plate of bacon and eggs in one hand and a cup of coffee in the other.
He pushed back a chair across the table from her and sat down to his
breakfast. He had stopped by the desk on his way to the kitchen at
this early hour and had found the note from Emmett in his box. He
laughed and swore quietly to himself. "Son-of-a-bitch!" He had
already learned of the new smokestack going up on the *Belle* this
morning when he checked the Blue Line waterfront to make sure that
White House guests were being accomodated. Now the news of the
defective stack was anti-climatic and Andy Ross seemed relieved.
"We'll have to win the goddamned thing on the up and up—which
is the way it ought to be, anyway." He shoved the note into his pants
pocket and headed for the kitchen and his breakfast.

"Good morning, Rose."

"Good morning, Mr. Ross."

"It's going to be a hot one today."

"Yes, I know." She sipped her coffee.

"See John last night?"

"Yes."

"He's going to win that race today."

"Yes, I know. He says it's very important to him that he wins."

"It's important to both of us, Rose, for different reasons."

"He'll win," she reassured herself.

"I have some things I must do this morning, but I'll see John
before the race. I wish I could go along for the race, but I'll be needed
here at the hotel this afternoon." Andy began to eat his breakfast.

" I wish I could go, too," Rose sighed. "I guess we'll both have to
watch the race from here." She had finished her coffee and began to
get up from the table. "I've got to get to work now, Mr. Ross, but—
but I'd like to thank you for our talk yesterday morning. I—I haven't

had anyone to talk to about that or tell me what to do. I'm glad you spoke to me like you did."

Andy looked a little embarrassed. "I'm sorry if I was rough on you. But I'm glad if things are better now."

"They are." She turned and started for the dining room door. Andy watched her go. Then she stopped, looked back, started to say something and apparently thought better of it. Andy watched her turn and push open the swinging doors and disappear into the dining room.

He sat alone, finishing his breakfast and brooding over the large mug of coffee. The race was on his mind and he was trying not to worry. He reached into his pocket, unfolded the crumpled note from Emmett and read it again. He would see John later this morning, but perhaps he should tell Emmett what was happening on the *Belle*. He smiled as he sipped his coffee. He knew where he'd find Emmett Markham on this Fourth-of-July morning. When Emmett was a youngster, his father would take him down to the beach early in the morning of each Fourth of July where they would cook breakfast and sit on the rocks along the shore. And when Emmett had come back to run the newspaper alone, he'd still head for the beach each holiday morning to cook breakfast and look out at the quiet lake. When he began to see Hillary, she joined him for the early-morning outdoor breakfast. Yes, he'd be down at the shore again this morning, cooking his breakfast—alone.

19

THERE WAS A QUIETNESS about this Fourth-of-July morning that Hillary Blair found particularly peaceful. Tiny rays of early-morning light pried their way through the cracks in the worn window shades of room 215 of the White House, and Hillary was thankful that their rooms were on the west side of the hotel. She remembered how early the brightness came into the rooms across the hall which faced toward the lake each summer day. Hillary lay still in her bed, watching the various forms in the dark room take shape as the first glimpses of gray light appeared through the drawn shades. She did not move. Perhaps she was afraid to break the stillness. Or was the peace which she felt now the precious tranquility she had been searching for ever since she had left St. Louis? She stared at the crack in the ceiling, a long fine line wavering across the plaster as if it were mapping out a river route across the white desert. She looked at the crack a long time before her concentration was broken by her sleeping husband who jostled her ever so slightly as he rolled over on his side to an apparently more comfortable position. The movement snapped her mind back to the moment. It would not be long before little Jamie would want his breakfast. He would awaken soon, and Emily would be along shortly to tell her mistress that it was time for another feeding.

More awake now, but reluctant to shake off the comfortable drowsiness of this early hour, Hillary's thoughts moved to more unpleasant, more pressing matters—her mother! She didn't want to think about it. Yet, she could not prevent the happenings of the night before from forcing their way back into her mind. And Hillary was upset with herself now for being so calm last night, for not losing her composure when she and Jim followed the chambermaid back up the stairs to the third floor where she found Emmett and Frances. How could she have kept her emotions under control as Emmett spat out the angry words that told her and Jim what Frances had subjected herself to. How could she have kept such a level head as they helped Minnie and Madge dress Frances in fresh clothing. Hillary remembered how she and Jim had helped Frances out of the warm third-floor cublicle and back down the stairs to her own suite without anyone seeing them. Thank God her father had decided to play cards in the Captain's Bar downstairs! Thank God!

Hillary was also thankful that her mother was too exhausted and upset to talk. She had helped undress Frances and get her into her own bed without waking the two boys in the next room. What would she have been able to say had her mother spoken to her? "I'm sorry, Mother," would have seemed so incompatible with the consequences which Frances had chosen. There was no need for worry. Frances had dropped off to sleep almost immediately, while Hillary sat watching from across the room. Then she slipped out the door and across the hall to her own quarters, to wait for her husband who had gone back downstairs to detain Mr. Blair. There was no need to worry. He was having a good night at the poker table.

The Stockton's room was lighter now, but Hillary's mind was still cloudy. What had Emmett said before he walked out last night? "You had damn well better tell your father about in in the morning, or I will!" At least the words had made clear to Jim Stockton what he had only assumed before, and Hillary was relieved that Jim finally knew for sure who was the real father of Jamie. Her thankfulness for his understanding last night, as always, was marred only by a gnawing resentment deep within her that he had not displayed the slightest jealousy or bitterness in the revelation that had been kept silent this past year, the only reason for their living as man and wife.

In the quiet of the second-floor room, Hillary suddenly became inwardly panic-striken. She would face her father this morning and tell him the truth. She consoled herself. It would be a relief, the end of a terrible secret she had been living with. In the next instant she was convincing herself that she could not tell her father what happened. Perhaps Jim would help. No. It was not of his doing. Emmett! Yes, Emmett! He was a favorite of her father's. Yes. She must talk to Emmett. She slipped out of bed and across the room to the closet. Yes, a simple frock and a light wool shawl would do in the early morning air. She hurried. Quietly. Only little Emily in the next room with Jamie heard Hillary leave. Barefooted, Hillary stole down the very back stairs that Emmett and Frances had climbed the night before. Then she was out into the warm, calm morning, heading for the Excelsior beach.

There simply wasn't a better aroma anywhere than freshly-ground coffee beans boiling over a beach fire. Emmett propped the gray speckled enameled coffee pot on some small rocks over part of his beach fire, and watched the thick slices of bacon fry in the black skillet over the main fire. He had bought a bacon slab at Bullock's store on Saturday, and took enough coffee out of Mrs. Palmer's larder for this morning's breakfast on the shoreline.

Emmett Markham was not an outdoor man. Yet he enjoyed cooking this holiday breakfast. While the bacon sizzled he sat on an old Indian blanket at the edge of the sandy beach with his knees pulled up and his arms holding them close to his chest. It was still quiet, but there was much more activity and sounds in the air than there had been earlier when he packed his Dad's old mess-kit from his service days and headed down the grassy slope from Mrs. Palmer's boarding house toward the Excelsior beach. He sat there, looking out across the lake toward Big Island. The lake was still, but it would not be long before steamboats of all sizes, charters, excursion boats, launches, and the big sternwheelers would begin to churn up the water carrying holiday passengers.

This morning's breakfast was different from those past holidays, however. Emmett had been just as busy cooking over the fire he had started here on the beach. But he was alone. As a boy, he had helped his father with the holiday breakfast, first by gathering the wood for the fire. Then he was allowed to make the coffee, an honor his father bestowed upon him with great importance. "Coffee is the most important part of this whole breakfast," his father would say. And Emmett had been proud to kneel along side of his father and watch the coffee while the bacon and eggs were frying. When Emmett came back to Excelsior as a young publisher, he invited Hillary to eat this Fourth-of-July breakfast with him. He had learned the ritual well, and he had allowed her to help, little by little, just as his father had given him some of the minor responsibilities for this special outing. As fond of Hillary as he was when they first met, and as much as he loved her as they grew to know each other, their relationship was not unlike the relationship between Emmett and his father each holiday morning. They talked about the future, about what was happening in the world, about people, and what they should, or might be able to do about it. There was never anymore than the squeeze of a hand or a knowing smile between Emmett and Hillary Blair while they enjoyed this early-morning treat. Now Emmett sat there alone—and he missed her.

He rubbed his right hand—it was bruised and sore from last night's encounter with Bertram. It was time to put the eggs on, and he reached into the old knapsack for the four eggs he had brought along. When each had been cracked into the cast-iron skillet, Emmett looked up from the fire to follow the smoke which trailed overhead and off toward the grassy shoreline which led to Excelsior Bay and

173

the municipal docks. Then he saw her. She was standing at the top of the hill in a pale blue cotton dress with a shawl around her shoulders. It was Hillary. She stood watching him. And Emmett noticed she was barefooted.

The boat landing in front of the Lafayette Hotel on Holmes Bay was crowded this morning with visitors arriving from all parts of the lake, and with hotel guests departing for Excelsior and Wayzata to celebrate the Fourth and to see the race between the *Belle* and the *City*. Mrs. Walter Chase had risen early this morning, had a leisurely breakfast in her spacious bedroom overlooking the lake, and hummed softly to herself as she dressed for the day.

Louis drove the buggy around to the side entrance of Fairmount and waited for Mrs. Chase, who came along shortly, followed by Mattie. This was to be a very special day and Jenny had requested that both Louis and his wife accompany her to Excelsior for the holiday festivities. When they arrived at the Lafayette Hotel, Jenny and Mattie waited on the rolling front lawn of the hotel while Louis drove the team back to the hotel stable where he would leave the horses and buggy for the day. Then he hurried back to join Mrs. Chase and Mattie and the three moved down to the docks where they waited for the mid-morning steamer to Excelsior.

When the steamer, *Hattie May*, arrived, the hotel docks were kept clear for the arriving passengers. The big white sternwheeler bristled in the bright sunlight. It was the third largest steamer on the lake and a favorite of the hotel guests from the Lafayette. Smoke churned out of its twin stacks as deck-hands made fast the mooring lines and passengers docked. They would spend the day being entertained by a band concert near what seemed to the longest outdoor bar in the world where drinks would quench the dry throats of sun-baked visitors through the afternoon and into the evening as they waited for the hotel's own private fireworks display.

Jenny and her two servant-companions waited patiently until the last arrival had stepped from the dock to the long walk up to the hotel, and then joined hundreds of others who had been waiting to board the *Hattie May* for the trip to Excelsior. Some would get off at the Lake Park Hotel at Tonka Bay, but most would remain until the sternwheeler pulled into the Excelsior municipal docks where it would remain until after the big race that afternoon. The trio moved to the top deck where they found empty deck benches. Jenny sat near the deck rail while Louis and Mattie found a bench directly behind her.

Would Pinky be angry when she arrived in Excelsior this day? He had insisted that he visit here at the Lafayette or at Fairmount—that she would not like Excelsior. Why? There was no apparent reason. He was not reluctant to be seen with the lovely Mrs. Chase at the Lafayette Hotel. Yet he always said, "No," to any suggestion that Jenny come to Excelsior. It was as though she was permanently exiled from that bustling little community, locked out of the hub of summer activity on Lake Minnetonka, relegated to the quiet and serenity of the sparsely-settled North Shore and of the isolated Fairmount estate. The deep and tragic memories of another day were replaced now only by the weekend visits of the handsome gambling man. But it had been a one-way street. There were to be no visits to Excelsior by Jenny. That is, until today. This Fourth of July would mark the beginning of a new relationship between Jenny Chase and Pinky Wolfe. There would be no more "Sundays only" for them. He would not object, at least not for long, nor with much enthusiasm. Although Jenny needed him, needed him badly, she was convinced now that Pinky Wolfe also needed her. Things would be different for them. Starting today.

"There isn't much doubt about it, John, the only way we are going to win the goddamned race now is to get to Wayzata and back faster than the *Belle*. There isn't any 'insurance' or any hedging, or any other way to win the bet except to win the damn race." Andy Ross was pacing back and forth in John Stark's cramped captain's quarters. His hands were shoved in his pockets, and although he spoke with a firmness, Andy's voice was soft, almost inaudible to John, who stood near the same porthole he had looked through just two days ago when he and the manager of the White House had made their bet with Pinky Wolfe. "It's for the best, anyway, John. We made the bet originally because we thought you could win. And, by God, I still think you can. You must think so too."

"I do, Andy. I do." John continued to stare through the porthole down the line toward the *Belle of Minnetonka.* "It's just that it would have been so easy to fix it. So easy." His voice trailed off to a whisper.

"It wouldn't have been right, though. And you know it. It just wouldn't have been right."

"It wasn't a question of right or wrong. You know that the Navigation Company owns us all, anyway." John paused, then turned away from the porthole. "Of course you're right, Andy. It would have been wrong. You know it. I know it. And Emmett knew it, too. That's why he sent Mose down here to see me." Both men just stood there for a moment. Then John spoke again, almost as though he were simply thinking out loud. "How in hell did that boozin' old Loos ever find out about the stack"

"I don't know, John. I don't know."

John realized that Andy had come down to the shoreline from the White House to make sure that he was all right, particularly in view of what was happening down the line on the *Belle.* But it was Andy who was down now. And there wasn't any reason to be. What the hell? What were they worried about? Of course the *City* could win it—with John Stark at the wheel. John knew he could win. Andy should know it.

"We'll win it all, Andy," John assured him. "We'll win it all. So get the hell out of here and let the ship's captain get his work done or we won't be ready to pull up the gang-plank in time for the fun!"

Andy smiled. "You're right, John. I'll get the hell out of here. I've an errand to run yet, and I must get back to the hotel. It's going to be a busy day for all of us."

The two left the cabin and moved along the deck to the gangplank. There they stopped, shook hands, and spoke for a brief moment.

"Good luck, John."

"Don't worry, Andy. Just keep that guy Wolfe around so's we can collect when it's all over."

They both laughed, and Andy left the boat. Instead of heading back for the hotel, however, or in the direction of downtown Excelsior, he turned right and started down the pathway along the Excelsior shoreline toward the beach. Andy noticed the sun had risen a little higher in the clear sky now, and it was already beginning to get warm. It would be a scorcher by afternoon. He looked out at the lake as he hurried along the path. It was too early for any steamer traffic, but it wouldn't be long before the boats and charters began to arrive with the holiday visitors. The only boats on the lake this morning were the white rowboats with the blue trim, the boats belonging to the Blue Line Cafe. They were manned by fishermen, and they would probably all have their limit and be back for breakfast before midmorning.

Andy passed the Excelsior Commons and headed up the hill and then back downhill again in that last block to the beach. Then he came up over the last knoll—and stopped short. On the beach, Emmett Markham was embracing a pretty young woman. It was Hillary Blair. Andy decided that he would talk to Emmett later.

20

THAT THE SMALL VILLAGE of Excelsior would be host to nearly ten thousand visitors this holiday was not apparent at dawn on this warm Fourth-of-July morning. The main street was deserted at this early hour except for the five or six teen-age boys who were helping Dr. LaPaul put up the American flags along Excelsior's Water Street, as they had done each morning over this holiday weekend. They would be back again this evening to take down the thirty-eight-star flags as the day's celebration came to an end. The boys were members of a young people's group from the Congregational Church and had offered to help Dr. LaPaul in this patriotic task during the three-day weekend. For their services, they would be treated to a dinner at the LaPaul House Hotel next week—and be given twenty-five cents each. The money would be pooled and saved toward a new Edison concert phonograph for the Congregational Church.

An hour later, the early-morning traffic consisted mainly of farmers and their teams and wagons, and special runs of the local dray lines servicing the hotels for what would undoubtedly be the biggest business day of the season. At the Sampson House alone, the hotel guests and dining visitors would eat three hundred chicken dinners, a half-dozen bushels of potatoes, and gulp down six hundred cups of coffee and enough iced tea to satisfy the whole contingent of the GAR gathered for the Fourth-of-July parade.

At the Bennett Livery Stable, thirty-six buggies—singles, doubles and some very fancy surreys were being readied for hire. Another twenty-four rigs were about ready for the day at the White House livery, and buggies and teams at a half-dozen smaller liveries were preparing for the busiest day of the year.

Another troop of horses and buggies was beginning to marshal forces at the M. and St. L. Railway depot to meet the incoming trains for the day. Four such taxies had already pocketed their first fares of the holiday when the first of twelve arrivals had pulled into Excelsior at 5:51 this morning and then went on to the Lake Park hotel at Tonka Bay, arriving there at six. By noon, there would be more railroad cars lined up at Tonka Bay than in the railroad yards of downtown Minneapolis, Another six sets of cars would arrive on the Minneapolis, Lyndale and Minnetonka road, coming into Excelsior with nearly a thousand fishermen who would spend their holiday pulling thousands of fish into their rented rowboats or on to the docks and wharves reaching beyond the shallow water of the shoreline. The lake would be invaded from all sides—hundreds and hundreds more visitors riding from Minneapolis to Lake Minnetonka via other railroads into nearby Deephaven and along the north shore via the Great Northern trains.

Some of the smaller steamboats had already left on early-morning runs to Wayzata, Crystal Bay, the Narrows, Spring park and Minnetonka Beach, as the first arrivals of veterans from the Grand Army of the Republic began to filter into Excelsior for the day. By eleven o'clock, the contingent of the GAR would be just about complete and old Colonel W.T. Whitaker would have his hands full, keeping some of his men together at the Slater House where they were treated to breakfast as they arrived. Those who had brought their wives and children were perfectly happy to settle for breakfast and a restful morning on the hotel grounds which overlooked the lake and the steamboat landing. But the navy-blue woolen uniforms began to get warm, and then hot. For those who had come alone, and were somewhat free for the day, the opening of the Fred Hawkins' Saloon was the signal to begin the Fourth-of-July celebration. They would be in no condition to march in the one o'clock parade this afternoon.

Colonel Whitaker's GAR would be the most imposing group in today's parade, but there would be other units that stirred as much excietment and offered as much color to the line of march. The Iowa State Band, performing at the Lake Park Hotel, would arrive by steamboat in time to take part, and the Minnesota Band from Minneapolis would step off the 12:44 from the city in time for the parade. Later, the band would play at the waterfront for the start of the race between the *Belle* and the *City*. Marchers would include the members of the Minnetonka Yacht Club in their navy blue coats and white trousers, while the Methodist Church's Ladies Aid Society would line up all in white dresses and carry parasols. The Excelsior Volunteer Fire Department, led by Fire Chief Joe Simms, would march ahead of the brigade's two most proud possessions, a hand-drawn chemical rig, and a horse-drawn hook and ladder. The brigade didn't own a regular team of fire horses and the rig was drawn by the first team to arrive at the fire barn when the fire bell was sounded. It was usually a race between Frank Hoag and Bill Vernon to see whose team would get the duty. Occasionally, a team from nearby Lyman Lumber or the Bennett Livery barn would be on the scene first. Other horses in the parade would be those drawing two of the Minnetonka ice wagons owned by H.A. and John Morse. And there would be two or three buggies from the Bennett Livery Stable carrying the town officials and visiting dignitaries. The honored guests would include Captain Loos and Captain Stark, both of whom would look uneasy in the Bennett carriage, and wishing they were back onboard, ready to start the race. The honor of being the first musical unit in the parade would go to the Excelsior Boys' Fife and Drum Corps, a unit of nine

180

young boys under the direction of Dr. T.T. Hayward whose dentist office was located over the Newell Drug Store. They would lead the procession as the official escort for the parade marshal who had yet to arrive on the scene for the parade today—the honorable George Bertram.

Emmett had left his cooking fire and ran to meet Hillary at the top of the grassy knoll and it seemed only natural for them to embrace. It was Emmett who broke the long kiss, realizing that this was not last year, or the year before, or the year before that. This was now, and Hillary was no longer Hillary Blair. He had pressed the matter to see her yesterday afternoon in her suite of rooms at the White House, and they had ended their conversation there in an embrace. This simply could not go on, and Emmett knew it. He stepped back, still holding her hand and looked at her questioningly and puzzled.

"What are you doing here, Hillary?"

"I had to come," she replied. She looked at him for a brief moment and then her eyes turned away and looked at the ground as she spoke. "I wanted to tell you how sorry I am about last night. I wouldn't have had that happen to Mother for all the world. I just never thought it would come to this—until I saw her lying there in that little third-floor room, and heard you speak the truth to Jim and me."

Emmett turned and led her by the hand back toward the beach and his little fire. "I meant what I said last night. If you don't talk to your father today, I will. Your mother has suffered enough, and there is no reason for you and your husband to live this lie any longer, at least not with your own family." Emmett was surprised at his own calmness as he spoke. He was angry when he had verbally blasted Hillary last night, and he had remained angry through the rest of the night. He could have even overcome his distaste for violence last night when he left the hotel. Perhaps it was because he had broken the ice with his encounter with Bertram, but he had even given a

181

second thought to going back up there to the third floor and punching Jim Stockton right in the mouth! It had taken him a long time to get to sleep last night. Yet here he was, speaking to Hillary with such composure that he could have been her clergyman instead of her jilted lover.

"Go home and tell him, Hillary. It's as simple as that."

"I had convinced myself last night that I would, the first thing this morning." She looked away from Emmett again and off toward the lake. "But his morning I was as confused as ever. I couldn't ask Jim to speak for us. And I can't do it myself, Emmett. That's why I've come here this morning. I knew you'd be here. I've come to take you up on your challenge. I want you to talk to my father and tell him."

There was silence. Emmett reached down to snap off a blade of grass and toss it into the slight breeze blowing off the lake now.

"I'll do it, Hillary. But it should come from you, not me."

"I can't!"

"You should. You must. Please give it a try."

Her voice began to break. "I just don't think I can."

"Try. Please! Try! Try—and if it doesn't work, then I'll speak to him." He paused. "One of us must relieve your mother from any further punishment. We owe her so much more."

"I'll try," Hillary assured him. But there was little confidence in her voice. "I'll try—today."

"Good girl." Emmett put his arm around her waist and turned her, half guiding her back up the knoll. "You cannot stay, you're going to be missed, and very soon."

"I know."

"Then go. It's difficult enough, Hillary."

"I'll go."

"Did anyone see you come?"

"No. I don't think so. I'll just say I went for an early morning walk. It'll be all right."

"You'd better go." Emmett stood there awkwardly. It seemed unnatural not to have her stay. Then he kissed her gently. "Goodbye."

"Goodbye, Emmett." She turned to leave, stopped and looked back at Emmett. "I wouldn't be truthful with myself—or you, if I didn't tell you that I didn't come here just to ask you to speak to my father."

"Oh?"

182

Her voice began to fail again. "I—I knew you'd be here this morning—and I—I missed you." She turned quickly and left.

Emmett watched her as she walked briskly back toward the Excelsior Commons in the direction of the docks and the White House. In one brief instant it had felt good to hear her tell him that she had missed their holiday breakfast. In the next second his heart weighed a thousand pounds as he watched her leave. He turned back toward the beach, kicking a few small stones and some dirt as he slowly walked back to the fire.

"My God!" He spoke out loud, but there was no one to hear him. He looked at his breakfast in the skillet. The eggs were slightly overdone to say the least—black around the edges, and the yolks had shrivelled up to four little hard, yellow marbles staring up at him. The bacon looked like four little pieces of burnt string.

Emmett laughed to himself. He'd forget the breakfast and just have the coffee. The coffee was the most important part of the breakfast anyway.

The diploma on the wall of the office read:

The Board of Regents Of
THE UNIVERSITY OF CHICAGO
on the Recommendation of the Faculty
Have Conferred Upon
EDWARD MARTIN PERKINS
The Degree Of
DOCTOR OF MEDICINE
With all its privileges and obligations
Given In Chicago in the State of Illinois
The Seventeenth Day of May, Eighteen Hundred Fifty-Five

It was not unusual to find Doc Perkins in his office on a holiday. During the summer months, one day was just like another to the good doctor, and with visitors, hotel guests, transients and the local townspeople to minister to, seven days were hardly enough in one week to take care of the calls he was asked to make. His office, like that of the dentist, Dr. Hayward, was located over Newell's Drug

Store, and by the Fourth of July, the upstairs office of Dr. E.M. Perkins had accumulated enough heat to remain warm throughout the rest of the summer. The office included a small waiting room with a black and white tile floor with small floral designs, and an inner office furnished with a large mahogony desk and high-back swivel chair, a black leather medical examination table, and an old roll-top desk which Doc used to store his medical bag and any other instruments he kept in his office. The walls of the inner office were plastered and painted a dull gray, and the inner-sanctum and the outer waiting room were separated by a partitioned wall with translucent glass from about four feet from the floor all the way to the ceiling. The outer office was furnished with some old wicker chairs and a wicker table covered with old newspaper editions and some year-old magazines.

The waiting room was empty this morning and Doc Perkins was just finishing up with his only holiday patient.

"You're going to be fine, George," the doctor assured his patient as he washed his hands in the gray enamelled wash basin on the small commode by the front window of the office. "There are no fractured ribs, and your jaw will be tender for a few days, but there's nothing broken. You put some more of that salve on those bruises around the eye tonight and again tomorrow. In a few days the soreness will leave and you'll feel better."

George Bertram sat on the edge of the examining table, one hand holding on to the black leather upholstery and the other rubbing his swollen cheekbone. "You're sure there's nothing broken, Doc?"

"Yep. You're just damn lucky that horse didn't kick you an inch higher, George. He'da kicked your eye out."

"I guess you're right, Doc. I don't know what got into 'em. I just reached down to check the harness and the whipple-tree and whango! He caught me a good one, and I just fell in between that damn horse and the buggy. Next thing I knew, he'd kicked hell out of me. And for no reason!"

Doc Perkins wiped his hands on a small towel which had been draped across a high bar on the back of the wash commode. "You're just plain lucky, George. Go get yourself a drink and try to forget about it. That's the best prescription I can give you. There just ain't

184

nothin' else to do for it, except to go back to the Bennet Livery Stable and kick hell out of the horse!"

George Bertram slid off the table, rubbed his jaw again, and started toward the door to the outer-office. 'Thanks again, Doc. I appreciate your comin' up here on the holiday and all."

"Don't mention it, George. I may be in trouble with the law some day and need a good attorney, on a holiday."

"You can count on me, Doc."

The door shut, and Doc Perkins moved across the room to his desk to make a note of his Monday morning caller in his records. Yes, Bertram was a damn good lawyer. But he was also a good liar. Someone had beat the hell out of him last night. He'd probably fooled around with somebody's wife and this time was caught at it. There'd be no way of knowing who it was unless someone came in with a sore hand during the next couple of days.

21

WHEN FRANCES BLAIR was a little girl, her family used to visit an aunt and uncle who owned a farm near Lamoni, Iowa. All day long Frances and her young cousins would roam the farm, enthusiastically pitching in to help with the chores, hitching a ride to town on a hay wagon, or riding along the county road. In the wintertime, they would ride on the back of a bobsled drawn by a strong team of black horses, and after supper, Frances would lie down on a straw-filled mattress spread over the woodbox in one corner of the large kitchen, while the folks discussed the happenings of the day and finished their coffee. The heat from the big, black, wood-burning range kept the entire kitchen warm and Frances would pull a light comforter over her and lie still, listening to the crackling fire separating the drone of coversation of her parents and her aunt and uncle. She would drift away, yet never quite going over the brink of consciousness into the sleep which seemed so close at hand. And the voices—the voices were heard, yet without distinguishable words—just voices. It never seemed to bother Frances Remington that she could not understand just what it was they were saying.

Frances thought about those childhood days this Fourth-of-July morning. She lay still in her double bed on the second-floor suite of the White House Hotel, hearing voices and yet not really caring who the voices belonged to or what they were saying. She had experienced that same feeling last night, the warm comforter, voices, the drifting away and yet the sounds of the voices coming and fading away—Emmett's voice, the chambermaid's coarse, yet gentle tone. Conversations . . . Hillary . . . Emmett . . . Jim Stockton . . . . Sleep. Dad coming to bed . . . . More voices . . . .

If T.J. Blair was the night-owl in the family, staying on in the Captian's Bar until the last poker hand was played, he was also the early-bird. He had been up for an hour, had shaved with his straight-edged razor in a basin of cold water on the commode in the private bathroom, and had made one trip down to the desk in the lobby to order breakfast for himself, Frances and the two boys. The order had been promptly delivered to the White House kitchen, and there had been a scurry there to make sure that the breakfast trays were just right before they were carted off by the handsome young bellhop who had delivered the wine to Mrs. Blair on the afternoon of her arrival. He was helped by one of the waitresses from the Marine Dining Room, Rose Fortier.

There was a light knock on the door of 212. Tom Blair moved to the door, opened it, and waved the young man and young woman carrying the breakfast trays into the room.

"Right over there on that table by the front window," he commanded.

"Yes, sir," the young man agreed.

"It's going to be a lovely day," Rose added as she carried the tray across the room.

"Yes, I know," replied T.J. Blair. "I was downstairs earlier and I can smell the lake breeze coming through the front windows now."

Rose Fortier quickly spread a white cloth over the table and the two hotel employees set the table and left the dishes covered on the table near the window. "There you are, Mr. Blair. I hope you enjoy your breakfast."

"Yes, yes." He hesitated a moment. "Oh, here. Here's something for you two to share for being so prompt and bringing the breakfast up here for Mrs. Blair and myself." He handed a half a dollar to the young bellhop. Surprised, they both thanked him, reluctantly, and left quickly.

The conversation in the living room of the hotel suite had sounded far away to the dozing Frances Blair. She could distinguish voices, and she couldn't. Yet, her husband's voice sounded real. It was real. He was standing alongside her bed. "Wake up, my dear. Do you want to sleep away the whole holiday?"

"Good Morning, dear." They were the first words that Frances had spoken since she had stood in the middle of George Bertram's room the night before and watched the chaos around her.

The Blairs decided to let their two young sons sleep a little longer this morning and the two of them enjoyed a quiet breakfast near the front windows of their hotel room. They looked out over the Excelsior waterfront, Excelsior Bay, and the early-morning activity along the docks of steamboats and the ramps at the Blue Line where most fishermen had already shoved off for a morning on the lake. Some had such good luck that they were returning with a boatload of bass, sunfish or pickerel. Frances appreciated this quiet time. It reminded her of breakfasts of another time, when she and Tom were first married and there were no children. But that was a long time ago. The silence was only temporary. The activity, the noise, the hustle and conversation of a family dining together would be with them again as soon as lunch time, or certainly by the dinner hour tonight. Yet this respite came at just the right time.

Another knock on the door of room 212 interrupted the Blair's breakfast. Tom Blair had finished his oatmeal, a breakfast menu he enjoyed everyday of his life, when the knock at the door came.

"I'll see who it is, dear."

"No, Frances. Sit still." He called out. "Who is it?"

"It's me, Mr. Blair." It was Jim Stockton's voice.

"Come in, Jim. Come in."

188

Jim Stockton opened the door and spoke almost before he had entered the room. "Have you seen Hillary this morning?"

Frances and Tom Blair looked at each other, then at Jim who moved across the room to the breakfast table. "No, we haven't, Jim," Frances answered. "Isn't she with you?"

"She was. Earlier. But I woke up a few minutes ago and she was gone. At first I thought she was in the other room with Jamie, but I found only Emily and the baby there. She's not there. I just thought she had come across the hall to your rooms."

"Sit down, Jim," Tom Blair commanded. "Don't get all worried. Hillary probably went downstairs to order breakfast to be sent up. I did the same thing a little while ago. She'll be right back."

"But she's been gone too long for that," Jim explained.

"We've finished our breakfast, Jim, but have some coffee with us." The invitation came from Frances. "If Hillary isn't back by the time we finish our coffee, we'll go downstairs and find her."

"You won't have to look for me, I'm here!" The trio turned to see Hillary standing in the doorway. "I've been for a walk. Now I would like to have a talk with my father."

The twin stacks of the *Belle of Minnetonka* stood proud, soaring into the air, commanding the long and busy waterfront along Excelsior Bay. Painters were putting the finishing touches on the new replacement, giving the tall black metal stack a hurried coat of bright red paint to match the other smokestack, as if the two would not work together unless they were the same color. Other workmen were hoisting the last section of the burned-out pipe onto a waiting barge of the Navigation Company. The job was finished. The defective section had been replaced. The *Belle* would be ready for the holiday race this afternoon.

Lamont Loos looked at his watch, then replaced it in his vestpocket. They had made good time. It was only 10:30 and the race wasn't scheduled to start until two o'clock! He issued orders to his chief officer to step up the stoking of the furnaces on the boiler deck as they were switched back to both smokestacks. Below, fireman Henry Carlson was already shoveling the coal into the second furnace firing a hot bed which would produce the steam power that would move the giant sidewheeler out on to Lake Minnetonka in the afternoon with tremendous power. The captain was pleased with the emergency service, the new smokestack, and the general condition of his ship. It was ready to race.

Rose Fortier had a short break between the late breakfast crowd and the beginning of the luncheon trade in the White House dining room. She hung her apron on one of the wall hooks in the kitchen and skipped through the back door and across the lawn toward the docks and the *City of Saint Louis*. As she approached the *City's* own dock, she could see her John Stark standing at the head of the gangplank at the very bow of the big steamboat. Her light skip turned to an easy run just as John looked toward shore to see her coming across the grass. The two met at the foot of the gangplank and embraced. His arms felt good to Rose as he held her. There was a new feeling, a good feeling that Rose knew was her newly-found peace of mind, gained only by her talk with Andy Ross and her promise to end her relationship with George Bertram.

"I only have a few minutes before I go back to the dining room, but I just had to come down to wish you luck."

"I wouldn't have sailed until you came." John continued to hold her.

"I know you can win, Johnny. I just know you can do it. And I want to tell you that I'll marry you whether you win or lose—if you'll ask me."

"Let's wait until after the race, shall we?"

Rose's face was flushed. She was a little embarrassed as the two stood there for a moment. Then John put his arm around Rose and started back across the grassy waterfront toward the hotel. "Come on, I'll walk back to the White House with you. I've got to eat before the race, anyway. We'll talk about all that marrying after the race today."

As they crossed the lawn, John looked down the line to the *Belle of Minnetonka*. Workmen were just finishing the painting on the new section of smokestack. Yes, it would be a fair race, and John was still confident that he could win, new stack and all.

Two soft-boiled eggs. That's what the waitress at the White House's dining room brought to Pinky Wolfe for his breakfast on the morning of the Fourth of July. It was not unusual. The gambler had two soft-boiled eggs for breakfast every morning, along with toast, a side-order of hash-brown potatoes, and black coffee. And a Brownie for dessert. It was also not unusual that Pinky Wolfe was the last hotel guest in the dining room for breakfast each morning and his routine would not be changed simply because this Monday morning happened to be a holiday. The rugged, yet handsome, man had already finished a half-grapefruit before the rest of his breakfast arrived. Now the waitress set the plate of eggs, potatoes, toast and coffee in front of him. He straightened the napkin on his lap where he had placed it when he first sat down to the table by the window. It was automatic for him to place the napkin in his lap as soon as he sat down. He remembered his boyhood years when his mother and father used to take him out for dinner at the Atlantic City hotels. "Place your napkin in your lap as soon you sit down, George," his mother would tell him. After while it became a game and he would see if he could catch one of his parents who would occasionally forget about the napkin. It was another in a long series of lessons that George Wolfe learned about etiquette. His mother insisted that he stand when a lady approached their table, or when an adult entered a room. When he was five years old he knew enough not to leave the spoon in his soup bowl, to always say "Yes, sir" and "No, sir", when talking to his elders, and how to order politely from a menu. As a result, Pinky Wolfe was the best-mannered gambler ever to sail the Mississippi. He was as much at ease with the exclusive clientele of the Lafayette Hotel or the beer-drinking crowd at the Blue Line Cafe's bar.

The *Hattie May* steamed into Excelsior Bay on the end of its morning run from the Upper Lake and churned toward the shoreline and the Excelsior docks as George Wolfe finished his breakfast. He asked the waitress for a second cup of coffee as the landing ropes were thrown ashore and lashed to the docks. It was while he was enjoying his coffee that he gulped, choked and spilled the hot coffee on his shirt-front and his lap as he looked down on the docks and the arrival of the *Hattie May's* load of passengers.

My God! It's Jenny! It's Jenny! And that's Louis and Mattie with her. What the hell are they doing here? Pinky shoved his chair back and the table forward, keeping his eye on Jenny Chase as he rose from the table, spilling more of the hot coffee on his pants. He left some change on the table as a tip, knowing that the hotel would add the breakfast to his bill, and in less than two minutes he had rushed out of the Marine Dining Room, out the front entrance and down the steps, across the lawn and through the crowd of passengers disembarking from the sternwheeler.

"Jenny! Jenny!" Pinky had spotted her in the crowd and he armed his way along, side-stepping and skipping his way through until he had caught up with her. "Jenny! What are you doing here?"

"Good morning, Pinky." She seemed so calm. She smiled, and Pinky felt better.

" What are you doing here?" He asked again, "I had no idea you were coming to——"

"Excelsior?"

"Yes, Excelsior," he agreed. Already he was feeling guilty for demanding an explanation from her. After all, she was an adult and had a perfect right to go anywhere she pleased. It was just that she hadn't said anything about it to him yesterday and he was surprised. "I mean . . . I—I—I guess I am just surprised to see you, that's all." His demanding tone had already been transposed into one of apology. Jenny was aware of it. She knew it! She knew it right now! She had won! It was going to be even easier than she had imagined. He had not let her down. She knew he loved her right now and that everything would turn out just as she had planned.

"I wanted to surprise you," she said as she smiled and then laughed a little. Pinky smiled, too, although he wasn't sure why. He had been upset when he saw her coming off the steamboat. Yet he

192

felt good that she was here. He might as well admit it. "I'm glad you're here," he said. Then he put his arm around her waist and the two headed up the hill toward the main street.

"Jenny! Jenny! Someone was calling her name. It was a man's voice. Jenny turned and looked over the crowd. She turned again, stopped, and then called, "Over here!"

Pinky turned to see who it was and had he been holding a cup of coffee, he would have spilled it all over himself again. He had not met the man who was heading toward them through the crowd. But he knew who he was, and, suddenly, he knew that he had lost the game—or won it—depending on how one looked at it.

"Pinky, I don't know if you have ever met the Reverend Mr. Horton. Father Horton, this is George Wolfe."

The bespectacled clergyman smiled and extended his hand. "It's a pleasure to meet you, Mr. Wolfe. You're the man I've heard so much about. And Jenny here has told me some mighty nice things about you."

Pinky Wolfe stood staring at the man in the clerical collar and the black suit. He had not only lost the game, he'd lost the deal, too. He automatically shook hands with the Reverend Mr. Horton. "I'm pleased to meet you, sir," he answered. "I've heard some fine things about you, too—and Trinity," he added.

Jenny was smiling. Pinky Wolfe looked at her. No, she wasn't smiling. She was grinning. And so were Louis and Mattie, standing behind her.

"But I didn't realize that you and Jenny knew each other," Pinky questioned.

" Oh, yes, Mr. Wolfe," replied the clergyman. Jenny and Walter were married in my church in the city and were parishioners of mine until they moved out here to the lake. Since Martha and I moved to Excelsior we only see her a couple of times a summer, and we miss her. She's a wonderful lady."

"Yes—I know," Pinky agreed.

"And I understand that you two would like to sit down with me and have a serious talk. I think it's wonderful and I was delighted when she sent me a note last night that she would be over today so that the three of us could visit about your future together."

It came as no surprise to George Wolfe by this time. Jenny had made some decisions for both of them—some decisions that Pinky had known were inevitable and yet had been postponing for a long time. It was right. And Pinky admired her for going ahead and doing what had to be done, doing what he should have done himself.

"Come on. Let's walk over to my place," said the Episcopal clergyman. "Martha will be disappointed if you don't stop by and have some coffee while we talk."

Jenny and Pinky nodded in agreement and smiled at each other as they followed the clergyman up the street. Pinky turned back once and saw Jenny's two servants still standing there. He was right. They were grinning.

194

22

"HOW THE HELL do you suppose that goddam Loos found out about the smokestack?" Andy asked. He and Emmett Markham leaned over an iron railing along the waterfront docks by the Blue Line Cafe, watching early arrivals board the *Belle of Minnetonka* for the Fourth-of-July racing trip to Wayzata and back.

"I don't know, Andy. I'm sure that Mose White didn't tell anyone. And nobody else knew about it, at least not until I left that note for you."

"The note. Yes—the note!" Andy turned to Emmett. "Who did you give the note to last night when you stopped by the hotel?"

195

"That young Rashel boy was working behind the desk," Emmett answered. "I gave him the note—it was folded—and asked him to put it in your mail box."

"The Rashel boy. It figures."

"I watched him, though, Andy. I watched him and waited until he had placed the note in your box. He made no attempt to open it, wasn't the least bit hesitant. In fact, I was impressed with his courtesy and his prompt action."

"The little sissy bastard. He's the one who looked at the note. He's the one."

"But Andy—I watched him. I saw him——"

"He's the one, Emmett. He's the one. His uncle is old Captain Loos."

"His uncle? Lamont Loos?"

"Yes. His mother was a Loos."

"Where the hell have I been all this time," Emmett asked. "I thought I knew just about everybody in town. But I didn't know that?"

"Not too many people do, Emmett. Some of the oldtimers would know. The Rashels and old Loos aren't on speaking terms, haven't been for years. But the kid looks up to his uncle. Probably the only bright spot in his life. At least until he came to work for the hotel. He used to work in the kitchen. Then he bellhopped for awhile and then grew up so fast, at least in appearance, that I put him on as a night clerk. He's done real well, too, except most of the staff stays clear of him. He's so goddam nosey. Know's what's goin' on everywhere."

Emmett shook his head. "If I'd only known. I . . . ."

"It's all right, Emmett. But that's what happened just as sure as hell. That young Rashel read the note and high-tailed it down to the waterfront to tip off his uncle. Christ! At least, he's got some loyalty to his own kin. Though I suppose he also figures there'll be something in it for him. I told John about it this morning and——"

"And we both agreed that perhaps the best way to win this race today is to simply go out and win it." The voice was John Stark's. He had walked up behind the two men after taking Rose back to the hotel.

The two greeted John. "Mose came to see you yesterday, John?"

"Yes, he did. But he might as well have stayed away." Stark

nodded toward the smokestacks on the *Belle*."

"Yes," Emmett agreed.

"At least it put any foolish thoughts you might have had out of your mind."

"You're right, Emmett. Except I'll never know, now, whether I would have really gone through with my plan or not." John turned to Andy. I knew that Andy had talked to you, Emmett, the minute that Mose told me why he had come to see me." Then he smiled. "But it really doesn't make any difference. We're going to win it all anyway."

"I think you're right," Emmett replied.

"We're not going to win if we're not ready to sail, though. I've got to get back to the *City*. We're beginning to load passengers and we sail in two hours." John shook hands with both men and they wished him luck. John walked a few steps, stopped and turned back. "I know one thing, gentlemen. I'll never make another wager as long as I live."

They all laughed and John Stark was on his way.

Andy turned to Emmett. He wasn't quite sure whether he should mention seeing Emmett and Hillary earlier this morning at the beach. He decided not to say anything about it. "I must be on my way, too, Emmett. I'm sorry I can't make the trip this afternoon, but it's almost impossible for me to be away from the hotel this afternoon of all afternoons. John will do just fine without me around. I just wish to hell I had your job so I could sit around onboard and have a few drinks this afternoon." He loved to kid Emmett about the newspaper business. "Yours is the only job I know where you work the first three days in the week and then take off the rest of the week"

Emmett nodded and smiled. He knew he was being joshed by his friend, and past experience had taught him to simply say nothing, or to agree with Andy."

I have to go. Stop in when you get back, and we'll celebrate," Andy said.

"I will, Andy. I will."

The hotel manager left Emmett at the railing along the waterfront. Emmett turned back toward the lake. Both the *Belle* and the *City* were taking on passengers now. Emmett would ride the *City* today during the race. He didn't know just why, but he decided that's where he would be. Perhaps he had some feeling of guilt about not being onboard the *City* should it lose today's race. It would be difficult to face John in that case, far more difficult than it would be to face Andy. Emmett thought about it. The race, the wager—it had brought about a change in John Stark. He had known John ever since they were youngsters, and John had always played hard, but fair. But John had been willing to risk all of that—his job, his reputation, everything, to win today's race. It wasn't like him. Maybe there was simply too much at stake—the money, the chance for his own boat, Rose Fortier. No, John would to the right thing. He was hot-headed and short-tempered, but he'd do the right thing. And he was probably right, he'd win the race anyway.

It was funny, Emmett thought, that John, the quiet one, would be prompted to even think about any devious plot to win the race. If anyone should be expected to make such plans or suggestions, he thought it would come from Andy. Not that Andy was dishonest. No, he was just the opposite. He was too honest. He had always said just exactly what he thought. If he thought you were a bastard, he said so. And it didn't make any difference if you were a railroad executive, a wealthy hotel guest, or a stable hand. He swore, he used bad language all the time, but he didn't do it on purpose. It was just his way. Yes, it was funny how today's race, the wager, had affected the two young men. Yet, if the *City* lost today, Emmett knew that Andy would somehow take it in stride. He'd swear a lot. But he'd go right on.

Emmett looked at his pocket watch. It was noon. The parade would begin at one o'clock and the race would start at two. He'd better get some lunch and then get aboard the *City* for the race. He'd see the Blairs and Hillary later today to make sure that her father had been told the truth. He would like to see Frances, too. And maybe—maybe Jamie.

His name was Harold Todd MacDougall, but he'd been called "Mac" all his life. Most didn't even know his first name and some thought that Mac was his first name. For such a long name, however, he was a very short man. Mac was a southerner, born in Shreveport,

198

Louisiana. He grew up in New Orleans'and started hanging around the waterfront when he was twelve or fourteen. He was small for his age, though, and no one would give him a job. He finally hooked on a short-haul steamer as a cabin boy for the crew. After that, Harold Todd MacDougall tried just about every job there was on a riverboat—fireman, mate, engineer,pilot and finally a captain. His only claim to fame was as one of the pilots aboard the Robert E. Lee when it beat the Natchez in the famous race up the Mississippi from New Orleans to St. Louis. After that, job offers came fast and took Mac away from the Robert E. Lee and away from the Mississippi to the Ohio River. When Mac left the Mississippi, his wife left him and went back to her home in New Orleans. He went back after her once, but she refused to leave the South. Mac found her carrying on with some waterfront characters, and damn near killed one of Reba's gentlemen friends with his bare hands when he came barging into her place while Mac was there, asking her to come back with him to Ohio. After that he boarded the next boat North and never looked back.

Mac's hair had always been a bit thin. Now, at fifty-seven, he was almost bald. Still, he was a handsome man with a resonant tone to his voice and a commanding manner about him. He had disliked the trip to Excelsior, especially the train ride from Chicago. Now he stepped off the train at the Excelsior depot.

"Where does the Lake Minnetonka Navigation Company put up its crews?" he asked old Herb Johnson.

"Most of 'em stay at the Sampson House," he was told.

"Perfect. Send my trunk up there soon as you can. Now I'd like to get down to the waterfront right away."

The depot agent helped the newcomer find a taxi rig and Mac climbed into the front seat of the buggy with the driver.

"Looks like a big celebration today?" he questioned.

"Yessir. This is just about the biggest day of the whole year here."

"There goin' to be a parade?"

"Yessir. It'll start pretty soon, now, and when it's over, the big race will begin," the driver explained.

"A race?"

"Yessir."

"What kind of a race?" Mac inquired.

"Between the *Belle* and the *City*."

"You mean a STEAMBOAT RACE?" Mac's eyes were shining.

"Yessir? The best damn steamboat race you'll ever see. That old Captain Loos is finally going to get his when John Stark beats him with the *City*."

"You mean the *City of Saint Louis?*"

"Yessir."

Harold Todd MacDougall smiled. And he sat up just a little straighter as the buggy wheeled along Excelsior's main street and down to the waterfront. Mac paid the driver twenty cents, twice the regular fare, thanked him for the lift, and promptly headed for the docks and the *City of Saint Louis*. He could see the beautiful gleaming red and white steamboat now, and somehow this small, handsome man knew that he made the right decision to come to Excelsior as the captain of the *City*.

It had been a long time since Tom Blair had gone for a walk with his daughter. When Hillary was young, they would often find time for a walk along quiet streets in the neighborhood or down to the park where they could share a bag of peanuts with the squirrels and talk about school and the family and things. Tom Blair liked to think that he wasn't so busy back in those days. But the truth of the matter was that he was busier then than ever. Come to think of it, there was no good reason why he couldn't take the time to go for a walk. And when Hillary insisted, her father surprised himself—and agreed.

Although the main street and the road along the lakeshore were busy with visitors and buggies and taxis, the lanes and roads which led through the residential areas were quiet and peaceful. Hillary and her father walked slowly down the middle of the road lined with maple and elm trees which bent over the street, protecting the dusty road from the sun climbing high into the sky. Hillary had already gained new confidence. At least they were this far. He would have to listen to her.

"Well, come on, Sis. What's so important that it calls for a private walk for just the two of us?"

200

"I'm afraid that what I have to say is not going to be very pleasant, Dad."

"It's all right. Out with it. After all, it's a holiday. What's the matter? You and Jim still having some differences? That's bound to happen during your first year of married life."

"No, Dad. It's far more serious than that. It's something that I am responsible for and now I'm afraid that it has affected all of us."

Tom Blair put his arm around his daughter as they walked along the shady road. "Oh, come on now, Hillary. I don't seem to have been affected by whatever it is you've done. I still have two arms, two legs, all my faculties, and all of my friends. Nobody has suggested firing me, at least not lately."

"You're joking with me, Dad, and it's no joking matter. If it were a joke, I could have told you in the lobby and we would have skipped all of this."

"Then out with it, Sis. What's the trouble?"

"I'm not sure where to start. It seems to get more involved with every step. I guess there's no easy way to explain except to simply tell you——"

"Tell me what, Sis? That you're not happy here and you want to go home? I know you haven't felt good since you arrived, but after a few more days of rest you'll feel better."

"It's not that simple, Dad." She was going to lose him if she didn't spit it out.

"If it's about the race this afternoon, my dear, I've already talked to Jim and he's willing to go, even though he doesn't like the lake. As a matter of fact, we'd best be starting back or we'll miss the boat ride and old Captain Loos' triumphant finish over that young Stark fella."

"Father. I don't love Jim."

"Of course you do. You just think you don't." He answered her, but his tone of voice had not changed. He simply went right on with the conversation. "I can remember when your mother and I had been married about a year——"

"I lied to you about the baby, too."

"There was a time when we were both unhappy, before your older brother was born. But after the first offspring, everything was different."

Hillary was losing the fight, and she knew it. It had to be now! He must listen! "He's not the father of my baby, Dad! Emmett Markham's the father!" She had swung around in front of her father and blocked his path. He had to listen. "Jamie is not mine and Jim's! He's mine and Emmett's!" She was shouting!

Tom Blair had heard this time. And the understanding tone in his voice had evaporated quickly. "Are you sure you're all right, Sis? You don't know what you're saying! You can't be serious!"

"It's the truth, Dad. I have made a number of mistakes. One was in not telling you the truth to begin with. Yes, Emmett's the father, the real father. And when I found I was pregnant, we were back home and I couldn't . . . I just couldn't let that happen to the Blair name."

"Hillary . . . you're not mak——"

"So I took the easy way out. I married Jim Stockton. Oh, he knew about the baby, but he married me anyway. And everything would have been fine, just fine, if you hadn't insisted that we all come back here this summer." Tears were streaming down her face now, and before she could go on, her father grabbed her by the shoulders.

"You and Emmett Markham? You and young Markham? Hillary, how could you? And I suppose everyone knew about it except me?"

"No, Dad. That's not true." She was still sobbing. No one else knew, not even Emmett. Only Jim and Mother."

"Frances knew? And you wouldn't tell me?" Tom Blair couldn't believe that all of this was happening.

" No one in our family has ever let you down, Dad. No one. And I couldn't let this happen to our family. I just couldn't let this happen! All your friends . . . your job . . . your . . . Oh, Father!"

Tom Blair gathered his daughter into his arms in the middle of the shady road and stood quietly. He didn't know how all of this could happen or was happening. But it was apparent that he had been oblivious to everything that had been going on. Somehow he had lost touch with his own family. "Good God!" was all he could say. As he held his daughter, he looked over her shoulder. They were standing in the street in front of Trinity Chapel. And it seemed only natural that they start across the road and up the steps to the small church. Somehow the holiday and the race didn't seem so important now.

There was a knock at the door of the captain's cabin and John Stark quickly opened the door as he spoke. "Come right in and—" The figure of Harold MacDougall startled him. He did not recognize the handsome face. The two men stood for a moment. "Yes——?" asked John.

"Are you John Stark?"

"Yes, I am." John was in a hurry. He didn't have time to visit today. Passengers were already crowding on for the race, and he would have to get a move on. "I'm in a bit of a hurry. Is there something I can do for you?"

"I'm Harold MacDougall," the man answered as he stuck out his hand.

"Yes. I'm pleased to meet you, sir. But I'm awfully busy. We're about ready for our annual Fourth-of-July race, and——"

"Yes, I know," the stranger answered.

"Then perhaps we can talk some other time. Right now——"

"I'm the new captain from Pittsburgh."

It was as though John Stark had received a hard kick in the groin from Captain Loos. First the new smokestack, and now this. How could the Navigation Company do this to him? Of all the times to report for duty. He was speechless. He simply stood there, staring at the intruder who blocked the doorway with his small frame.

The balding man smiled. "Don't look so worried. I would no more think of taking over command of this boat today than I would try to fly across the bay out there. No sir, young man. You go right ahead. I don't intend on reporting for duty until tomorrow."

John took a deep breath and blew a sigh of relief. But before he could speak, the newly-arrived visitor spoke again. "I'd just like to ask one favor of you, however."

"You name it, Mr. MacDougall. It's yours," John replied.

"Just for the fun of it—I'd kinda like to ride along this afternoon. Just as another passenger—if you don't mind."

23

IT WAS TRADITIONAL that the mayor of Excelsior serve as Grand Marshal of the Fourth-of-July parade and it now seemed traditional that George Bertram serve in that capacity whether he was mayor or not. For the occasion, the Hotel Lafayette had sent over its grand carriage, replete with a magnificent team of shining black horses with special show harnesses and bright red plumes atop the bridle harness. The driver, too, was resplendent in his bright red coat, white breeches, glossy black boots, and top hat. To complete the image, George Bertram wore his very best white suit, he had three such ensembles, and, on this special occasion, a white straw hat. A black string tie fell carelessly against a white shirt that was already stained with perspiration. What would normally be a politically triumphant day for George Bertram, however, was marred somewhat by the appearance of his usual broad smile. He was smiling, all right, but it was difficult for him with the bruises to his cheekbone, a scraped nose, and a slightly darkened left eye. The cuts inside his mouth were not visible, but they were even more painful to the Grand Marshal this day. Doc Perkins had told him to leave them alone and they would heal by themselves; but in the meantime, Bertram had discovered that his usual whiskey and water were simply too strong for the abrasions on the inside of his mouth. As a matter of fact, he didn't even feel like watching the parade, let alone serving as Grand Marshal. But there he was, Mayor George Bertram, coming down Water Street in that magnificent carriage, heading for the municipal docks at the foot of the main drag where he would fire the gun that would start the two giant steamboats on their way across the lake toward Wayzata.

The carriage followed the colors, the American flag with its thirty-eight stars, for the thirty-six states which had survived the Civil War along with the two new states, Nebraska and Colorado, that had joined the Union since that terrible conflict ended, and the flag of the Grand Army of the Republic. They were flanked by two middle-aged men in faded blue uniforms that seemed about two sizes too small around their bulging middles and husky necks. Slightly short sleeves were tight on the arms of the two color guards who carried Springfield rifles, the standard field weapon for the Union infantry.

The two Blair boys sat on the edge of the boardwalk at Water and Second Streets watching the parade swing down toward the waterfront. And it went almost as planned. The local boys' Fife and Drum Corps came along behind the Grand Marshal's carriage, and then the main unit of the parade, the Minnetonka contingent of the Veterans of the Grand Army of the Republic, about one hundred strong, led by Colonel W.T. Whitaker. They were followed by all the rest of the traditional units, the Ladies Aid Society, the Fire Brigade, and the only other musical unit in the parade, the Iowa State Band, loaned to Excelsior for the parade by the Lake Park Hotel. The Minnesota Band was also scheduled to march, but when the train pulled into the Excelsior depot shortly before one o'clock, there was no band on board. The only other carriage in the line of march was the rig from the White House livery stable which carried Captain Lamont Loos and Captain John Stark, the two opposing skippers for the steamboat race which would follow.

John Stark was uneasy. He had great confidence in his boat, and in himself, but Lamont Loos had simply been too cordial to him. They made small talk as they rode along in the carriage behind the Iowa band, and the captain of the *Belle* was just too damn friendly.

"Quite a crowd here today, Stark," said the old captain as he surveyed the long line of faces along the boardwalks. "Maybe the largest crowd ever."

"Yes—I think you may be right," John answered.

"I'll have about two thousand aboard this afternoon, Stark. How about you?"

"I told the purser to stop the boarding at fifteen hundred."

"That's good," the captain nodded. "Yes, that's just about right for the *City*. I know your boat's in good shape—and I want you to know that mine is, too." He looked out at the crowds again and a faint smile crept across the sunburned face.

"Yes. We're all set," replied John. "I slept on board last night. Not that anything would happen. I just felt better, that's all."

Loos nodded again. "Yes, I know just how you feel."

The crowds didn't make John nervous, but he just didn't like being on display. He would be glad when they reached the waterfront. Old Loos was too confident again, and it bothered John.

"Lucky thing for you, young fella, that the new skipper didn't show this week. I frankly would have been a little disappointed if you would have had to step down for some stranger just before the best race of the year."

John wondered where Harold MacDougall was at this moment. He thought back to their meeting this morning in his captain's quarters. And all of sudden, John Stark was no longer worried about Loos or the *Belle*.

Red, white and blue bunting bedecked the band stand in the park at the foot of Water street adjoining the Excelsior municipal docks. Perhaps two thousand visitors crowded the shoreline, many of them disappointed that they could not get passage on one of the two steamboats in the race today. The parade had not taken long. Yet it had been an impressive line of march. The Iowa band had assembled on the small white bandstand and had so overcrowded the tiny structure that there was hardly room enough for Mayor Bertram to shoulder his way up the steep set of stairs to start the race. While the last-minute preparations were being made on board the two steamers, the vendors, hawkers, and the barmaids at the Blue Line Cafe and the White House Hotel were doing a land-office business with the holiday visitors who would have to be satisfied with watching the start and the finish of the Fourth-of-July race from the Excelsior shoreline.

On board the two steamboats, the engines were idling, noisily, rumbling with anxiety to get on with it. Captain Loos appeared calm as he stood outside the door of the *Belle's* wheelhouse, far above the decks and the crowds along the shoreline. The old captain sucked on his pipe and smiled. Fourth-of-July races were nothing new to him. He had been through all of this before and he seemed to gain new confidence as he glanced up at the new smokestack which was already billowing black smoke into the clear Minnesota sky. Two docks down, John Stark was also in the wheelhouse aboard the *City*, but he was too busy to watch the crowds. He was still going over last minute adjustments and changes as the gang-plank was pulled aboard and crewmen slipped the knots off the landing ropes. All that was left now was the short speech by His Honor, the Mayor, and the signal— the gunshot that would send the two steamboats on their way.

The mayor made his speech, including a welcoming of visitors to Excelsior and to the day's festivities along with the hope that they would stay through the day and come back again soon. Old-timers watching the proceedings were surprised at the brevity of the mayor who usually took every opportunity to enhance his political position and mention his law practice. But the mayor was not in the best physical condition, and the inside of his mouth hurt him something awful. As a result, the address was short, and with little fanfare, he wished both captains luck, raised the pistol over his head, and pulled the trigger. The sound of the pistol shot was almost drowned out by the blast of the steam whistles on board the *Belle* and the *City*. Crewmen hopped across the widening span from the docks to the moving steamboats with the last of the docking ropes; ships' bells rang and the roar of the furnaces on the boiler decks could not be heard because of the rumbling of the engines swinging into action. Black smoke belched from the twin smokestacks of the two magnificent steamboats as they backed out of the municipal docks into a half-circle before steaming out of Excelsior Bay to head north toward Wayzata. The race was on!

Jim Stockton and his wife had boarded the *Belle of Minnetonka* about a half-hour before the race started and had missed the holiday parade down Excelsior's main street. The two sat quietly in a corner of the barroom at a small table, Hillary sipping on a lemonade and Jim gulping down a shot of whiskey. It had been easy to talk until they felt the big steamer move away from the dock and heard the crowds outside and the steamboat whistles. Then the passengers had flowed into the large barroom like water into a sinking ship. It was noisy, and yet, Hillary and Jim seemed to be able to continue their conversation without too much difficulty.

There was a quiet but pleasant sound to Hillary's voice. "I'm glad we came alone today, Jim. I was surprised when you said you'd go even though the folks had decided to stay at the hotel. I know how much you dislike the water."

"It seemed the thing to do," he replied without looking up from the table. "Besides it's the first time we've been alone, I mean really alone, since we came to Excelsior."

"I know," she agreed. "And I'm sorry for all that's happened. Everything that I was afraid would happen, has happened. And it's all my fault."

"Let's not go back over it again, Hillary," Jim interrupted. "I've heard all of th——"

"No, Jim. I won't go over it again." She paused. "It's just that I know what a terrible mess I've made of all of this. It was all wrong from the start. I never dreamed that it would end up like this, like it did last night with Mother——"

"Let's go home, Hillary!" He spoke as though he had not even been listening to her. "Let's go home tomorrow. We'll take Jamie with us. Emily can stay with your folks and the boys. But let's leave, while we still have something to salvage out of all of this." He looked back down at the table again. "I know now what I had guessed all along about Emmett Markham. And it isn't going to get any better,

Hillary. It can only get worse. You know how I feel abut you, how I've always felt about you. That hasn't changed at all. I still love you, Hillary. That's why I think we should leave. Now! While we still have a chance! I don't want you to make the decision—nor your dad or mother. It's my decision, and I think we should go. We must go, Hillary, if I am to have any respect left for myself. If you are to have any respect for me."

There was silence at the small table, a sort of vacuum, surrounded on all sides by the noise of passengers yelling, drinking, singing and cheering. Jim Stockton ordered another whiskey.

Aboard the *City of Saint Louis*, John Stark was at the wheel himself, as the big steamboat passed the southernmost tip of Big Island and headed down the line toward Wayzata some five miles away. Everything felt good, the giant wheel in his hands, the ride of the *City* on the smooth surface of the lake, and the feel of the big boat. It was quiet up in the wheelhouse and John smiled as he looked across at the *Belle* which trailed off the starboard bow by about two lengths. The smaller boat had been able to get into high gear much quicker than its bigger and heavier rival, but John knew that old Loos would have the *Belle* fired up to pull even with him before they reached Wayzata. In the meantime, there was nothing to do but keep the *City* at full blast and John intended to do just that, from the minute he left the Excelsior docks until he reached them again.

On the lower deck in the *City's* ornate dining room, Pinky Wolfe and his new fiance, Mrs. Jenny Chase, were enjoying a light lunch. They, too, had boarded early and had immediately gone to the dining room, missing the parade and the mayor's speech. And they, too, had other things to talk about besides the race. Pinky wasn't quite sure just why they had decided to go aboard the *City* for the race this afternoon. There was nothing he could do about the outcome of the race, or about the wagers he was already committed to. And he had already committed himself to something far more serious, and permanent, since Jenny arrived in Excelsior this morning . . . .

"More coffee, Mr. Wolfe?" inquired Martha Horton.

"No, thank you," replied Pinky Wolfe.

"Will you have some, Jenny?" asked the clergyman's wife.

"Yes, thank you," Jenny said. "You have a lovely home here, Mrs. Horton. I'm sure you will miss it when you leave."

"Yes," she answered. "I'll miss it. But when you're the wife of a clergyman, you learn to enjoy each home while you're there, and then to go on to the next parish and take up where you left off. We're going to miss Excelsior—and Minnesota. We're both from Missouri, you know, and it's going to be quite a change for a couple of mid-westerners to start over again in the east. And West Point is going to be a lot different from any parish that Henry ever had before."

Martha Horton was a pretty woman. She had been a nurse when she first met her husband and had kept working at her profession when they were first married. It was curious that his first parish had been in Excelsior Springs, Missouri, and that his last parish before going to West Point would be another Excelsior parish, in Minnesota.

The Reverend Henry Horton entered the room again from his small study off the front parlor.

"July twenty-third will be just fine," he said as he entered the room. "You let me know what time you want the service, and I promise I'll be here," he beamed.

"Yes. July twenty-third will be just fine, won't it, George?" inquired Jenny.

"Yes—just fine," nodded Pinky.

"Good!" And as an afterthought, the clergyman added, "I don't think we need any kind of rehearsal or anything."

"No, they'll do just fine," added Mrs. Horton.

" I think we should go now, said Jenny. "We've taken up enough of your time, and it's a holiday."

"Yes, we do thank you for your help," Pinky added. "And we'd hope that you will come over to have dinner with us at Fairmount before you leave for the east."

"Yes, of course," they agreed. "There'll be plenty of time after the wedding before we leave," said Martha. "We'll come. . . ."

Pinky shook his head, just thinking about the morning just passed. He sat there across the table from Jenny in the dining room of the *City of Saint Louis* and wondered how all of this had happened so fast. Then he looked up at Jenny and knew that it was right. And, as usual, luck had been with him once again.

He smiled at her as she read the menu. "Let's order."

Young Tom Blair and his brother David had not expected to be aboard any boat this day. They had watched the parade swing down the main street of Excelsior and were about to get permission from their parents to go to the Excelsior Commons to watch the start and finish of the steamboat race when Emmett Markham had come along.

"I suppose if Mr. Markham, here, wants to put up with you two boys, it's all right if you go aboard the *City*," said their mother. "I'll tell your father."

"Yes, ma'am," the two youngsters chimed in unison.

"And you be sure to find us up at the hotel the minute you get off the boat after the race," she added.

"I'll see to it that they get back here safely," Emmett assured her. "I'll be careful with them, Frances."

Frances looked at him for a moment without saying anything. Then she caught herself, and smiled. "I know you will, Emmett. I know that Tom will appreciate your taking them along." She hesitated for a moment. "He had a long talk with Hillary this morning, and he's just not up to the parade and race and all."

"I can't say I'm sorry he knows," Emmett tried to explain. "I'm only sorry that it has all turn——"

"He's been hurt, Emmett. Not only by what's happened, but because he feels everyone else knew about it but him. The mere fact that he wasn't told right at the beginning by his favorite child makes it even worse for him."

"I'd like to talk to him someday soon, Frances."

"Not right now," she answered. "Perhaps later, when he's had an opportunity to think it all out. Perhaps then."

"I understand," Emmett agreed. "But we'd better get going or we're going to miss the boat." He shoved the two boys toward the waterfront and the three of them were off and running to catch the *City*.

But they ended up on the top deck of the *Belle*. It was an excellent vantage point, and Emmett told the boys they were lucky to have found such good seats after being the last ones to jump aboard before the gangplank was pulled away from the dock. Emmett would have preferred they ride the *City* this day, but it was already filled up to capacity and the boarding gate had already been closed off by the time Emmett and the boys reached the municipal docks. So it was down the shoreline to the *Belle*. And they had just made it.

The *Belle* was moving along, but was trailing its sister boat by a little more than a length as they passed Swift Point on the right and steamed into the wide expanse of the Lower Lake toward Wayzata Bay. The crowd became boisterous as they began to pull abreast of the *City* but quieted when they slowed and swung wide as the two steamboats rounded the specially-installed racing buoy at the north end of the lake. The *City* was only a length ahead coming out of the turn, now, and Emmett could see the figure of John Stark in the pilot house. They were approaching the northernmost tip of Big Island again on the return trip home and Emmett could feel the power of the *Belle* as it began its back-stretch surge to overcome its smaller and lighter rival! If John Stark was going to win today, he'd have to win it along the west side of the island, he thought. There'd be no burned-out smokestack to help him today. And Captain Lamont Loos was not about to give John a chance to escape the menacing challenge of the larger *Belle*.

Emmett strained to look again at the bristling white steamboat ahead of them and could still see the figure of John Stark in the pilot house on the hurricane deck! What he could not see were two well-dressed men who had now slipped through the crowd on the top deck of the *City* and had started down the steps, brushing by the holiday passengers who were crowding their way topside for a better look at

212

the final stretch of the race! The short one, with the heavy sideburns and beard, was shoved aside at one point midway down the stairway into the enclosed deck and he paused to touch his chest to make sure that the pistol was still in place under the brown flannel coat. He reached the lower deck and waited for his partner, a younger and taller man, and then the two of them set off along the starboard side of the *City*. They stopped just outside one of the entrances to the ship's bar and asked directions. And a crewman pointed the way.

"You'll find the purser's office just down that companionway— about four doors. It's on the right."

24

THE HOLIDAY CELEBRATION was in full swing along Excelsior's shoreline and down the little town's main street. The two thousand passengers onboard the *Belle* and another fifteen hundred riding on the *City* didn't even make a dent in the crowds which had come to spend the day. The walking paths along the shoreline were so jammed that visitors who had hoped for a stroll along the lakeside were caught in the tumultous throng that spilled out over the green grass which would look like a plowed field by tomorrow morning. Hawkers had set up their little transient stands along the road, selling everything from the latest Minneapolis newspaper to special souvenir ribbons and pillows. People were everywhere. Some young couples down along the shoreline couldn't wait for darkness to make love, while older and more affluent couples with such inclinations were jammed in standing-room-only bars in local hotels, trying to edge toward the exits and the stifling hot third-floor rooms rented for the day.

Frances and Tom Blair had walked a few blocks away from the lakeshore and the crowds, and stopped at a smaller hostelry for a light lunch. The Donaldson House was one of the older hotels in Excelsior and was known for its "home-cooked" meals. In contrast to the celebration going on just blocks away, the atmosphere at the Donaldson House was quiet and intimate. There were a few families and one younger couple, guests of the hotel, enjoying a late lunch. And there were the Blairs. Frances Blair was her usual self— elegantly beautiful, tastefully, but simply, dressed, and looking perhaps a little tired. Yet she smiled as she visited with her husband at a corner table in the small hotel dining room.

Tom Blair, on the other hand, was not himself this afternoon. On any other Fourth of July, he would have been surrounded by his entire family aboard the *Belle of Minnetonka*, leading the holiday festivities, betting on the outcome of the race with the gentleman at the next table, and ordering food and drink for everyone in his own party without even asking whether or not they wanted it. Yet, today he was more quiet and reserved than his lovely wife. He spoke in soft tones, in quiet terms, and with a sense of devotion and love in every word. Through the lunch hour, the two of them talked about Hillary—about her childhood, her growing up, of past days in Excelsior, of home, of their family, their friends, Tom's job, their successes, the joys and heartbreaks of raising a family.

"I just never dreamed that I was so demanding, so—so overbearing in my desires to have my family just the way I wanted it to be," Tom said as he looked down at the near empty glass of brandy he had been holding. "I should have known that everything couldn't always be my way." He shook his head as though to disapprove of some inner thoughts. "My attitude toward others—the people I do business with, my own associates, my employees, the people at the hotel—that's bad enough! But to think of how I have looked and acted with my own family is unforgiveable!" He paused and then looked up at Frances. "Especially to you, my dear." He reached across the table and took her hand in his.

"Nothing has changed, Tom," she assured him. "We're still the same family. We're still just as proud as ever of our children. Even more proud of Hillary, now. What's happened can't be changed. That's already in the past. But we must all think of Hillary and Jim now, and of little Jamie. They're the ones who need our love, our compassion, and understanding. We have to let them live their own lives, Tom. Starting right now!"

The two of them talked some more, agreeing that Hillary and her family should do whatever they thought best. Perhaps they would decide to leave for home before the rest. It would be understandable. Yes, that would be wise. And Tom would find time to talk to Emmett. He still liked the newspaperman. There would be time to mend fences, to change course, to set things right.

Had Tom Blair known about George Bertram's blackmail scheme and the midnight episode with Frances, there would have been only time for murder!

There was still a full dining room of guests at the White House as visitors enjoyed their mid-day Sunday dinner—on Monday. The choice tables, of course, were always those next to the screened windows along the waterfront, but they were especially sought-after now. The view of Excelsior Bay and the finish of the race would be excellent from the Marine Dining Room and it was nearing the time! At first there would be a rumbling in the crowd along the shoreline, a low murmur that would be magnified into cheers when the first sight of the smokestacks of the two big steamboats came into view from the far side of Big Island. From there it was a straight line south to the Excelsior docks and the finish line. The captain and crew of the winning steamboat would be the toast of the town tonight! For the loser, it would simply mean getting ready for the regular daily schedule again tomorrow. The Fourth of July was not the end of the world, or even the season here on Lake Minnetonka. There were still two months of vacationers, resorters, parties, moonlight cruises, singing, dining, dancing, gambling—and seducing. Yes, tomorrow would be another regular working day for both the losers and the winners.

Andy Ross had some time to relax this afternoon. His staff had worked their way through the busy morning and the overcrowded lunch hour.The bar was beginning to thin out now as the time approached for the climax to the race. After that, the hotel would be full again, catering to its own guests and visitors in the dining room and bar until late into the evening. Andy and his staff had already flushed three whores out of the lobby. One, an attractive blond, had been put out three times since ten o'clock this morning and Andy finally suggested that she try the Sampson House down the street for a change. Then he found a small table in the back corner of the dining room and gulped down some lunch. Before he was through, he received word that some of the hotel guests were unhappy because the buggies they had ordered still had not arrived at the south entrance. So it was off to the hotel livery stable to make sure that the delay was simply from a busy afternoon. Or else "the goddamned help was celebrating the Fourth on company time!"

He was walking back to the hotel across the back lawn when he saw Rose come out of the servant's entrance. She saw him and waved. Andy waved back and called to her. "Wait up, Rose! Wait a minute!"

She paused, turned back to him, and waited. "I'm on my way 'round front to watch 'em come home," he said as he approached her. "Come on! Come on with me and we'll watch from the front porch. You'll never be able to see anything from down along the shoreline with all those people down there!"

"I'm through work for the day," she explained apologetically. "I just didn't think I had time to get out of this uniform before the boats get back."

"It's all right. There's no reason why a couple of hotel employees can't watch the race from the front porch, is there?" He laughed. "At least on their own time."

"If you don't mind the uniform," she hurried to say.

"Rose, you'd look good in almost anyth——" he stopped, kicked himself mentally, and went right on. "Come on, they'll be along almost anytime now."

217

The two hurried around to the front lawn of the hotel and crossed the porch to the far end where they could see the lake and be a little away from the crowd. No noise from the shoreline crowd, yet, and no sign of the smokestacks coming from beyond the tip of Sunrise Point. They leaned against the porch railing.

"I hope John's all right," she said worriedly.

"He is, Rose," Andy assured her. "He'll do just fine. After all, he's got a lot more riding on this race than anyone else. Sure, we'll both win some money which will help us both do the things we want to do. But he's countin' on that money for his whole future, for his own boat—and you."

She looked down at the porch floor. "Yes, I know. But the race isn't that important to me—only to him. I'd marry him regardless of the race or what boat he's on."

Andy looked out over the lake. Maybe if he loses, he'll just have to accept that. He'd be a damn fool if he didn't"

They both were silent for a moment. Then Rose turned to Andy. "I want to thank you again, Andy, ah—Mr. Ross."

"Forget——"

"No, I want to thank you for what you did to help me yesterday. I know you are right and I'm ashamed of what's happened. And I'm so grateful to you, not just because of what you said, but because you've been kind to me, and understanding, and you've given me someone that I can talk to about these things. I feel comfortable talking to you. Yes—I feel comfortable."

John Stark looked off his port bow to keep an eye on the Big Island shoreline which the *City* was hugging as it glided along toward Williams Shoal. Then John glanced back to check the position of the *Belle* which was now off the pace by just a hundred yards.

The two big boats were approaching the end of Big Island now and they would soon swing out to clear the shoal and the red and black buoy, then swing to the portside and head for home a mile away. There'd be some wind as they got out into the open waters of Excelsior Bay and John knew that his bigger and heavier rival would be churning at full speed and would be less affected by the wind and wave currents than his own craft. He needed the hundred yards he now had and perhaps a little more if he could get it. The *Belle* was offshore by another hundred yards, too, and if the *City* could just keep that advantage as well when it made the turn into the homestretch, John figured he could hold on. The colored buoy was really a safety buoy, but was used as a race buoy for such events as today. The sand bar it marked had built up at the end of the island opposite the entrance to the old narrows. Recently, a second bar had formed beyond the old one but the Navigation Company hadn't bothered to move the buoy. Of course, everyone knew about the second bar and steered clear of it. A shallow channel existed between the bars at the buoy and small craft used it as a shortcut when rounding the island.

John had asked Harold MacDougall to watch from the wheelhouse and Mac was standing quietly in the background by the screen door, watching the young skipper navigate along the island shoreline and head toward the safety buoy. He admired the way John Stark ran his boat and was impressed by the efficiency of the *City's* crew. He hoped that they would work that well for him when he took over tomorrow. What he couldn't understand was why the Lake Minnetonka Navigation Company would want to bring him all the way to Minnesota when they had John Stark to run their ship for them.

John was thinking about the channel. His boat was forty-feet wide and the *Belle* was sixty. The *Belle* could never make it through there but the *City* might!

In the wheelhouse of the *Belle of Minnetoka*, Captain Lamont Loos eased up as he prepared to make his turn. He was quite relaxed. He knew the *City* would falter in the strong head wind on the last leg of the race. Then, he would bring his powerful, sharp-nosed boat passed her at Sunrise Point and give the shore folks, as well as his passengers, a little show. Loos waited for the *City* to swing to the starboard and leave the shoreline for deep water. Stark would have to make his move soon or he'd be in there too tight to the shoal. The veteran captain knew about the shoal's channel and he knew it wasn't big enough for the Belle, not for the City, either. The City did not change course, however, and Loos realized there wasn't enough time now for Stark to move starboard. If he did, he'd hit the second sand bar for sure. By God! He didn't intend to, thought old Loos. He's going for the channel! I'll be damned, he's going to try it! If he makes it, he'll be on course for Excelsior before we round the shoal. Another minute will tell. Well, if Stark gets hung up, he can stay there. The Belle would play it straight and head for the finish. Someone else could come out and get 'em off the hook! Loos rubbed his chin—another thirty seconds and the bastard would be through there.

John Stark held his breath as he piloted the big sidewheeler through the inner channel himself, flags flying and huge clouds of smoke trailing from the belching smokestacks. On the main deck, passengers could look over the side and easily see the sandy bottom of the lake as it rose on either side of the channel. Another twenty seconds and the City would be home free! Then John Stark could feel the drag on the big flat bottom steamer, and Harold MacDougall could hear the crunching. The City's hull was scraping the bottom of the channel! The giant paddlewheels were digging up sand and spitting it out behind now! John kept a firm grip on the wheel and the engines were still at full power as the City crunched its way along the narrow channel. They were losing speed! They were no longer gliding through the water! The creaking was louder, now! John could see the sandbar just below the water on the portside! And the Belle was gaining! The City lurched, the scraping and creaking stopped, and the paddlewheels bit into deep water again! They had made it!

The Belle was approaching its last turn beyond the buoy now, but Loos' eyes were on the City. Stark was already heading for Excelsior and there was no way the Belle was going to catch her now in that last mile. The passengers didn't know it, but Lamont Loos knew, that though he still had to bring the Belle home, the race was over!

It was only a matter of minutes before the news had spread throughout the Belle. From crewmen to bartenders to waitressees to passengers came the whispered rumor, "The Belle has lost the race!" The whispers spread to low undertones, "The City is on its way to winning!" The murmurs broke into shouts as passengers headed for the railings to watch the finish! Yes, it was all over but the shouting. There was no way the Belle could catch the winner now. Captain Loos had just given the order to "turn the corner" and head for home! But unfortunately, the *City* had cut the corner and was already on its way across Excelsior Bay for the municipal landings. The *City* had won!

Emmett had taken the two Blair boys to the top deck to watch the last lap of the race past Big Island and on to Excelsior. They moved around to the starboard side to get a good look at the *City* which was now churning up the water two hundred yards ahead as if it were spitting back the whole lake itself into the face of the *Belle of Minnetonka*. Emmett could see thousands of holiday visitors pressed along the shoreline as if some invisible wall was holding them back from falling into the lake.

On the deck below—the second deck, Jim and Hillary had just stepped out from the stairway and into the open air so that they, too, could see the finish. They were among a few hundred passengers who were now jamming the passageways from the bar and restaurant, all with the same purpose, to get on deck to see the last mile of the race. It all happened so fast that no one was even aware of the accident. As the crowd pushed onto the deck and swarmed toward the railings it picked up the added force of arms and legs, of pushing and shoving, and then there was the sight of a man being pushed over the starboard side. Jim Stockton fell head first, hitting his head on the top of the starboard paddlewheel and then into the water where his body was like a pebble caught in the paddles of the giant wheel. Hillary screamed! Other women screamed! And then Emmett heard the cries from the deck below, "Man overboard!" When he looked down, he saw a man's body being smashed against the catchplates along the water level. Then the form disappeared, just as he heard the sounds of the *Belle's* engines grinding to a halt. The hysterical words were an automatic braking device to every steamboat on the lake, and it was not the first time that Lamont Loos had shouted the brisk order to halt his ship in an attempt to salvage another human life from a tragic death!

The giant *Belle* listed to the starboard as the mass of passengers on deck rushed to the rails to see what had happened. Crewmen tried to push back the crowd while others tried to see where the form of the man had gone after it was pulled underneath the waterline by the big red wheel. Then Emmett caught just a glimpse of a suitcoat! An arm! Then the coattails! Then nothing but the white churning water.

221

There was no time. No time for throwing out a lifebuoy or a line! The form had gone under again, amidst the screams of women along the rails of all three decks! Emmett turned to the young Blair boys and shouted, "You two stay right here! Don't move until I come for you—do you hear?"

He didn't wait for their answer nor did he see them nod in frightened agreement. Without hesitating, he climbed over the rail of the top deck and dove into the churning water some forty feet below! Now he was underwater, along side the *Belle*. No sign of anything there! He turned back, toward the sidewheel, but couldn't make it all the way before he came up for air. There was fresh air and noise, and he was once again in the silence of the lake below. Toward the bottom of the wheel, he saw the inert form of a man—dangling from the paddles at the very bottom of the cycle. Emmett swam down and grabbed his arm. He pulled hard but the man was caught in the wheel. Emmett got a better grip and tugged and pulled, finally ripping him away from the paddlewheel, leaving fragments of his coat still caught!

Emmett put his arms around the man and kicked his feet as hard as he could. He was no longer a kid playing underwater tag along the municipal docks now. There was a life at stake, and he shot upward toward the foaming, glistening water level, and fresh air. When he reached the surface, he was exhausted. It was all he could do to hold on to the man he had rescued from the paddlewheel. Two men jumped overboard to help, and they lifted the lifeless body out of the water and on to the boiler deck into the hands of waiting crewmen and passengers. Emmett simply held on to the gunwale along the hull of the *Belle*. Suddenly he was too tired to even climb back on to the deck. He just held on, gasping for breath.

25

JOHN STARK was being congratulated by those in the wheelhouse high atop the *City of Saint Louis* as it made its final dash for home and victory. Crowds jammed the shoreline less than one hundred yards away now as the *City* prepared to land at the Excelsior docks. It was the victory that John had dreamed of, the one he had waited for, and now it was his. He gave his final orders to Dick Blake who had been at the wheel for most of the race, and amidst pats on the back, John told his crew that he would go below on his way to the bow of the ship to receive the Holiday Racing Flag of the Minnetonka Yacht Club which was presented annually to the winner. Mayor George Bertram

223

would be at the docks to present the flag to the winning captain on the main deck of the winner.

"I'll stop in the captain's quarters," John told his crew in the wheelhouse. As he turned to leave, he saw Harold MacDougall sitting at the rear of the cabin. "Come on, Mac," he motioned to him. "Come on along. You're going to be running this boat starting tomorrow." He laughed as he started down the passageway with Mac right behind him, smiling as though he had won the race himself. They moved along the companionway on the portside, heading for the captain's quarters with John leading the way. It was less crowded on this side of the deck, and they were just about to pass the purser's office when two men bolted out of the door and right into the arms of John Stark. The taller man almost knocked John down trying to get out of the way, and he was followed by a short man in a brown suit who carried a satchel in one hand and held his other hand up underneath his coat lapel. When the two were jostled by John, the coat flew open and both John and Harold MacDougall saw the gun. John slammed the tall man against the cabin wall, knocking the wind out of the intruder with one sickening thud. But the short man had wheeled around before Mac could reach him, and as Mac lurched for the satchel, the short man with the sideburns and beard flashed his pistol and opened fire!

Two shots rang out, both of them catching Mac in the shoulder, spinning him around and into John Stark. Then the assailant turned to run, but found the passageway too crowded to make it forward. As he turned to head past the fallen MacDougall, the door of the purser's office flew open again with a staggering officer calling for help! The door jostled the short man with the gun and John Stark swung his right arm to the plump mid-section and followed with a hard left to the beard. The gun flew over the side-rail, and the man careened to the floor, still clutching the satchel. In a matter of seconds, he was being held by passengers and crewmen while John turned to Mac who was lying on the deck. He was bleeding profusely from the chest.

John turned to a crewman, "Do the best you can for him... we're pulling in ... I'll get a doctor." He was off, down the companionway stairs to the main deck, just as Dick Blake pulled the *City* alongside the municipal docks. John rushed along the deck toward the bow of the steamer, bumping into passengers and sliding past others. Mayor

George Bertram was there, waiting with the flag, but John Stark never even stopped as he passed the mayor and jumped from the deck to the docks and started pushing his way through the crowd. "Is there a doctor here?" he shouted, but there was too much noise from those watching on shore who were unaware of the shooting. John Stark reached the street and headed for the White House—and a doctor.

On the porch of the White House, Andy and Rose had watched the final moments of the race. When they saw the *City* pull away from the *Belle* as the two steamed into Excelsior Bay, they threw their arms around each other and danced in a circle on the crowded front porch of the hotel. They shouted and laughed and hugged each other!"

"I'm going down to the shore to meet John, she shouted as she turned and headed for the front steps. "Come on!"

Andy hesitated. "No—I'll be down later. I'd better check inside to make sure everything's all right." Just then he heard someone in the lobby shouting for a doctor. Andy hurried inside. He knew Doc Perkins would be in the Marine Bar.

At the other end of the long White House porch, Tom and Frances Blair were standing arm in arm, watching the festivities from the porch railing. The *Belle* had also docked now, and it would be impossible to reach the shoreline or to sort out Emmett and their two sons. There were just too many people milling around the docks as the passengers began to go ashore. The Blairs watched for a few minutes more, and then decided to go back inside. As they turned, they were confronted by Emmett Markham, standing on the side steps to the front porch. He was soaking wet.

"Don't be frightened," he said as he raised his hand slightly. "There's been an accident! The boys are safe. But I'm afraid Jim Stockton is dead!"

"Oh my God!" murmured Frances as she wilted in her husband's arms.

Pinky Wolfe had found Andy in the hotel lobby following the race and made arrangements so that Genevieve Chase could stay over until tomorrow morning before returning to the north side of the lake. Andy also made sure there would be accomodations for Louis and Mattie, too.

Pinky looked at the clock in the lobby and headed for the Marine Bar. It was after eight and he would have to hurry to settle his business before meeting Jenny for dinner. It had been a hectic day. First the arrival of Jenny, the race, and the two tragic accidents. Doc Perkins said that young Stockton had died from drowning. It was awful, Pinky thought. The guy didn't even like the water, and then to have that happen—with his wife standing there. It was awful. And then the robbery and the shooting aboard the *City*. Doc had said the new man would pull through, however. But it would probably mean that John Stark would have to stay on as captain until the new captain had recovered. What a hell of a way to start off a new job!

Pinky turned the corner of the lobby and headed for his favorite table in the bar. Sure enough, George Bertram was there, looking a little rough with his swollen jaw and some other cuts and bruises on his face.

"I knew you'd be here, Mr. Mayor," said Pinky.

"Yep. I'm here and ready to settle our wager," replied the Mayor. He handed an envelope across the table to the gambler. Pinky took the envelope and slid it into his inside breast pocket.

"Aren't you going to count it?" asked Bertram.

"No, George. I trust you," Pinky assured him. "You may be an old reprobate, but you and I have never had any trouble in paying off our gambling debts, have we?" The mayor tried to smile, but it was too painful. He simply nodded and shook hands with Pinky Wolfe.

"There'll be another day," he assured the gambler. Then he left.

Pinky knew the money was all there. And with the envelope that Lamont Loos had sent by messenger late in the afternoon, he now had all the money he needed to pay off John Stark and Andy Ross. Yet, he couldn't write the day off as "just even." A lot of things had happened to Pinky Wolfe since Genevieve Chase stepped off that steamboat this morning.

He ordered a Scotch and was still thinking back over the happenings of the day when John Stark and Rose Fortier appeared in

226

the doorway. They were hand in hand as they approached the table.

"We didn't mean to press the matter," said John. "We just looked in and——"

"That's fine," Pinky assured them. Then he pulled out an envelope from his coat pocket and counted out the money. "It's all here, John, both yours and Andy's. You ran a good race and you won it fair and square before all of that monkey business started out there." Pinky smiled. "I'm glad you won it, John. Take it and go settle with your partner."

John Stark took the money, thanked Pinky, put his arm around Rose, and left the bar. Pinky laughed to himself for a moment, pulled his pocket watch from his vest and checked the time. There'd be time for one more Scotch before he met Jenny.

Out in the lobby, John and Rose sought out Andy Ross. He was in his office and he hugged them both as they entered.

"We've come to settle up, Andy," said John, shoving the money across the desk to Andy.

"I've been meaning to talk to you about that, John. I've been doing a lot of thinking and as long as I'm not out anything, I don't think I want any of the goddamned money. I talked to Tom Blair last night and he's agreed to recommend me to some hotel people in New York. So what do I need the money for anyway?"

"But half of it's yours, Andy."

"I know, I know. But I don't want it. I've changed my mind, and I don't want it. Consider it a wedding present to you both. I mean it. You can give me a free ride on your own steamboat someday. Just make sure that some bastard doesn't try to shoot me!"

John Stark knew that it was useless to argue with Andy Ross.

"Besides that," Andy continued, "you won't have enough money if you don't take it all."

"All right, Andy," John finally agreed. "But I'll take it only as a loan. I'll pay you back! I won't forget this." He shook his hand.

"Neither of us will forget it—ever," Rose added. Tears streamed down her face as she put her arms around Andy and held him close. "We both want you to be the best man at the wedding." She paused, stepped back, and looked at him. "Will you?"

Andy was speechless. For the moment. And then he lost all of the brashness in his speech and replied in a quiet voice, "I'd be proud to." They looked at each other for a moment without a word. Then John shook Andy's hand again and turned to Rose. "Come on, Rose. Andy's got work to do. Let's go."

The office was silent. Andy sat on the edge of the desk and drummed the desk top with his fingers. Yes, this summer would be his last here at the White House. And he'd speak to Tom Blair in the morning about seeing some people in New York this fall. As Andy left his office and came around from behind the front desk in the main lobby he noticed a familiar figure starting up the stairs and then out of sight at the turn in the landing. It was Emmett Markham.

Frances Blair had already boarded the last Pullman car on the M. and St. L. passenger train, which stood steaming and ready to leave the Excelsior depot for Minneapolis and all points south on this Tuesday afternoon. She had taken the tiny Jamie with her to the Blair's private compartment of the special car. Tom Blair would stay over another day and accompany the body of Jim Stockton back to St. Louis. And Emily and the two Blair boys would stay the extra day, too, and return home with Mr. Blair.

Suddenly it seemed like another time, another year, to Emmett Markham as he stood face to face with Hillary Stockton. They held hands and had little to say. They both remembered the same goodbyes of just a year ago. A lot had happened since then. Now this parting was equally as difficult for both of them.

"I'm truly sorry, Hillary."

"I know, Emmett."

"As much as I love you, I wouldn't have had this happen for the world."

"Somehow, it will work out, Emmett. I know it." She hesitated for a moment. "I just haven't had time to think it all out yet. There'll be time for that now."

"I'll see your father off tomorrow."

"He'd like that." She paused again. "A lot has happened to him, too, in the past few days."

"He had to know sooner or later."

"Yes. I was wrong not to tell him at the beginning."

"That's all past now," he assured her.

"Will you write?" she asked.

"Of course. And I'll be in St. Louis to see you this fall when the summer season is over here."

"Mother said you're welcome to stay with us."

"Yes, I know." There was awkward silence. "I still love you, Hillary. Honestly."

"And I've always loved you, Emmett. You know that. It's a terrible thing to say after all that's happened. But it's true. Jim was always . . ." Tears welled up in Hillary's eyes. She bit her lip. She could not speak.

"I know, Hillary. Just remember that I love you—and Jamie. Remember that. And we'll talk about it again when I come to St. Louis."

"All right, Emmett," she replied. "I'd better get on the train. As mother always says, 'Your father may be a vice president of this railroad, but . . .'."

"Goodbye, Hillary." He kissed her cheek.

"Goodbye, Emmett." And the two embraced.

Hillary turned and swiftly boarded the last car on the train. Emmett stood there watching as the conductor made his final call and swung on to the steps of the last car just as the train began to move ever so slowly. Emmett watched as the train pulled away from the station and rounded the bend at the east end of town, the clicks of the iron wheels fading in the distance. It always seemed so silent after a train had left.

Emmett turned and started back toward Excelsior's main street. He had a newspaper to get out yet this week. It would be a memorable edition. Then he remembered his vow of just a year ago and he knew that it would come true. No, he would not let her go the next time.

THE END

About Excelsior

THE *CITY OF ST. LOUIS* sailed on Lake Minnetonka through the 1880's and into the 1890's. In 1895 the big steamer was rebuilt and continued in service until 1899 when it was dismantled. The *Belle of Minnetonka* ended its lake service in 1890, but it was eight years before workmen wrecked the giant riverboat in St. Alban's Bay, across from Excelsior.

Most of the hotels were destroyed by fire, while others were simply taken down. The White House, through the years associated with owner F.E. Bardwell, was eventually closed in 1921. It was known as the Sunshine Home into the thirties and forties and was torn down in 1946. The large bluff on which it once stood was removed to make way for Excelsior's expanding commercial district. The Blue Line Cafe became famous for summer dining into the 1940's, and fishermen continued to rent boats there until it was destroyed by fire in the early morning hours of March 4, 1958.

The Lake Park Hotel continued its operation through the turn of the century and was closed in 1911. The Hotel Lafayette was destroyed by fire in 1897 and the well-known Lafayette Club now stands on the same site. The Sampson House in Excelsior continued to serve as a hotel into the middle of the twentieth century and was taken down in 1962. An apartment building stands on the same property today.

The Minneapolis and St. Louis Railway provided passenger service west through Excelsior into the middle of this century. The steam engine gave way to the diesel, and the railroad became a modern freight line. A wholly new railroad station was dedicated in Excelsior amid a civic celebration in 1952, replacing the original depot where Emmett Markham once stood, waiting for the arrival of the beautiful Hillary Blair. The line through Excelsior has now been discontinued and the railroad tracks were removed in 1981.

Excelsior remained an attraction for summer visitors into the early 1900's as new steamboats replaced the older and more famous steamers to carry passengers and visitors to the Big Island Park constructed in 1906 by the Twin City Rapid Transit Company. The amusement park was closed in 1911, but in 1925, a new Excelsior Amusement Park was opened on the shores of Excelsior Bay and the F.W. Pearce Corporation operated the park as one of the better-known Minnesota summer attractions for almost 50 years. Two restaurants and a new housing development occupy the property today.

Excelsior and the Lake Minnetonka area are now suburbs of the Twin Cities, but the community still retains its small-town atmosphere with some of those main-street buildings and some homes from those earlier times still standing. The famous bell from the *Belle of Minnetonka* is now displayed in front of a modern Excelsior Library building as a memorial to another era. Excelsior is now part of the Minnetonka School District but offices are located in the old Excelsior school building built in 1899.

The steeple of a new Excelsior Congregational Church towers

231

over the community. In the early 1900's, Trinity Episcopal Chapel was moved to a new location on a high bluff in the heart of Excelsior village to make way for the new street-car right-of-way. A new chancel and trancepts were added to the Chapel in 1949 and a new Trinity Church was constructed on adjacent property in 1970. But the old Chapel remains in use throughout each week and every Sunday morning.

The Excelsior Commons and beaches remain largely untouched by modern-day progress, and families, mothers and dads, children, and young lovers still crowd the shoreline to watch the fireworks and thrill to the excitement that others experienced back in 1887 on the Fourth of July.